D0848839

REGION OF WATERLOO LIBRARY
3 6501 00413 4859

CARAVAN THIEVES

BY THE SAME AUTHOR

Fiction

August

I'll Go to Bed at Noon

A Curious Earth

Poetry

Householder

After the Deafening

Island to Island

We Were Pedestrians

CARAVAN THIEVES

Gerard Woodward

Chatto & Windus
LONDON

Published by Chatto & Windus 2008

2 4 6 8 10 9 7 5 3 1

Some of these stories have previously appeared in the following publications: British Council New Writing Series 12 (Picador) and 15 (Granta); *Manchester Stories* (City Life); *Hyphen* (Comma Press); *You Are Here* (Redbeck Press) and *New Welsh Review*.

First published in Great Britain in 2008 by
Chatto & Windus
Random House, 20 Vauxhall Bridge Road,
London SW1V 2SA
www.rbooks.co.uk

Addresses for companies within The Random House Group Limited can be found at: www.randomhouse.co.uk/offices.htm

The Random House Group Limited Reg. No. 954009

A CIP catalogue record for this book is available from the British Library

ISBN 9780701177607

The Random House Group Limited supports The Forest Stewardship Council (FSC), the leading international forest certification organisation. All our titles that are printed on Greenpeace approved FSC certified paper carry the FSC logo. Our paper procurement policy can be found at www.rbooks.co.uk/environment

Printed and bound in Great Britain by
Clays Ltd, St Ives plc

Contents

Rape

WITHOUT lifting his body, Phil parted the curtains of his twin-berth Fleetwood Marauder and saw that the world had changed.

From his pillow, he should have been able to see the green tips of the leylandii swaying gently back and forth, as they did every morning. A regular of Glenmore Caravan Park for nearly twenty years, Phil had known these trees since their sapling days, and had followed their progress like a rarely visiting uncle, surprised by their growth each time. Recently they had reached a stately, deep-green maturity, so bulky with foliage that even in the strongest winds you felt a sense of stillness beside them. On hot days they cast a wedge of shadow so thick it was like a private patch of night-time.

But this morning there were no trees. They had gone. Instead there was sky, cement grey and flat, a few birds flapping lazily across it.

Phil glanced across the two feet of space that separated him from his wife's bed, just to reassure himself he was in the right caravan. Even though nothing of his wife was visible, apart from a sprig of white hair somewhere near her pillow, he was quite sure it was Joyce. And, as he looked around the caravan – its orange-check upholstery, its ash and wild-cherry trim, its Karisma cooker and fitted cocktail cabinet – he had no doubt that he was in his own Marauder.

Phil thought of the caravan as his, even though he and Joyce had bought it together, after a visit to the caravan show in Earls Court. Their old Agrarian, faithful home-from-home for more than twenty years, having nurtured their children from puking babies to sullen teenagers, had eventually rotted away on its steadies outside the house. With Phil's lump sum and retirement nest egg, they'd decided on a brand new replacement, something that represented the latest in caravanning luxury, something, now the kids had gone, they could indulge themselves in and share for the rest of their lives. And caravan design had come a long way in twenty years. The new Marauder was so well equipped it was like hitching up the car to the living room and simply extracting it from the house. That first holiday last year, they'd had to make themselves leave the caravan, it was so comfortable, so like home.

Phil lifted his head a little higher. Still no leylandii. Was he sleeping back to front? Had a strong wind in the night turned the caravan around?

A sudden blast of snoring came from Joyce, which stopped when she quietly choked herself with her tongue, shifted position a little, and went on with a kind of distant whistling noise instead. She had never made noises like that in their first years together. She had slept like an angel, or like the princesses you see in fairy-tale books, with their heads resting on praying hands. He would sometimes look at her while she slept, unable to believe the golden symmetry of the face that rested on the pillow beside him, that was his alone to look at, for ever.

Now she gave nocturnal cries, snores that rattled from the back of her mouth, from deep down in her throat sometimes where the soft tissues shook and flapped, as she lay on her back. Out cold. Too much chocolate. Too much gin.

Joyce had a gut. Phil had a gut as well, but he could carry his. Joyce tried to keep fit but it was a losing battle. He'd seen what she could do with a slab of Dairy Milk in front of the telly on a Saturday night. She could get through the whole block in fifteen minutes. Then she would wonder where it had gone, as though she'd eaten it in a trance. She would blame Phil for not stopping her.

But Phil was just as bad. Since his early retirement from a lifetime in the post office (from postman on the walk to manager of his own sorting office), he had grown steadily fatter. People from his days on the postal always said the same thing when they saw him – 'You've put on some weight, my son, look at you!' But they weren't disapproving. In fact they seemed to have the opposite view, that he'd done something admirable, that he was doing exactly what he was supposed to do in retirement – indulge himself.

So nearly every evening Phil and Joyce indulged themselves in a small banquet of chocolate and gin. They'd never been great drinkers before, but they'd developed a real taste for gin recently. They considered it their reward for doing everything properly – working all their lives, raising a family, never burdening the state. They had done exactly what we expect of human beings and nothing more. They had earned it.

But Phil was unable to avoid thinking occasionally – *Is that it?* A lifetime of hard work and all I've got for my reward is a slab of chocolate, a tumbler of gin and a night in front of the telly? But then he couldn't think what else he was expecting. He was a man without hobbies or interests, apart from caravanning, which didn't really seem to count. He was not one of this world's gardeners or birdwatchers. He wondered if he was supposed to build the Taj Mahal out of matchsticks, or (even harder) take up golf. Amateur dramatics. Watercolour painting. Nothing appealed. A bit of DIY now and then was the best he could manage, and he wasn't even very keen on that. He'd recently thought about getting a carpenter in for something he could easily have done himself.

Perhaps they should have tried a different caravan park. Perhaps they should have tried a different part of the country, or even a different country. (They'd been abroad only once in their lives together, to a little resort on a peninsula that jutted out into the Adriatic. They hadn't liked it.) Joyce was keener on trying somewhere else, but Phil had always felt himself drawn back to the lawns of Glenmore and its now magnificent trees. They needed a change of scene, Joyce said. A change of scene would do them a world of good. A change of scene was what they needed. Now, as Phil lifted his head further, propping himself up with difficulty (where had those stomach muscles gone?) on his elbows, he realised a change of scene was precisely what they'd got.

The trees had gone – from their roots to their swaying tips, vanished. Moreover, so had all the other caravans. Over the summer, the little tree-transepts of Glenmore Caravan Park became small communities for the three or four tourers that occupied each one. Phil had enjoyed numerous afternoon chats with Pete, who'd arrived two days after Phil and Joyce and pitched directly opposite, up snug against the firs. Often they shaved side by side in the washrooms and Phil was amused by how Pete, a Brummie, was such a clumsy exponent of razor skills, nicking himself frequently, especially under the chin, where a hammock of fat hung. Sometimes, in the morning, the blood was running down Pete's face as though he was sweating the stuff.

But Pete's caravan had gone. So had Bob and Diana's. So had Bernard and June's. All the caravans had gone.

Phil sat upright, startled, pushed his face right up against the Triplex. The trees had gone, the caravans had gone, even the grass had gone. Instead of grass there was a dazzling, glaring yellow crop of flowers that extended almost to the horizon. A subluminous sea of vividness. They were in the middle of one of those vast fields you see sometimes, those stark, yellow quadrilaterals that seem inserted into the English landscape with a scalpel, that children think is mustard, but which Phil knew wasn't mustard – but what was it? The name escaped him.

'Love,' Phil said urgently. Joyce stirred. 'Love.' He repeated the word more loudly: 'Love.'

Joyce, sensing the panic in her husband's voice, suddenly jerked her head upright.

'What?'

'Someone's been buggering about.'

Phil was sitting up now on the edge of his bed. It was possible to join the couchettes of a Marauder together to form a double bed, but Joyce and Phil found it easier to have two singles. Phil leaned across and parted the curtains above his wife's bed. The same field of yellow flowers, almost to the horizon.

'Someone's been having a joke, love. The campsite's gone. We're somewhere else.'

'What do you mean, "somewhere else"?'

Phil turned his attention to the back window, tugged gently at the silk rope and, like a minor royal opening a hospital, unveiled a vista of limitless yellow flowers swaying gently, some black crows sailing above it.

'We're in the middle of a frigging field. Take a look. We're in the middle of a load of yellow stuff.'

Sitting up, Joyce had to put her hands over her eyes. It was as though someone had shone a torch in her face. Then, carefully lowering her hand and squinting into the yellow, lit by a sudden burst of sunshine, she gave a weak, husky, sobbing sort of cry.

Phil walked to the front end of the caravan, passing the galley and the bathroom, to the loungette. The whole place tipped slightly.

'The steadies haven't been put down properly,' he said, in a mildly complaining tone, as though annoyed that whatever agency had brought them here hadn't even done its job properly. He parted the last set of curtains. The same view of uninterrupted yellow. No car. Whatever vehicle had towed them here was gone.

Joyce was out of bed and looking around her with a panicky, jerky watchfulness. It was as though she hoped every time she looked out of a different window the view might change. But it didn't.

'What is that stuff?' said Phil, irritably. 'It's everywhere, but what's it called?'

'I can't remember,' said Joyce, 'But it gives you headaches. That's what they say. Allergies.'

The field in which they found themselves was enormous, its limits marked by gappy, overgrown hedgerows perhaps half a mile away in every direction. Beyond those boundaries were more fields, equally vast, made visible by the slight upward tilt of the land. This was the world, as visible from the caravan. There was little sign of anything else. In one direction Phil could see, very distant, a line of pylons. They looked like a row of children with skipping ropes. A clump of trees in another corner of the field could possibly have concealed a farm building of some sort. Little flocks of small, brown, sparrow-like birds dipped in and out of the crop as merrily as a school of dolphins.

'Unbelievable,' said Phil, shaking out the legs of his trousers, then stepping into them. 'Frigging unbelievable.' Then, turning to his wife and about to vent some anger, he softened, because she was crying.

'I don't know why I'm crying,' she said.

'It's the shock,' said Phil.

Joyce gave a loud sniff, drawing all the loose mucus back into her head, then fumbled about with her pillows.

'I can't even find any tissues.'

Surprising herself, she found a scrunched-up piece, carefully uncrumpled it, then blew her nose violently.

'I told you it gives you allergies, this stuff,' she said, wiping her nostrils one after the other, as she always did after blowing her nose, as a way of concluding the whole messy process. Then she suddenly turned to her husband and blurted, 'Phil, how did we get here? What's happened?'

Phil, buttoning up a summery, short-sleeved shirt over his string vest, answered thoughtfully.

'I think we've been stolen, love.'

Stolen. Phil remembered how he once thought of his wife as something he'd stolen, right from under the nose of that greasy chip-shop owner she was shacked up with at the time. Tony whatever-his-name-was. Skin like a gherkin, eyes like pickled eggs, nose like a split saveloy. There he was, scooping up chips from his drainer and wrapping them like a newborn for Phil while Phil was shafting his girlfriend. What looks they'd exchanged over the chromium brim of the deep-fat fryer. Tony so obviously proud of her – Look what a catch I've got, and she's working for me! Joyce's lacquered beehive was like a polished trophy balanced on top of her head. She looked like the FA Cup given human form. And he snatched her away from Tony who didn't suspect a thing until they were off down the A2 on Phil's Lambretta and had gone into hiding in Margate. That was it. Phil had stolen Joyce.

'What are you doing?' she said.

'I'm going outside.'

'Do you think you should?'

'We can't stay here for ever.'

He opened the door. Its rubber seal yielded, as always, with the faintest air of truculence. The flowers were right up to the step. They nodded as the door pushed past them, then bobbed inwards, as though taking a peek at the inside of the caravan. Phil withdrew, as though afraid they might sting. Then, as if to banish this impression, he took a half-hearted kick at them. Yellow petals fell on to the floor.

'You're not going to leave me here,' said Joyce, standing up, still wiping her nose, 'not on my own.'

'Get dressed then, we'll both go.'

'Go where?'

Phil waved his hand vaguely at the view, slightly exasperated by Joyce's question.

'We'll just set off in whatever direction looks most promising. We're bound to come to somewhere sooner or later.' Though there was no sign of civilisation in any direction. Only the pylons. The oddest thing about the whole situation, Phil now realised, was that there seemed to be no tracks left by the vehicle that had towed them to the field. No flattened flowers, no sign of any disturbance in the crop. Maybe the plants were so robust they simply sprang back into position as soon as they'd been passed over, but to Phil it looked almost as if he and Joyce had been dropped into the field from above, conveyed there in the vortex of a kindly tornado, or in the traction beam of a flying saucer.

Joyce was pulling on some clothes, straight on top of her nightie.

'Wherever you're going I'm coming with you,' she said. 'Don't even think of leaving me. Supposing the maniacs who stole us come back? You hadn't thought of that, had you?'

'Why should they?'

Phil had taken a cautious step out into the flowers. It was like stepping into a lake of liquid gold. The flowers came up to his waist. He pushed through them a few paces and stopped to take in the view all around. His caravan – dazzling white and streamlined – seemed in every way normal and undamaged; it looked, in fact, remarkably clean, as though it had just been through the wash, and was now standing in the middle of a field of yellow flowers – with no sign of how it had arrived there, or how Phil and Joyce could have possibly slept through what must, in its last stages, have been a bumpy ride.

He checked around the base of the caravan. The electricity and water hook-ups had been carefully disconnected and the covers replaced. The same with the TV input. The gas bottle had been turned and the tap tightly shut. The water-closet cassette was still in place, a quarter-full. The car coupling showed no sign of hasty use, everything was carefully tightened and nothing loose left hanging. One of the steadies had not been lowered to the full extent. That was the only thing.

Joyce appeared at the door, scanning the field as though to make sure there was nothing lurking among the flowers before she set foot in them. She surprised herself by letting out a giggle of childish excitement. For a moment, she seemed to think the whole business rather fun, but within seconds she was frightened again, and swished her way quickly through the crop towards her husband. When she reached him she held out her arm and grabbed his shoulder, anchoring herself there.

'Unbelievable liberty,' said Phil, straightening his back (he'd been inspecting the tyres), 'I've never heard of anything like this.'

'How could they have done it, Phil?'

Phil shook his head slowly, disbelievingly.

'They must have just crept up in the middle of the night, put everything away very quietly, hooked up the car and driven off. Perhaps they were going to steal our car and our caravan in one go, then changed their minds about the caravan. Perhaps they hadn't thought it through – what they would do with us – but then why go to the trouble of driving all the way out into a field like this?'

Phil's hypothesising brought tears to Joyce's eyes again, as she imagined the silent brutes who must have done this, and what a lucky escape they'd had. '*What they would do with us*', Phil had said. What had they thought to do with them?

'Oh, Phil,' said Joyce, 'I'm scared. I'm scared.'

'No need,' Phil whispered soothingly, using a voice he hadn't used for years, 'No need, love. They're well away, whoever they were, well away.' He patted the hand that was still firmly latched to his shoulder and was struck with a curious sense of accomplishment when he found that his actions had considerably calmed Joyce's anxieties, to the extent that she began smiling.

'Stupid to think they could still be around here, waiting for us,' she said. Then, turning her attention to the flowers that previously she had thought might conceal their abductors: 'Oh, I really wish I could remember what they're called.'

'They're not an English crop, I can remember that much,' said Phil, 'they might look pretty but they're not English.'

'What are they then?'

'I don't know. German, probably. Continental. It's thanks to the EU we have to grow so much. And they're not food, either. They're grown for some other use.'

'I thought they were mustard,' said Joyce, wistfully. 'I know they're not, but I used to think they were.'

She reached out to touch nearby petals.

'They look like a type of pea,' she said. 'You look closely at the heads. They've got the same shape as sweet peas, but yellow, and smaller. And look, Phil, they've got pods, like pea pods.' She broke one off and held it aloft, triumphantly. Phil couldn't feign interest, and was looking around him for clues as to which would be the best way to walk.

Bees floated haphazardly from flower to flower.

If Phil had been a birdwatcher he would have had a pair of binoculars to hand. As it was, he only had his eyes, which couldn't make out any promising details. There was a clump of trees in the distance that might have been concealing a chimney stack, but then it might just have been a pollarded treetop. And there were no telephone wires leading to the trees. It didn't look promising. In another direction, there seemed to be a gap in the hedge that might have been a gate, or it might simply have been an absence of hedge. Binoculars could have picked out details like those. It surprised him, unsettled him, that there was not a single building evident in such an expansive view. In a country so overcrowded, they seemed to have been delivered to its emptiest part.

'Well,' said Phil, putting his hands on his hips decisively, 'are we going to set off?'

Joyce was still absorbed in contemplation of the plant pods. They were thin and flat and, as though vacuum-packed, bore an impression of the seeds within. She split one open; inside were round, black seeds, five of them. She picked another and split it. Five more round black seeds in a row. Rather daringly, Phil thought, she lifted them to her nose and smelt. She looked puzzled, sniffed again, then shook her head, as if unable to identify the smell. Then she did the same with a flower head.

'They smell really nice,' she said, 'really sweet. Have a smell.' She held out the flower for Phil. Phil laughed at the pointlessness of the offer, as he was surrounded by countless flowers that he could just as easily pick for himself. But he took the flower anyway, and sniffed. It was a nice smell.

'OK,' Phil said, having settled on which direction to walk (towards the clump of trees), but he then felt compelled to observe his wife. She looked truly terrible, as she always did after crying. Her face was red and puffy, her pores had opened, her hair was sticking up at all angles. She would normally never set foot outside the caravan in such a state. He wondered whether he should tell her to go back inside and tidy herself up before they set off. He decided not to, and they started walking together through the flowers towards the distant clump of trees.

It was hard going. The ground was rutted and invisible beneath the foliage. There were big flinty stones hidden down there as well, and they continually stumbled over them. After a minute's walking they stopped and looked back. They were both shocked by how small the caravan looked, and yet they hardly seemed any nearer the clump of trees. Joyce was already breathless. The clouds had broken up and there was hot sunshine coming through. The sunlight seemed to set the field on fire; all the flowers turned up their brightness and gave out rich honey breath that was almost choking in its sweetness. Bees and butterflies were lunging across the landscape. Phil felt the sweat prickle out over his bald pate. They pressed on.

After another minute, they stopped again and turned to look at where they'd come from. By now the caravan was a tiny white particle adrift in a sea of yellow, its open door a dark little gash in its side. At least now the trees were nearer, they were on their way; but it began to look as if there were no buildings among the trees after all.

'I'm sweltering,' said Joyce, and, crossing her arms, pulled her hastily donned sweatshirt up over her head, exposing her cotton nightie beneath. Her large breasts swung and flopped beneath the thin fabric as she tied her sweatshirt around her waist. Phil found himself ogling them like a teenager, just as he'd ogled them over the deep-fat fryer in the chip shop – though then they'd been firmly, rigidly held in place by an underwired brassiere, and buttoned up beneath the white, nylon, fat-splattered tunic she'd had to wear. He remembered their journey down the A2, when, as pillion, she'd grasped him tightly around the waist so that her breasts had pressed into his back, had nuzzled against him all the way down the road to Margate. Looking for somewhere to eat their spam sandwiches, they'd made a long detour through hop fields and orchards, and found a field. A yellow field, like this one, but of a traditional English crop that time – barley, or wheat, or corn, he couldn't remember what it was. He'd parked up the scooter and they'd sat in its shadow, in the warm, sweet stink of its two-stroke engine, and they'd made love there and then. In the field. A field like this one. It was their first time. And Joyce had unbuttoned that puffy little dress to reveal a black brassiere, two conical cups full to overflowing, and they'd lain down in the corn, or the barley, or the wheat, or whatever it was, Joyce on her back, Phil on top, and the sunlight on top of both of them. And when Joyce had lifted herself up he saw that her back was criss-crossed with red – the impression of the crop she'd being lying in, details of ears of wheat patterned all over her, as though she'd been woven, like a basket. And there was the crop itself, splinters of wheat, whiskers of barley, something like that, sticking to her skin, picked up by it. And then they'd done it again, Joyce on top this time, and he could remember the crunching sound the crop made, the creaking and grinding of the corn stalks as they flattened them, Joyce's magnificent tits bobbing in front of his face. Somehow he'd imagined they would always make love in cornfields, for the rest of their lives. But they'd never done it outdoors again, not that he could remember. It was their one and only time.

These thoughts occupied Phil for almost the whole journey across the field towards the trees. The memories aroused him. He took sideways glances at his wife. The nipples were showing through. The rest of her body may have begun to sag and thicken – in places horrifyingly – but her breasts had somehow retained their voluptuous shape, their firmness. What would she do, he wondered, if he were to take her now, push her down into the flowers and make love to her? For a moment he was quite convinced she would succumb, yield, open herself and allow him in. Even now, with her running nose (she had started sneezing halfway across the field), lit from below by the yellow glare of the flowers, with the dust of pollen drifting past her and the sunlight dabbing at her unbrushed hair, she seemed something beautiful that he needed urgently to capture and consume.

He made a reach for her, but stopped. She was oblivious, wiping her nose and pushing through the scraping flowers, her double chin quivering, trying not to sob, as she was still very frightened. He thought he could imagine the reaction. 'Get off! What are you playing at? Are you mad?' Then a tussle while he groped at her and she tried to break free. It could all go so horribly wrong. He could pin her down but she could kick him in the groin. He might be driven to pick up one of those huge flints and break her skull, just to make her keep still. Just to shut her up. But he would be too stupid to aim the blow properly, he'd break her nose instead, she'd scream the rooks out of the trees while he hammered at her again and again until she went quiet. Phil was always frightened that he was capable of violence, and that he would use it one day. In fact, he hadn't hit anyone in his life. That made it all the more frightening, in a way. What would happen when the moment came?

They reached the trees.

'There's nothing here,' said Joyce, confirming what they'd known for some time. The woods were just woods, full of ivy-strangled trees and strutting pheasants. But there was a hedge nearby and, when they peered through a gap, they saw a lane. It took them a while to push their way through nettles and brambles, but eventually they made it.

'Which way?' said Joyce, 'left or right?'

'You choose,' said Phil, looking at the stings and scratches on his arm.

Joyce did choose, and they set off in that direction.

Seagulls

I'D moved back to the city after ten years in the south, and I was trying to set myself up as a puppeteer. I wasn't having much luck. I'd lost touch with all my old contacts in the puppetry society, which seemed no longer to exist. I felt as though I was having to start again from scratch.

The city was an industrial one. I found it noisy after the quietness of the suburbs I'd left behind. People's voices were much louder than I was used to because they worked in noisy factories. They thought nothing of blasting music at deafening levels through thin walls, and seemed genuinely surprised if you complained. Sometimes, in the street, you could listen to the shouting coming from different houses and follow several conversations at once. Everyone kept bow-legged, thick-jawed dogs who shat with arrogant indifference all over the children's playgrounds and barked as repetitively as engines for no reason. The women wore their hair pulled back so tightly their eyebrows were lifted, giving them permanent looks of surprise. People were either shockingly thin or shockingly fat. The thin ones were on drugs, I was told, and the fat oncs weren't.

They were capable of quieter moments of tenderness and contemplation, however. On Sundays they flew brightly coloured kites in the playing fields. The men went fishing on the canals, often with no more equipment than a single rod and line. Most of the families seemed to own small green songbirds with bright red beaks, which they kept in cages in their front windows, and which came, I later found out, from a single pet shop run by a very old man.

MY first attempts at re-establishing myself as a puppeteer involved contacting local schools. They all replied that they already had regular visits from a puppet troupe called Small World. This outfit sounded impressive. They conducted puppet-making workshops, and playwriting workshops. In the afternoon they would put on an hour-long performance of a play the children had written, using puppets the children had made. Small World, it seemed, had the city's puppet scene sewn up.

I managed to scrape by as a children's entertainer for a while, doing birthday parties and special occasions. Bookings were scarce, and it was heartbreaking work. The children were usually out of control by the time I arrived and would tear down my theatre before I'd even finished setting up. They would demand magic tricks, but I wasn't a magician. In the end, the parents would suggest I put on a video. So I was paid a hundred and fifty pounds to push one of their own cassettes into their own VHS player. And the children did calm down, and seemed to value and relish the video all the more, simply because I had put it on.

My applications to the local offices of the regional arts board were fruitless. Every grant, award, prize or theatre residency had already gone to Small World. These people had a complete monopoly, a stranglehold on puppeteering. I suggested to the arts board that this was unfair. Their reply was to the effect that there was really only room for one puppet troupe in a city of this size. If I wanted a future as a puppeteer I should consider contacting Small World. Joining them.

I found out that Small World gave weekly public performances in one of the city's central squares, behind an old Georgian church, blackened with soot.

I had to admit it was an impressive show. Small World, as its name suggested, fused the puppetry styles of many cultures: Javanese, Japanese, African, Eastern European . . . They even had a scaramouch, whose heads were nested in its body. The finale of the show was a skeleton called Georgina, who did a spectacular dance of death during which her skeleton disassembled itself bone by bone, down to the smallest vertebra, until the stage was a crowd of bobbing, dancing bones that would, bone by bone, reassemble itself into a skeleton once more. The audience of tubby toddlers and orange-haired tots loved this, and screamed with delight at the rollicking skeleton. I was all the more amazed to find, at the end, that the whole show was performed by just two puppeteers, a husband-and-wife operation.

I have to say that, for some reason, my nerve failed me and I didn't introduce myself to the puppeteers of Small World. Instead I observed them silently from a corner of the graveyard as they packed away their stage. Mrs Small World was a fortyish woman with girlishly long hair. She was wearing a diaphanous tie-dye blouse over sky-blue cords. Mr Small World was quite different, however. A much older man, in his late sixties, I thought, a pallid, cadaverous, lumpy sort of creature with porridgy hair and biscuity skin, a lipless visage and sad, melting eyes. He wore nothing but grey – a damp, mushroomy grey – right down to his socks. I wondered for a while if they were father and daughter, but it soon became apparent they were not. Once they'd lugged all their cases and boxes to their Dormobile, they gave each other a parting, lingering lip-kiss before the cadaverous one drove off in the van leaving the girl behind.

IT was shortly after this that the scandal of the songbirds broke. The old man in the pet shop was discovered to have been painting ordinary sparrows with green and red enamel paint, the sort kids use on plastic model aeroplanes. No one knew how he'd managed to trap these sparrows, but it raised a debate in the pages of the local paper about the continued decline of that species. The sparrow population had fallen by 75 per cent in some parts of the city. Surely one man couldn't be responsible, they said, while others pointed out that sparrow decline was part of a national trend.

I wondered what the bird owners did with their songbirds now they'd discovered they were fakes. Did they remove the paint and continue their domestic entrapment of ordinary sparrows? Contributors to the letters pages asked the same question. Most people, it was believed, kept the birds as they were, green and red, having been told that removing the paint would harm the birds and it would eventually flake away. Others suggested the birds would die a natural death long before the paint flaked off. There were calls for them to be released back into the wild to rebuild the sparrow population. This sparked further debate as to whether painted sparrows would be able to find mates, except with each other, and then would they recognise their young?

I had not got used to the way people looked at you in this city. They would stare at you, but with faces of dreamy indifference, as though their thoughts were elsewhere, or as if they didn't have any thoughts at all. It was the look of blissful unawareness that you see on sleeping faces.

I remember the night after my first encounter with Small World. Someone turned over all the brave, packed wheelie bins in the alley beside my house, spilling their rancid loads. They looked like the fallen, disembowelled dead of some medieval battlefield.

THE next time I saw Mr and Mrs Small World at the graveyard, I realised I actually knew the man. Just before I left the city, he had joined the puppetry society of which I had been a member. I think his first meeting had been my last. He had been distraught, as I recall, because his father had just died.

I hadn't had the opportunity to speak to him on that occasion, but I had noticed his sickly pallor even then. I also remembered the general twitchiness, the continual but short-lived looks of shock and pain, as though an invisible assailant was continually sticking pins in him. I remembered overhearing him telling other members of the society, 'My father died last week. I'm having trouble talking . . .' He wouldn't elaborate further, thinking his own manner sufficient testament to the level of grief he was experiencing.

I remembered thinking it odd: your father dies (a cause of great sorrow), and the next thing you do is join a society of puppeteers. Did he hope to derive some comfort, perhaps, from manipulating the strings of a father-homunculus?

This time I spoke to them. Mr Small World, whose name was Seamus, claimed he didn't remember me. I couldn't say this was surprising as we'd never really met. Yet I felt inwardly annoyed that he should have made a so much larger impression on me than I on him.

I tried fishing into their lives, hoping for a bite of something that I could use to draw myself closer to them. But Seamus remained very distant, secretive even. He said almost nothing about himself, while his wife said nothing about anything, busying herself with the packing away of the puppets and their theatre.

We did find common ground when we talked about the society of puppeteers to which we'd both belonged. Many of the familiar old names had left puppeteering altogether. Small World now worked with a whole new set of names, acting, it seemed, almost like an agency, contracting out puppetry work that couldn't be done by Seamus and his wife to individuals or teams. And then I mentioned Henrietta.

'We haven't seen her for a long time,' said Seamus, 'though I think she's still around. She's changed her name though.'

'What to?'

Seamus thought hard.

'It was a city, I think. She called herself after a city.'

'Chicago,' came his wife's voice from the back of the van.

'That's it – Chicago.'

'Henrietta Chicago? It's a bit of a mouthful.'

'No, just Chicago. She had it done officially via deed poll. She won't answer to anything else.'

TRY as I might, I could not think of Henrietta, that small, sad vampire of mine, as Chicago. Absurdly, even though we hadn't spoken for more than ten years, I felt a little bit hurt, as if she'd been my daughter and I had chosen the name Henrietta for her. It must, after all, be hurtful to parents to have their child reject the name given to them, the name their mother and father had spent nine months or more deliberating over, that they'd argued about in Mothercare, or over ice creams on a final walk of freedom on the playing fields. Name-changing, I supposed, was a type of linguistic cosmetic surgery – removing or altering something one is born with, replacing it with something of one's own choosing. A nose – a name.

Henrietta and I had had a very brief affair when I'd lived in the city before. It couldn't have lasted more than a month, though I seemed to remember it had a long, moth-eaten tail – no sudden cutting-off, just a series of ever briefer, ever rarer meetings and phone calls, until it faded away altogether. When I left the city, we wrote to each other a few times, but her letters were always politely formal and full of irrelevant news – her brother passing his exams, her sister passing her driving test. What really annoyed me about them was the way they always ended with the phrase, '*Sorry, must dash now.*' Henrietta, that little gothic finger puppeteer, never dashed anywhere.

I could remember the turning point of our relationship distinctly. It was during a weekend we spent together at a B&B near Hadrian's Wall. Somehow it all went wrong over breakfast. I ate all mine – a generous dish of the traditional fried meat and eggs – while she only nibbled at hers. Somehow, during the eating of that breakfast, she'd fallen out of love with me. I wondered (though never said, it would have sounded too silly) if my carnivorousness had somehow repelled her. She wasn't a vegetarian, as far as I could tell, yet our romance had come unstuck over a Full English Breakfast. She must have looked at me tearing into those rashers and sausages and thought, 'My God, he's just an animal . . .'

I found her way of eating rather cute. Although not possible, it seemed to me that she made a shape with her mouth exactly matching the shape of whatever was on her fork, then simply slotted it in, like one of those children's puzzles. Decorous, that was Henrietta's eating.

EVENTUALLY Seamus remembered who I was and we spent quite a while sharing reminiscences of the puppetry society members. 'They used to talk about you a lot,' he said, 'once you'd moved down south. You were much missed. People round here even began to feel a little bit betrayed. They spoke as if you'd sold your soul to the Devil, attracted by the bright lights of the capital. How did things work out for you down there?'

Not too good, was how I replied. But Seamus didn't share these small-minded thoughts, and almost straight away he started giving me work. I helped with public shows and school workshops. I met some old acquaintances, some of whom looked openly displeased to see me back. 'He thinks he can swan off down south and then come back when things don't work out, and expect us to greet him with open arms and balloons – who does he think he is?' At least, that's what I imagined they might be thinking. The puppetry society had disbanded shortly after I left, and some people clearly blamed me for that. It had allowed Seamus to form Small World from the rump of the society, and get his subsequent stranglehold on the city's puppetry.

I began to think I might meet Henrietta again, that she might turn up for one of the shows, or that we might find ourselves teamed up for a school workshop session. But her severance from puppetry seemed complete. Chicago, as I was never able to call her, had put her ten fingers to more productive uses. I just wondered what they were.

I did glimpse her once, from the top deck of a bus. She was leaning against an advert at a bus stop, looking worried. At least, I think it was her. I couldn't be sure.

THINGS were going too well. I was getting regular work through Seamus and his Small World. Then I was invited to dinner at his house to hear some bad news.

I knew it was going to be bad because so little preparation had been put into the dinner. They'd expended the least possible amount of effort, to the extent that when I arrived I half sensed they'd forgotten about the invitation. Mrs Small World answered the door and took a second to comprehend my presence. I met Seamus walking down the hall with two milk bottles full to the neck with water.

'Our plants get very thirsty,' he said, pouring the water into the pots of various succulents. Feed the plants first, I thought. Get your priorities right.

The dinner was cold, intentionally. Quiche and couscous with a helping of salad. The meal was punctuated by Mrs Small World suddenly looking at her fingers in alarm, as though something had just bitten her. Then she would put the back of her hand to her mouth, and nibble her nails. She did this all evening.

I was very surprised to see one of the painted sparrows in a cage by the window. I couldn't tell if the Small Worlds knew that it was painted. Even from a distance I could see that the colour on its beak was beginning to flake, the green of its feathers beginning to fade back to its natural brown.

'The thing is,' said Seamus having chewed insufficiently, so his every word revealed a different arrangement of the food in his mouth, 'we're not sure we can use you in Small World any more.'

'Why not?' I said, shocked by Seamus's bluntness.

'There's a question of fairness,' said his wife, drawing herself away from careful contemplation of her fingers. 'There are people in this city who would give their right arm to be in your position.'

'Good puppeteers,' Seamus added, 'good men and women who've been loyal to us and to the city. I'm afraid your position with us has upset a great many of our loyal friends. Much more than I had expected . . .'

'We are both great admirers of your work but, like I said, it comes back to a question of fairness . . .'

Just then their nine-year-old daughter appeared. Up until then, she'd been playing games on a computer in her bedroom. On her arrival, everything in the room changed. Her parents stiffened noticeably and looked concerned. Even inanimate objects – books, cups, pictures – seemed to react to her presence.

The daughter was cross, red-faced. She stamped around the room telling her parents they were stupid. Something had gone wrong with the computer. It had run out of memory. Seamus, it transpired, had been promising to buy new memory for the computer for months.

'I'm sorry, I keep forgetting, darling –'

'You're so pathetic, Daddy!' she screeched.

'And memory is very expensive,' said her mother.

The little girl shivered with rage, clenched her whole body and shrieked at the ceiling, 'Why can't you be richer?'

And then she stamped out of the room.

I felt as though, reluctantly, I'd been let in on a secret, the secret being their daughter's hideous temper and her parents' helplessness before it. No comment was passed on the incident, even though for several minutes the stamping and slamming could be heard somewhere high up in the house.

I finished my cold couscous and made to leave. I didn't think it was right that this couple should hold the careers of the city's puppeteers in their hands, but all I could find to say was:

'Your bird isn't real. Didn't you know? It's just a sparrow that's been dyed and painted.'

I left them in their dining room and let myself out. I can still picture the expressions of shock on their faces as they absorbed my news, looking first at each other, then at their fake songbird, then at each other. I could see it had all suddenly made sense for them – the fading plumage, the rasping tunelessness.

I carried on living in the city but I gave up puppeteering. I got a job as a postman. On my afternoons off, I wandered aimlessly along the canals. I never saw Chicago again, but I saw lots of seagulls, even though we're fifty miles from the nearest coast. They come all this way inland and congregate on the playing fields. Sometimes they rise up and circle about in a great rotating wheel of birds, hundreds of feet across. This will sometimes carry on for hours, so high in the sky that no one takes any notice. But sometimes I'll spend a whole afternoon watching them. As they wheel, they drift, so that, eventually, they are circling several streets away from where they started. Then an amazing thing happens. A few seagulls peel themselves away from the main circle and fly in a straight line back to where the circling started. After a while the rest of the gulls follow, unspooling from the main loop to return to the original circling. So for a while there are two circles connected by a straight line, just like a vast tape recorder made of birds, until all the seagulls have returned to the original location. Then the whole process starts over again. I see it nearly every day.

The Golden Boys

I'D just arrived for my interview for the position of manager at Rabbit & Pumpkin – London's largest children's bookshop – when I was suddenly struck by the odd and rather alarming thought that I hadn't passed water for two days.

In every other respect my preparation had been meticulous. I'd thoroughly researched the company (a subsidiary, I was interested to learn, of the American entertainment conglomerate Etna, which also ran a chain of bookmakers, and whose philosophy was summarised in its tag line – *Spend to Play, Play to Spend*), I'd picked the children's buyers' brains at the bookshop where I was currently deputy manager for what was hot in tot and teenage literature, and I'd reread the handouts I'd accumulated in attending countless management training courses. Sartorially I thought I had got it just right – smart but informal, colourful yet sober, wild yet neatly pressed.

But all morning I was bothered by the feeling that I'd overlooked some crucial detail. I felt as if I was at the airport without my passport, or had just finished a huge and expensive meal at a select restaurant only to notice the emptiness of the pocket where my wallet should have been. And it was then, as I strolled into Rabbit & Pumpkin itself, that I realised my visits to the bathroom for the last two days had been purely ablutionary, that I had used the lavatory only in its literal sense, as a place to wash.

It wasn't as if I hadn't been taking in water. Fluids had entered my body at their usual rate, of that I was sure, but somehow they'd managed to stay there, or else, by some mysterious metabolic process, had evaporated. It was rather like being told of the death of an old friend you hadn't seen for years and had all but forgotten about. It is only when they die that you remember them. I suddenly felt nostalgia for a bodily process. I missed that morning fall and splash. And then I panicked, imagining myself caught short during my interview: surely the build-up of water in my bladder must, any moment, tip over and weigh its accumulated volume for release.

But even as I browsed the three gleaming floors of Rabbit & Pumpkin, I felt no need to go. I forgot about my unusual condition as I took in the ambience of the store. Apart from the contents of the shelves and a purple rocking horse, grotesquely huge with pink spots, that occupied the entrance area of the ground floor, there was little to indicate that this shop had anything to do with childhood. In fact it struck me as a building designed to baffle, trap and even hurt children, rather than educate and entertain them. The shelves were of smoked glass, the floors mirror-smooth marble, the stairs razor-edged and banistered with hi-tension cables. Security guards in black neo-fascist garb stalked the floors.

I remembered reading somewhere about the philosophy underlying this hard-edged spartan design. It was meant to echo the purity of childhood. '*Our stores have the freshness of little children, unblemished of soul or body . . .*'

My interview was with three men – Bob, the manager whom I hoped to replace, Tim, the assistant manager, and Mike, the pre-school buyer. It was conducted in a cramped little room that housed assorted junk: piles of books were stacked everywhere like termite mounds, there were some big promotional cartoon cut-outs of Mr Toad and Mr Badger, and a bank of TV monitors occupied the two walls behind my interviewers. I found these monitors very distracting. They offered a seemingly limitless number of perspectives on the shop, each one flicking automatically to a different camera every few seconds, a caption identifying the locale (*rear entrance*, *teenage fiction*, *Pooh Corner*). Every time I was asked a question I found my attention drifting towards these screens; I noticed how still people became in bookshops, just standing there, browsing.

I was invited to remove my jacket. I declined, remarking that I wasn't hot. I then noticed that my three interviewers were all shirtsleeved. And when, later in the interview, Tim informed me that Rabbit & Pumpkin was very much a 'hands on, jackets off' kind of company, I realised I had stumbled at the very first fence.

'Do you have children yourself?' asked Mike, a man whose prematurely bald scalp was as waxed and polished as a showroom car's.

'I'm afraid not,' I replied slowly, wondering if they had the right to ask something like that. My slowness came across as guilt.

'Not a problem,' said Tim, the youngest and plumpest of the three, 'neither do we.'

The trio gave synchronised chuckles.

'"I'm afraid not," you say,' Bob said, 'but the truth is we find blokes with young families . . .' he paused, looked past me, looked at me, looked past me, '. . . they can get into difficulties working for a company like Rabbit & Pumpkin.'

'It's the hours,' said Mike, 'we had a guy here, he used to . . .' Mike began sniggering violently into his notes, shaking his head, 'he used to cry, do you remember, Bob? . . .'

'Yes,' said Bob, smiling fondly.

'. . . he used to go on about how he missed his little daughter . . .' Mike tried holding tears of laughter back by a finger and thumb pressed to his eyes.

'If your tombstone had room for only one word apart from your name et cetera, what word would that be?'

Tim, who'd asked this question with a stern face, crossed his legs twice, three times, settled his notebook on his knee, held a pen poised to record my response.

I looked passed him at a monitor and saw a woman in *Enid Blyton* slip a paperback into her coat.

I struggled to find a word. I had not expected to encounter my own grave in a children's bookshop. I could see it, but its marble face was blank. A stream of words was swiftly chiselled into it, but they seemed nonsensical – *cheese*; *corrugated*; *ice*; *hierophantically*. I could sense tall Bob, the one in the middle, smirking as I struggled to pick one. Eventually a usable word appeared.

'Honesty,' I said, then: 'Truth.'

The trio nodded with thoughtful approval.

'Honesty extending to matters concerning the ownership of objects?' said Bob, his eyes meeting mine only for a second.

Of the three it was Bob I found most unsettling. Not only did he refuse to meet my eye from behind his wire-framed spectacles, but he wore a permanent and ambiguous smile. The long length of his body was folded succinctly into his chair. His complexion was ruddy, smooth, blossom-soft. His hair was roughly cut, brass-coloured curls. His lips pouted grotesquely when he spoke. He seemed to sip his sentences before producing them. Most irritatingly he had a tendency to begin his sentences with the stub ends of mine.

'I'm not sure what you mean.'

'What I mean is personal integrity and security. Once or twice we've found a creature among us . . . it's an unpleasant path to go down. Money was disappearing from some of the tills. Now there are all sorts of things one can do: miniature cameras, money that leaves traces on the hands, all sorts of horrible things . . . And she was such a charming girl, the last person we suspected. She had some sort of habit to feed. She was led out in handcuffs and said tearful goodbyes to the colleagues she'd tried to frame for her thieving. We don't want a creature like that working here again . . .'

He tasted his lips, smiled.

'I'm not a creature like that,' I said and noticed a flicker of irritation cross Bob's roseate face as I unconsciously borrowed his sentence-borrowing habit.

'Your greatest failure?' said Mike briskly as if ticking through a checklist.

'My marriage,' I replied.

'Honesty,' whispered Bob to himself.

'All your fault?' said Tim, smiling.

'I wouldn't say that exactly . . .'

'Another man?' said Mike, lifting his eyes from his pad for the first time in ages.

'No . . .'

'Another woman?'

'It's confusing, isn't it, relationships and all that,' said Mike to Tim. Then to me: 'Did you ask her if she knew how to ride a bike?'

'I'm not entirely comfortable with this line of questioning, if you don't mind,' I said, flushing.

'Absolutely,' said Tim, suddenly looking worried. 'It's just that none of us three are married,' he waved his biro at the other two, 'you know, so it's interesting for us to hear . . .' His sentence petered out. Bob rekindled it,

'To hear about life in the world beyond bachelordom,' he said. 'You know, the worst thing about it was how she tried to pin the blame on her friends. She would come up to me and suggest I kept an eye on so-and-so. In the end you just didn't know who to trust. Well,' a quick double look at his two companions, 'interview over, I think.'

Closing rituals were observed, hands shaken, pleasantries exchanged, exits made. Further interviews were being held the following week. I wouldn't hear before then. Just as I was leaving, a sphincter somewhere deep in my body opened and a cascade of water tumbled through me, halting only at the last, tiny round muscle before the outside world.

THE company loo was as shiny and spotless as the shop floor. There were three stalls. I stood at the central one, unzipped, produced myself and waited. I heard the door behind me open and two men enter. As usually happens on these occasions another door deep in my bowels slammed shut and I couldn't go. I had hoped that the weight of accumulated wee would be great enough to overcome this annoying shyness, but evidently it wasn't. I stood there dry and mute while the two men flanked me, produced their members and peed with gusto. I sensed, out of the corner of both eyes, the two plump, pink lengths of flesh held with surgeon-like tenderness. To my right, the more powerful flow gave a sound of cup after cup of bone china being hurled at a wall. To my left, the stream came out at a steep fall and in pulses that quickly drained. Thin clouds of steam rose. I was the dry channel between these copious canals, having given up any hope of breaking the ramparts that now held my water supply. I'd left it too long to pretend I'd just finished (a quick mime of a shake) and too long to be waiting for the commencement. I was just standing there not going, my penis an unproductive lump in my fingers. Those few centimetres of nakedness seemed to unclothe me entirely. I had no option but to wait it out, huddle myself in a cocoon of personal space, hood myself in phallic self-contemplation and wait for my neighbouring floods to withdraw. I'd invested too much of myself at this central stall to leave it now. (At my foot was the trough drain, gargling on lemony rivers from both directions at once.)

It seemed an hour had passed before the man on my left gave his last pulse of pee, let a dozen or so drips fall, pummelled his piece with a technique I was unable to observe in detail, tucked himself away and zipped up. As he turned to leave I sensed him pause and look at me. I glimpsed the bland, smooth cranium of Mike. He hesitated, as if about to say something, and then left.

I was rocking back and forth on my heels as the flow to my right finished. I sensed this man too turn towards me. I then glimpsed the awful fact that he was holding out his hand towards me. I stole a shy glance to my right. It was tall Bob, the curly-haired, rosy-faced manager.

I folded my unused self away and reluctantly put my hand in his. He shook it firmly.

'You don't remember me, do you?' he said. He held on to my hand for as long as it was seemly to do so.

'You're the person who interviewed me just now.'

He laughed, revealing a new, complicated face.

'No, not just now. I mean from before then. From way back . . .' He said this as he walked towards the loo door. He was leaving without washing his hands. Since our conversation had become ambulatory I felt obliged to follow him out of the toilets and on to the shop floor, also without washing my hands.

'I'm sorry, I'm not sure I remember . . .'

During the interview Bob had seemed silent, quiet, uninspiring, but in motion, able to use and demonstrate his height, he gained a stature and authority that unsettled me. I felt like a pageboy carrying a king's train.

'St Nicola's,' he said over his shoulder, smiling at a customer, then turning to me. 'They called us the Golden Boys, you and me. We were five or six. The Golden Boys . . .'

But a customer with a complicated enquiry about a pop-up book intervened and Bob began a hunt for this book which I was unwilling to follow. I didn't speak to him again and left the shop puzzled, wondering if some coded signal of approval had been given, that I'd got the job. Or perhaps it meant the opposite.

How was I to interpret Bob's claim of childhood friendship? He did not dwell in any alcove of my memory. I felt certain of this. But then neither did much else from those times. It worried me. When I thought back to my first years at primary school it was like walking around the shop after closing. Everything was in place, the rooms were in the right order, the furniture was where it should be, but there were no people, or if there were, they were like mannequins, their faces standardised childhood faces – freckled, odd-toothed, tousle-haired. The longer I thought about them, the less defined they became, their features disappearing altogether, leaving bland, smooth membranes. There were Christian names, the huge faces of teachers, wooden clocks, buckets of grey plasticine, blunt cutlery and scissors, the odour of simmering tureens. But somewhere in the intervening thirty years, I had carelessly let the identities of my infant companions slip into a convenient abyss. I felt anger at my carelessness, to have not retained that information. So much of what I am today could have been moulded back then. Bob, who claimed a significant stake in those years – what gestures, linguistic tics, opinions and ideas that I now think of as essentially me might he have endowed me with as we maybe played marbles on sunlit drain covers endlessly?

I began to feel that the abyss down which those childhood memories had been tipped was the same one that now provided a bottomless reservoir for my water. There was a deep chasm somewhere down there which I could neither fill nor draw from.

MORE waterless, unflowing days passed. The whole rhythm of things had gone, yet I felt a lightness and energy I hadn't felt in years. It was this that prevented me from visiting my doctor. I felt vigorous, alert, clean and dainty. How could I call on my GP feeling so well? But, nevertheless, there was something out of kilter. It was as though the daily flow of water from my body, the daily filling and emptying of my cistern, had measured some essential cycle in me that, once switched off, kicked my life out of sync with itself.

A childhood memory did come to me during those days, but it was a later one. Staying with an uncle in a tiny Welsh village for two weeks. He had an outside loo that was alive with spiders, snails and woodlice. For the whole two weeks, I didn't defecate once. I was amazed by my body's ability to retain its products, and when I returned home I endured an hour of grinding agony on our own plush toilet. I had been conscious, throughout the two weeks, of the geological build-up in my bowels, the sedimentary strata slowly hardening, petrifying. And I knew that I was in for a difficult time when it came to removing them. But now, I had no sense of carrying around a week's build-up of water inside me, sloshing like a loaded petrol can. It just wasn't there. The twisted loops of my guts had a kink in them somewhere down which my liquid intake was vanishing.

There was an odd smell on my right hand that I couldn't wash off. A smell of fresh bread, warm yeast, wet seaweed.

NEARLY a week had passed since my interview. I'd been working late at the shop on an author event and had stayed for a few drinks at the Unicorn before taking the tube home.

Near the tube station is Tim's Kebab, a Formica emporium of skewered lamb, rum babas and rotating meat loaf at which I would often stop to satisfy a hunger pain after a late night. I purchased a special doner, a pitta envelope stuffed with ribbons of thin meat like a letter from an over-friendly pen pal. I gnawed at this warm bundle as I walked the empty lime avenues that connected my flat with the Underground station.

There was Bob walking towards me.

'Final interviews tomorrow,' he said, unsurprised to see me. Somehow I felt unsurprised at seeing him. He was starting to look familiar.

'Great,' I said. I had already decided I didn't want to work for Rabbit & Pumpkin.

'You should hear from us by the end of the week. That looks nice, where did you get it?'

'Tim's Kebab,' I said, swallowing underchewed doner, 'near the tube.'

'Really? I've never tried it. Lived here all my life. Mind you, I'm not that keen on kebabs,' he chuckled wetly. 'Anyway, see you.'

'Yes, see you.'

When I got home I found a little stalactite of cold, opaque fat hanging from the heel of my hand.

On Friday I received a letter from Rabbit & Pumpkin. It was handwritten in watery brown ink. It came straight out with it:

After careful consideration we have decided not to offer you the post of manager.

Our decision was a difficult one. In the end we felt that your personality lacked a certain quality we call 'knowing naivety'. We also sensed that you were uncomfortable with your age. You kept referring to your childhood as 'many moons ago', for instance, which only served to make you seem older than you actually are.

I hope you are not too disappointed. As a mark of gratitude for your taking an interest in us I am enclosing a complimentary copy of a book that is doing rather well in the tots section.

Yours sincerely

Bob

The book was a thick board book called *Raymond the Rainbow*, a peculiar tome describing a day in the life of a meteorological phenomenon. There was Raymond, all seven colours of him, sitting at his table having breakfast; Raymond going for a walk in the countryside, meeting his friends Sammy Sun and Ronald Rain; Raymond doing his tough day's work of being a rainbow; Raymond doing the gardening, watching telly, brushing his teeth, going to bed. Is there something missing from that list of activities? Yes, of course, the activity that is missing from all children's books.

A few nights later I was walking towards Tim's Kebab from home when I met Bob coming the other way with a wad of pitta and meat attached to his face.

'I thought you didn't like kebabs.'

'You were enjoying yours so much I thought I'd try one. Rather nice . . .' He gasped the words between difficult swallows. Chilli sauce was smeared around his mouth like clumsily applied lipstick. 'Listen, I hope you're not too upset about the job . . .'

I closed my eyes in a dismissive gesture, as if to say it was the least of my problems. Bob laughed, picked out a strip of meat and fed it to the red fish that was his mouth.

'Of course, it had nothing to do with your failure to recall our early life together. I hope you don't think that . . . You still haven't remembered, have you?'

I shook my head.

'I thought you might have remembered by now. We were best friends. We were famous throughout St Nicola's for our peeing games. We had contests among the trees in the corner of the playground, side by side, arches of pee – who could send it furthest? You always won. We'd rotate like lawn sprinklers' – here he performed an illustrative mime, the kebab serving as a penis – 'spray our audiences. They'd laugh. We'd cross piss swords, duel with them. You could pee so high and far the sunlight caught in its spray and made tiny rainbows. You were the boy who could piss rainbows. I thought *Raymond the Rainbow* might remind you. And the letter I wrote. It was in my own urine, mixed with ink. Thought it might trigger something. I was always envious of your superior jet, the way you made your pee fly. You sent yourself into the clouds. I was Robin to your Batman . . .' He paused, looked at his kebab as if it had suddenly transformed into a living thing and dropped it. 'Do you remember now?'

I didn't say anything as he took a handkerchief from his pocket, wiped his mouth and hands . . .

'I don't like kebabs,' he said, looking down at the burst pitta on the pavement, 'I've never liked them.'

I must have walked the lime avenues between Tim's Kebab and my flat several thousand times but that night I briefly became lost. It was midsummer and the trunks of the lime trees had bushed out, almost blocking the pavements in places. I found myself wandering in a maze of them, along roads whose names I didn't recognise. I found my way home only by chance.

This was two years ago. I haven't seen Bob since. Nor have I passed water.

I find myself bothered increasingly by trivial questions which I have to write down in a notebook in the hope that I'll be able to answer them one day. Here are just a few (I've numbered them):

47. How did the fish get to be in a lake two thousand feet up a mountain in Wales? Did they swim up from sea level?

279. What is the earliest surviving example of initials carved in a tree?

438. The noise made by pelican crossings – where does it come from? The lights? The push-button box, or somewhere else? You can't tell by listening (presumably because there is a stereophonic effect).

Caravan Thieves

As for my past, I have lost all interest in it. In fact, I genuinely feel I have no past. The present covers a period of the last three or four years; beyond that there is nothing. And the space of the present is shrinking. The puddle of my nowness is evaporating. Except for this smell I have on my right hand. It reminds me of something from way back. Biscuits, perhaps, from the oven in my mother's house. Or from the bark that was up against my nose when I climbed a tree in her garden. Something like that.

A Ford Mondeo

MARC and Cat were getting a lift from Rupert on Boxing Day. Cat's parents lived in a small village a few miles outside Oxford, and the whole family was converging on them, trying to make up for not being there on Christmas Day itself. Marc and Cat didn't drive, and couldn't have afforded a car even if they did. So when Tamara called Cat to suggest that Rupert pick them up on the way, as he was passing close to their part of London, Cat had been enthusiastic. Marc was angry at first, because he didn't like the idea of being given a lift by someone he didn't know, but Cat persuaded him. Public transport was a nightmare over Christmas and, anyway, it would give them a chance to get to know Rupert, her sister's latest boyfriend, without Tamara herself getting in the way.

When they woke on Boxing Day morning everything was set. They had two carrier bags of presents ready. They had some small talk prepared, which they hoped would last the journey from London to Oxford. There was just one problem. In the night, Cat had been woken by the worst nightmare she'd ever had. She'd dreamt she and Marc were in a car crash, that they were trapped upside down in a burning car, and that Marc was screaming for her to do something to save him from the flames that were slowly engulfing him, and the only thing she could think of doing was to end his suffering by clubbing him to death with a lump of metal.

She hadn't told Marc about that last bit. When, several times in the course of an hour, she burst into tears, she said it was to do with the horror of the car crash in the dream, the darkness, being upside down, the feeling of being trapped. She avoided being specific. It was just so horrible, she said, wiping away the latest crop of tears. So horrible. Marc asked if Rupert came into the dream at all. Cat said she didn't think so. But this wasn't true. In the dream she could remember seeing Rupert in the driver's seat. He was already dead.

'Shall I tell him you're not feeling well?' Marc asked, hopefully.

Cat shook her head, took a deep breath and closed her eyes.

'He'll see you've been crying,' Marc went on, 'you don't want to worry him.'

'He'll just think we've had an argument.'

'But I don't want him to think that.'

'I can't help it,' Cat said. 'Every time I close my eyes, I keep seeing it. I'll be all right once I'm in the car . . .' The word 'car' was too much for her and she brought up another spoonful of tears, and then sobbed for a minute.

Neither of them had mentioned the word 'premonition'. They didn't believe in things like that, and even discussing the possibility of prescience in dreams would have seemed ridiculous to them. But they couldn't help thinking about it, each privately. It was a cold morning. The weather reports were talking about ice on the roads. Wasn't Boxing Day notorious for accidents, because of all the people driving with hangovers? Or was that New Year's Day? And who was this Rupert anyway? That's what Marc wanted to know. What sort of driver was he?

Cat's sister had always gone for show-offy men. Big earners with big powerful cars. Rupert worked in insurance, they were told. At the top end. Tamara hadn't gone as far as giving them a complete breakdown of her boyfriend's finances, but she had dropped many hints that he was earning large amounts of money. He'd bought his own flat in Camden Town, and he was only twenty-three. He'd bought his younger brother a motorbike for Christmas.

'I can't say I'm ill,' said Cat, 'it'll just sound like I'm making excuses for not wanting to visit Mum and Dad. And then I can't tell the truth either. I can't say I don't want to get in the car because I had a dream last night. I can't . . .'

AND so, when Rupert arrived, they dutifully climbed into his car, each feeling as if they were giving their lives to him.

But Rupert wasn't that bad. He wasn't driving the big, show-off car they were expecting, but an ordinary saloon. A Mondeo. Marc noticed this word written in silver on the back of the car as they closed the boot on their presents. He wondered for a moment what it meant, and decided that it must be 'world' or something like that. From the Latin *mundus*, perhaps. A rather odd name for a car, he thought.

There was a brief quibble about who should sit in the front, which was conducted mostly through looks and angry, urgent glances exchanged between Marc and Cat. Before her dream, Marc had assumed Cat would sit in the front. Rupert was her sister's boyfriend, after all, and they would have lots to talk about. Now she adamantly refused, and Marc was lumbered with the task of conversation, or the greater part of it. Sitting next to Rupert in the passenger seat of his Mondeo, trying to think of things to say for an hour and a half, while Cat sat comfortably in the back, chipping in when she felt like it, Marc felt slightly betrayed.

For her part, Cat was relieved. She had been right: she did feel better once she was in the car. She looked around her. The interior was very different from the one in her dream. She couldn't be sure in what way, but the main thing was that she was alone in the back. In her dream, both she and Marc had been in the back seat. They were side by side, dying together. To be sitting seperately from Marc: this in itself was enough to reassure her, and to make her almost forget her dream.

Rupert seemed, at first, to be a careful driver. At T-junctions he stopped and looked carefully both ways before edging out, even if it was obvious there was no other car anywhere near. He signalled when changing lanes even on a completely empty road. But he also had a tendency to tailgate, which only became apparent once they were on the faster, busier roads at the edge of London. He constantly jostled for position on the carriage-ways, looking for gaps to slip into, following a few feet behind other cars, then expressing disgust at their driving when this led to near misses. In fact, he seemed engaged in a continuous dialogue (one-sided) with the other cars, which he conducted loudly.

'Hello, what's the Renault doing?' (a short blast on the horn); 'Now, Mr Taxi, what lane do you want? You don't really know, do you?' Once, in a jam, a car was trying to pull out of a side road but was blocked by Rupert's Mondeo. Edging forward, it seemed to expect Rupert to reverse in order to make room. Rupert seemed eager to show he wasn't intimidated by this. Talking loudly and casually in the hope that he could be heard through his open window, he said, 'Ooh, look, he's got a big shiny car. That's a nice big shiny car. I wonder what else he got for Christmas.' Then, when the other driver pulled back in order to drive around Rupert, 'Ooh, look, it's got reverse gears as well . . .'

Marc and Cat were not sure what to make of this commentary. It seemed provided for their amusement, but they found it hugely embarrassing instead. Rupert appeared to regard himself as a tired, bored schoolteacher and the other cars as a class of constantly misbehaving children. In this scheme of things, his own conduct was beyond criticism. Occasionally, having delivered some sarcastic comment, Rupert would glance in Marc's direction, as if for Marc's agreement, or approval. Marc wondered if he was expected to chip in with his own admonitions, but decided against it.

'So you're at uni?' Rupert said, after the long business of negotiating the London traffic was over and they were on the emptier motorway.

'Yes,' said Marc, rankled, as always, by the abbreviation. He disliked the way the uneducated used it to show a cocky familiarity with something they knew little about.

'What are you reading?'

Again the term 'reading' seemed to hit the wrong note. Only people who watched *University Challenge* still talked about 'reading' a subject.

'I'm studying for a PhD in social anthropology.'

Marc was expecting more cocky familiarity, but instead Rupert seemed completely floored by the statement. After a few minutes' thought, he had, clumsily and awkwardly, to concede defeat.

'It's a long word,' he said quietly, 'and I don't know what it means.'

Marc was wrestling with the problem of explaining the term to Rupert without appearing patronising, when Cat piped up from the back with a single word: 'Tribes.'

And Rupert nodded, while glancing gratefully into his rear-view mirror. His look seemed to imply that everything had fallen into place for him, not only the meaning of social anthropology, but why Marc and Cat didn't have a car, and appeared so uncomfortable in one.

'So there are still tribes in the jungle who've never seen a white person before, is that true?' he asked.

Marc had no idea, but felt he was expected to give a definitive answer, so said, 'A few.'

'So why is it,' Rupert went on, 'that they've lived that way in the jungle for thousands of years, and yet they've never evolved into a technological society like us?'

Marc's heart sank. There was no way of tackling this question without getting into deep waters. He longed for something to come up in the scenery around them to change the subject: an unusual car, a cathedral, a fairground glimpsed through trees. But there was just the almost empty motorway, stretching before them in a long series of gentle corners.

Marc tried smoothing over the issue with something about the perfect balance of man and environment negating the need for technological development. But Rupert wasn't satisfied.

'So you're saying that, because they can pick bananas out of the trees any time they want, there's no need for them to invent anything?'

'In a way. But technological development is driven by lots of social forces, not just need. There is trade, land ownership, migration, social structure, to name but a few. These all have to be taken into account when explaining why some societies develop complex technologies and others appear to remain static. For instance, the Romans could have had an industrial revolution – they knew about steam power. But they didn't because the slave economy meant there was no demand for steam-powered machinery. If you've got slaves to row your triremes, why would you want to bother with an engine?'

Rupert couldn't grasp the argument. It kept coming down to what he saw as an inexplicable indolence or apathy in primitive societies. A lack of drive, energy, ambition.

Cat changed the subject, calling from the back seat, 'So how was your Christmas Day, Rupert?'

This question seemed to cause Rupert a moment of discomfort, and he took his time before answering.

'My family have always had this thing about Christmas,' he said, as though making an excuse, 'ever since I was young. We've had this thing about presents. It's a rule in our family that we only buy each other one small present. I think my father was getting fed up with all the excesses.' He smiled and looked over his shoulder at Cat. 'Not really much fun, I suppose. But that's what it's always been like.'

'That's the way with wealthy families . . .'

Cat bit her lip after starting this sentence, and Rupert began a denial – 'Well, we're not really . . .' – but thought better of it.

Rupert had the baffling sort of face that Marc understood was attractive to women, but against all possible reason – long, broad nose, piggy little eyes, thick girlish lips, in roughly the proportions of an Easter Island statue. And lots of long narrow teeth that came to points. Lots of them. Marc could only take in Rupert's face in short, sideways glances, and even then he mostly had to make do with the profile. But he had a sense that he was sitting next to something smooth, streamlined and hard. Rather like a car. That was it. Rupert looked like a car.

THEY arrived at Cat's parents' house a little before midday. For some reason Marc found himself unable to relinquish his coat, which puzzled and amused Cat's family. He sat in one of the living-room armchairs with his anorak puffed up around his ears, and his hands in his pockets. Cat's grandmother was there. It was years since Marc had last met her, and she looked shockingly old. Embarrassingly old. But still she insisted on the ritual kiss: dry, downy, encrusted lips meeting his, followed by a brief conversation about what he was doing, and the inevitable feeling that what he was doing wasn't enough. 'She looks *so* old,' Marc couldn't help saying to himself. There could be no better illustration of old age as a type of disfiguring disease. It couldn't have been worse if Cat's grandmother had been delivered to the house scarred with leprosy, or elephantiasis. That we should all end our days like this, if we lived long enough, suddenly seemed to Marc the most intolerable thought. Especially when his attention was drawn to a picture of Cat's grandmother taken in her childhood. There, what was now dried-up and wrinkled was smooth and unblemished. What was now slow and tired seemed sharp and quick. And pretty. Pretty and intelligent.

Cat walked into the room.

'Are you cold or something?'

Marc wanted to reply that they were still alive, her dream hadn't come true, but he didn't. Somehow the presence of the grandmother made it seem irrelevant. Rupert was talking about his secretary. Cat's parents were appropriately impressed by the news that Rupert had a secretary. Even the grandmother seemed to prick up her ears at the word.

'You've got a secretary, have you?' she said. In all that long life of hers, no one of her acquaintance had ever had a secretary. Her husband had been a farm labourer, a quarryman, a postman, a soldier, a market gardener and had ended his career as a taxi driver (Nobby's Cabs). Marc had heard Nobby's story many times. He had been an honest, straightforward, everyday sort of man. Never troubled the state for anything. Never troubled the social geographers with a desire for upward mobility. Never desired anything much, so Marc thought. Baptised, married and buried, all in the same village church. Never lived outside the parish he was born into. Just like those people in the jungle Rupert had talked about.

'Do you think life is dependent on planets?' said Marc, out of the blue. 'I mean, did it all have to gather into one big lump before the chemicals could mix up and start self-replicating?' His remark was directed at Rupert, who was sitting in the best armchair with Cat's sister on his knee. 'Or could life have evolved in space, and be floating around freely?'

'Dunno, mate,' said Rupert, to a titter from Tamara.

'Imagine you looked down one day and the world had gone. What would that be like?'

'I think you should take your coat off,' said Cat, 'it's really hot in here.'

'You wouldn't start falling, because gravity would have disappeared too. You'd just hang there. And everyone else would be hanging there too, in a spherical formation. You'd be able to look down and see the people in Australia twelve thousand miles below you (there'd be no atmospheric mist to cloud the view) and then we'd all slowly drift off, I suppose, going our separate ways.'

'Only we'd all be dead, because of lack of air,' said Cat.

'Why don't we open the presents?' said Cat's dad, who didn't appear to be listening. There was a neat little pile of presents beneath the artificial Christmas tree, which was standing, as prim and as stiff as a ballerina, in the bay window. Cat's parents had, a few years ago, made their apologia for the artificial Christmas tree. In the course of it, they had so viciously attacked the idea of a natural tree that it had quite shocked Marc. They had spoken of 'stinking needles', of 'bitter sap', 'reeking resin', slugs and woodlice; they had so annihilated the very idea of a Christmas tree that Marc felt quite heartbroken, as though the magnificent larches that had towered above him in his earliest memories of Christmas, with their sweet odour and vivid electrical regalia, had been felled before his eyes, and the fragile bodies trampled and spat upon.

CAT was becoming troubled by Marc's behaviour. It was she who had woken in tears, pleading hopelessly for remission from this day of visits and gift-giving, yet somehow she suspected that Marc was taking advantage of her crisis. Sitting there in his coat, talking nonsense. He was on the edge, the very edge, of being offensive. She'd noticed how he pointedly wiped his lips after kissing her grandmother. He had even looked at his fingers as though there might be something horrible on them. But she too hated these residual Christmases. The Christmases that weren't really Christmases, but replays of the event in diluted form. There was roughly one gift each, and so the frugality of Rupert's Christmas Day was here reproduced. The thought made Cat smirk. She was sitting on the porridge-coloured carpet, feet tucked under her bottom, right at the feet of her own sister, Tamara, still perched trophy-like on Rupert's thick knees. He was talking about his car to an uncle of hers. The uncle seemed to know a lot about cars.

'It replaced the Sierra, didn't it? Like the Sierra replaced the Cortina. Everyone had a Cortina when I was a young man.'

Marc picked up this conversation from a distance and wondered about it. He was thinking as much about the word 'Cortina' as about 'Mondeo'. And 'Sierra'. An oddly Hispanic clutch of names. What the hell did 'Cortina' mean? He felt he should know. Some sort of Spanish chevalier, he supposed.

'The Cortina replaced the Consul,' said Cat's father. 'I had a Consul when I met Jenny. It was my first car.'

'You always remember your first car, don't you?'

They began opening presents. Marc's present from Cat's parents absolutely amazed him. It was *Flaubert's Parrot*, by Julian Barnes. It amazed him that this was what Cat's parents had decided would be the perfect Christmas present for him because Cat's parents were not book people at all. They never read anything. There was not a single book in their house. Nor had Marc ever said anything to them about Julian Barnes, or Flaubert. He hadn't read a book by either of them. He was not interested in them. Why had they done it?

Cat's present was a pot of hyacinth bulbs, little green thumbs-up signs protruding from dry soil.

Rupert's present, from Tamara, was the one that drew most attention, the most gasps and 'wow's. It was a huge object wrapped up in gold paper. It turned out to be a steering wheel. A big, black, leathery hoop that Rupert held up in his two hands and twisted and turned, a gleeful look on his face.

'Hasn't your car already got a steering wheel?' said Marc, from his chair on the other side of the room. This drew appreciative laughter, but Marc had not meant it as a joke. It was a genuine question. Rupert's car did have a steering wheel, so what did he need another one for?

* * *

AFTER lunch, Rupert and Tamara decided they wanted to go to the sales in Oxford. It seemed to go without saying that Cat and Marc would tag along. It was expected that the sisters and their boyfriends would want to shop together. So, Marc and Cat found themselves in the Mondeo again, driving the few miles of country lanes and A-roads to Oxford. Marc hadn't realised that the shops would be open on Boxing Day. The one morsel of solace he had taken from the day was that at least there would be no more shopping. But no, on Boxing Day, it seemed, the big stores flung open their doors in order to offload all their unsold goods at discount prices.

'I think they should leave it a respectful amount of time after Christmas before they start selling things again,' he said, from the back of the car, but no one seemed to hear him – although Rupert had in fact heard, because he replied, although it was after several minutes of silence.

'People need something to do on Boxing Day,' he said, 'otherwise they'd have to find something to talk about.'

Rupert and Tamara fell into conversation in the front seats, during which Marc was able to say, unheard by them, to Cat beside him, 'What are we supposed to be buying?'

She smiled and shrugged, not wanting to get into some sort of anti-consumerist argument.

'I mean, what *type* of thing? I just don't know. Clothes – is that it? Are we supposed to be buying clothes?'

Cat nodded.

'But I don't like buying clothes. Neither do you.'

'There are other things to buy.'

'Like sofas? Why are there so many adverts for sofas on television?' They were on the bypass now, and were skirting the edge of a retail park. Kingdom of Leather. Carpet World. Land of Sofas. A little solar system of soft furnishing.

A Ford Mondeo

It struck Marc how happy Tamara and Rupert seemed at the prospect of shopping together. Really happy. They giggled and cuddled each other. Rupert gave Tamara a piggyback all the way out of the multi-storey car park. They were as excited as children at the seaside. Yet what they were about to embark upon filled Marc with nothing but a deep sense of gloom. It was only now that Tamara was up on Rupert's back that he realised the couple were wearing almost the same clothes. Leather jackets and stonewashed jeans. Piggybacked and viewed from behind, they looked like a single creature with two bottoms. Marc wondered if he and Cat were meant to be as happy, and looked at Cat for guidance. She returned his look with a smile, and they both giggled at the two bobbing, stonewashed bottoms that were running away from them.

'Perhaps we should separate,' said Cat, who felt a little guilty after they'd been caught giggling at the piggyback episode. She hoped that Tamara and Rupert had seen the laughter as an attempt to join in with the general levity, but she suspected that they thought it was derisive. She felt even more guilty when she thought to herself that, actually, it probably was.

'That's a good idea,' said Rupert, 'let's divide up the city. You take the western half, we'll take the eastern half, that way we'll conquer the whole place. Claim it for ourselves.'

So they split up, agreeing to meet at a café near the Bodleian Library later in the afternoon.

'OK,' said Marc, 'we've got two hours to fill with shopping, and absolutely no money to spend.'

'It doesn't matter,' said Cat, 'we can just look around the city.'

'It's Boxing Day,' said Marc, 'nothing's open. All the museums are shut. The only places open are shoe shops.'

This wasn't true. There were some bookshops open. Marc and

Cat spent two hours in one of these. Marc immediately made for the languages section, where he looked up 'Mondeo' and 'Cortina'. He managed to find out that 'Mondeo' did indeed mean 'world', and that Ford had chosen the name to emphasise the fact that the Mondeo was a 'world car'. By which they meant, Marc supposed, that it could be sold everywhere in the world. America, China, Australia. There must be people driving Mondeos in Cambodia and Mozambique, he thought. There must be Argentinian honchos driving Mondeos across mountain ranges. Mondeos in Jamaica with boots full of sugar cane; Mondeos driving across the tundra; eskimos in their Mondeos skidding across the ice sheets, their back seats draped with seal skins. Mondeos overtaking camel caravanserais in Libya, or crashing through the undergrowth of the Mato Grosso. A goatherd in the Caucasus goading his goats to market in his Ford Mondeo . . .

The translation of 'Cortina' was slightly more puzzling. It meant, simply, 'curtain'.

THE two couples met at the café near the Bodleian at five o'clock. Rupert and Tamara were hauling big paper carrier bags with the names of expensive-sounding shops on them, looking flushed and exhilarated. Marc and Cat were carrying nothing apart from the bags they'd come with.

'Do you want to see the funniest pair of shoes in the whole of Oxford?' said Tamara.

'The funniest shoes in the south of England?' added Rupert.

'But they're really sweet as well, look.'

Tamara rustled about in one of the bags and produced the shoes. They were ordinary flat canvas shoes, except that they were covered in blue and black leopard spots.

'I bought a pink pair as well,' said Tamara rummaging again, then producing the pink leopard-spot shoes.

Marc and Cat hadn't been expecting the shoes at all, and were trying their best to find them funny. But they couldn't get past the thought that they were just ordinary, rather good shoes.

To their relief, Tamara and Rupert didn't ask Marc and Cat what they had bought in the sales. It was almost as if they'd been expecting them to arrive back at the café empty-handed. In which case, why suggest that they come to the sales at all? Cat felt a bit annoyed with how the day had gone. She'd hardly had a chance to speak to Tamara at all. Not a girl-to-girl talk. She felt she still didn't know anything about Rupert.

Rupert took a call on his mobile phone while they were waiting for their food. It was a friend from work. 'We've just been to the sales,' he said. 'Tamara's bought half of Oxford. And I bought . . .'(a faux-thoughtful pause) '. . . I bought a third . . .'

IT was pitch dark by the time they drove back to the village. Marc couldn't quite believe it was Boxing Day, the traffic was so heavy. Looking around him at the flow of traffic, Marc could see that every car was loaded with stuff. Boxes, bags, long things sticking out of windows because they wouldn't fit inside. Someone had a settee on their roof rack. It was as though a city had fallen, and these were the looters on their way home, laden with spoils.

It was quieter once they were beyond the bypass. But Cat was uncomfortable now, because she and Marc were in the back seat, and it was dark now, just like in her dream. And Rupert had inexplicably put on a huge spurt of speed, so that they felt pressed back into their seats. He was hurtling along the empty road as though he was late for his wedding. Tamara didn't seem at all bothered. The road was empty. Marc looked out of the window at the dark. So dark he only got a vague sense of things rushing past. Trees or hedgerows. They could be anywhere in the world, he thought. There was no sign. They could have been absolutely anywhere.

You Are Here

IT was a Saturday afternoon and Jake was on his way back from the betting shop, having just lost five pounds on a horse called It Takes Time, when he was set upon by a group of longbowmen.

The attack came from behind, so he wasn't aware of anything until it was too late. He heard a car pull up, he heard car doors opening. The first two arrows missed, though passed Jake closely enough for him to hear the dove-flutter of their flight feathers. Even when they clattered on the pavement many yards ahead, Jake did not realise what they were. The next three arrows struck their target. Jake felt no serious pain. It was more as though he had been hit by some small pebbles, forcefully thrown, landing with a quick thud-thud-thud.

Jake turned and saw three men climbing into a car. He couldn't be sure but they seemed to be dressed in the tights and codpieces of medieval fancy dress. Their weapons made entering the car an awkward manoeuvre. For a moment there was a comical tangle of men and longbows, and it took three attempts to close the doors. Then the car drove off, with tyre-screeching haste, two men looking out of the back window as they departed.

Still Jake hadn't quite realised what had happened. He shrugged to himself and walked on, though he began to feel an itchiness in his upper left arm. When he looked at it, he saw that something silver appeared to be attached to the tweed of his jacket. He stopped, looked closer. It was an arrowhead with a smear of bramble jelly at its tip. It was when he tried to pick this object off his sleeve, to find that it was still attached to the shaft of the arrow that had struck him, having entered his arm on the opposite side (from tricep to bicep), that the pain began to register. Craning his neck and twisting his arm, Jake could just see the arrow shaft, with its glossy red and blue feathers, sticking out behind him.

Then he became aware of the other arrows. He could feel one high up in his back, between his shoulder blades. There was another one in his left buttock. But he couldn't see them, no matter how much he twisted and turned.

He walked on calmly. Calmly, because there seemed no point in behaving otherwise. There was nothing he could do. The street was empty, there was no one he could turn to for help. He couldn't remove the arrows – their backward-pointing barbs saw to that – and besides, he'd heard somewhere that it can be dangerous to remove an object from a wound, it could be acting as a plug. Nor did he think it a good idea to run. That might loosen the arrows – and, he felt, might appear faintly ridiculous. He didn't want to draw attention to himself.

He was only a short distance from his house. He had just to make it down the street, turn right at the second turning, and he'd be home. Once home he could deal with the problem.

He could call an ambulance. He could lie down, check for bleeding, bandage himself, have a cup of tea. Just as soon as he got home.

JAKE kept thinking about the horses. He couldn't get them out of his head. Why had he decided, that day, to go to the betting shop? It was thanks to his brother, Ray, who'd paid him a rare visit the week before. They'd gone for a drink. Ray had told him all about his luck at the races. Jake had been surprised. He'd had no idea Ray was so interested in racing, or gambling of any sort. Ray was too careful, especially with money. He was the sort of person who would make a big fuss about being short-changed a penny. He was the sort of person who hoarded his loose coppers in giant whisky bottles. And when the whisky bottle was full, he wouldn't splash out on a treat for himself, he would put it in his savings account. But now Ray was telling him about his recent win – a complicated accumulator bet that had eventually won Ray enough money to leave his job and set up in business. Ray said he wanted to buy a dog track. This dumbfounded Jake. He was only just growing accustomed to the idea that his brother was interested in horse racing. Now he had to contend with the idea of a brother who intended to devote his life to gambling on dogs. Ray said he had every intention of betting on his own track, just like any other customer. He was staying with Jake so that he could have a look at the local circuits. There were two nearby. Jake hardly knew where they were, but according to Ray they were nationally famous.

Ray only ever visited if he wanted something. In the old days this meant that he visited almost every week, but he had pulled himself together over the last few years. He'd settled, living on his own after his second divorce, in a small northern town. He had a decent job, which he'd held down for ten years. Until this big win on the horses.

After Ray left, Jake thought for a while. Ray had given him lots of tips and advice, and had been so enthusiastic and persuasive – saying there was money to be made for people with enough nerve (or big enough bollocks, as Ray put it) – that after a week of dithering, Jake finally entered his local betting shop and took the plunge. He followed Ray's advice, placing small bets on favourites at first, just to get the feel of things, before trying anything more complicated like following newspaper tipsters (their 'naps'). It Takes Time was a favourite. Five pounds was, Jake supposed, a small bet.

He hadn't liked the betting shop. It stank of cigarettes. It was crowded and slightly threatening. Builders in hard hats were spending their lunch break in there. Jake peered over their shoulders at their betting slips. They were placing bets of ten or twenty pounds with hardly a thought. When Jake's race came up on the screen, the place fell silent. He was expecting expressions of excitement, but there was only a tense hush. As It Takes Time began to fade, one old Irishman in a filthy shirt did holler a 'Come on!', and when the horse finally fell two fences from home, there was a collective moan. Jake could hardly believe it: the silly puppet-sized jockey, dressed up like a playing card, tumbling in the grass then curling up in the foetal position while other horses thundered past him; It Takes Time carrying on riderless, craftily bypassing the remaining fences. If It Takes Time had won that race, Jake would have been hooked. He would have tried another five-pound bet with his winnings (he'd already picked the next horse he was going to back). But as it turned out, Jake wasn't going to waste another five pounds. He'd had enough. He felt stupid. He felt as though he'd fallen for the oldest trick in the book ('Trick No. 1 – get people to speculate on the outcome of an unpredictable event'). If It Takes Time had won, Jake wouldn't have been walking disconsolately home along Briar Lane at just the moment a car full of rogue longbowmen had been looking for a suitable target. This medley of thoughts about horses and archery gave Jake the vague impression that he'd been set upon by a herd of centaurs.

JAKE was embarrassed. His embarrassment at losing a bet seemed to extend into the embarrassment of being so publicly violated. He was glad there was no one else in the street. He was lucky in that way. No one to see the arrows sticking out of him.

For the first time, he was struck by the shabbiness of Briar Lane. The front gardens were wild, rambling. Several had let their privet hedges turn feral. They had become trees, sprouting white, lilac-like flowers. It had never before occurred to Jake that privet bloomed. One front garden was filled entirely by a car, a Ford Escort, its front smashed in, crumpled up, as though stifling a sneeze.

Work had been done to prettify the street, however. Trees had been recently installed. This was the result of local pressure on the council. Jake's signature had been added to a petition. The planting, which Jake had observed from his window, had been a remarkably quick and painless process. They had turned up with a truckload of almost-mature dwarf cherries, ornamental maples and rowans, and used a circular saw to cut small squares into the bumpy, patched-up asphalt. They then shovelled some compost into the raw earth exposed beneath and poked in each tree, bedding it down and sleeving it in a protective wire mesh.

Jake was a little disappointed with the trees. They were too small and would never get much bigger. He was hoping for trees that would grow into stately planes or limes. But councils didn't plant trees like that any more, only the little, titchy, harmless trees. To Jake, they didn't seem to belong in the street. Instead, they looked rather as though they had fallen from the sky, as though they had been stabbed into the pavements. He didn't expect them to last long. The local kids would soon tear them limb from limb, as they'd done to the little avenue of cherries that had been planted in Chapel Street Park. Those saplings, admittedly tiny and without protective cages, were all slaughtered in a single day. Just the trunks were left after the kids had been at them, pathetic knee-high stumps that still, heartbreakingly, put forth a few nervous leaves in the spring. Eventually the council took them out altogether and replaced them with bollards. A stolen car crashed into those.

The new trees of Briar Lane and the adjoining streets were doing well, however. Only one had succumbed to vandalism, its thin trunk snapped clean in half one Saturday night. The person who lived in the house overlooking this tree had made a touching attempt to save its life. They had taped a broom-handle splint to the trunk, as though the tree were an animal with a broken neck.

As Jake walked towards his own road, he felt a strange sense of fear. He saw that the woman who'd instigated the planting of the trees, the local resident who'd gathered all the signatures, a woman whose respectability and apparent affluence set her in contrast to the prevailing grimness, was coming towards him. He felt suddenly vulnerable, as though in a dream of being unclothed in public. He didn't want the progenitor of trees to see his arrows, to make a fuss. He didn't want to frighten her. Thankfully she didn't notice. She didn't even look at Jake as they passed each other. She probably didn't even know who he was. Afterwards, perversely, he felt affronted by her indifference. That she should fail to notice him in an empty street with three arrows pointing at him.

Jake was starting to feel pain. He'd begun to sweat heavily though he was cold. He was developing a headache. He sneezed into his hands and then noticed that his hand had caught blood. Even Jake could see that this was a bad sign. One of the arrows might have punctured a lung, or his stomach, perhaps. He could be bleeding to death inside. For the first time, he thought he might not make it home. Perhaps he should flag down a passing car and get a lift to hospital, or perhaps he should call at one of the shabby houses he was passing and phone from there. But he didn't. What worried him about flagging down a car was how he was going to sit in a car seat with three arrows sticking out behind him. Perhaps he could lie face down on the back seat, but would there be space? Jake was tall. As for the houses – they mostly looked empty. He could waste valuable time knocking at empty houses. He could be home before anyone answered.

When Jake got to the corner of Cornwall Avenue (now, thanks to the tree-planting, literally an avenue), he had to have a little chuckle. It was a one-way street. To indicate this, there was a sign with an arrow on it. There were two signs, in fact, one on each side of the road. A white arrow on a blue background, pointing to the sky. *I'll never look at arrows the same way again*, Jake thought. He paused for breath and stared at the one-way arrows for quite a long time. It occurred to him what a mean, cruel and terrifying instrument an arrow was – or rather, an arrowhead. Its backward-pointing barbs were such a nasty little trick, meaning the arrow couldn't be removed from its host without causing further damage. It travelled emphatically in one direction only, which made it an ideal symbol for directional signs. But it was a weapon of war also, of conflict. Wasn't that rather inappropriate? Would we be happy to have our directions indicated by little nuclear missiles or machine guns? Why couldn't we have pointing fingers on our signs, or birds in flight?

These arrows, Jake suddenly thought, were everywhere – on road signs, noticeboards, even on the lids of jam jars, medicine bottles, frozen TV dinners. It was as though a silent Battle of Agincourt was being continually re-enacted in the background signage of everyday life. Nevertheless, Jake followed the arrows home, though with difficulty. He found that he had to rest against the many vertical objects that furnished Cornwall Avenue – the one-way sign, a lamp post, a telegraph pole, a newly planted dwarf cherry. This made him realise he'd been a fool. He should have said something to the tree woman instead of hiding his arrows shyly from her. After all, she'd used him as a support, extracting from him that uniquely valuable thing, his signature, which he'd written on to her clipboard as though making a delicate incision with a scalpel. She owed him one. And she would have been just the sort of person to know what to do. She'd brought this little avenue of trees into being. She was good at organising things. Good at sorting things out. But it was too late to think about that now. Jake had to concentrate on getting home, from vertical to vertical. His was the tenth house on the left. By the time he reached it, Jake's sense of being in the world was beginning to fade. The world, in fact, had begun to seem like something thin and temporary.

He was also conscious that he was losing a lot of blood. It was dripping down his back, in between his buttocks where it pooled for a while before continuing down his legs and into his shoes. Jake could feel its constant trickle, and his shoes had begun to feel heavy and to make a sloshing, squelching sound as he walked. If Jake looked down he felt dizzy, but he knew that he must be leaving a distinct trail of red footprints behind him.

There was no tree outside Jake's house. This was because the pavement space was already taken up by a lamp post. Jake would have liked a tree, but they had to be spaced evenly along with other street features or there would be problems for car parking. So he was stuck with the street lamp.

'Not long now, not long now,' Jake said to himself as he struggled to fit the key in the lock, 'soon be inside, soon be on the phone . . .'

Once in, he collapsed on the doormat, but managed to pick himself up and get to the phone, which was at the other end of the hall.

He should, of course, have called an ambulance straight away, but when he picked up the phone, he caught sight of his brother's number on the memo pad where he'd scribbled it the week before. His brother wouldn't be expecting a call from him. Not for another three years would they be likely to make contact again. Jake thought it would be funny to phone him now. So he dialled Ray's number. Just a quick call, and then he'd ring for an ambulance.

His brother's phone was switched to the answering machine. Jake left a message.

'Hello, Ray. It's me, Jake. I'm just phoning to tell you I've tried your betting thing and it doesn't work. I put five pounds on It Takes Time, he was favourite in the two thirty at Cheltenham. He didn't come anywhere. I lost five pounds thanks to you. I don't know how you got so rich betting on horses. You must have some sort of special luck . . .'

Here Jake felt a peculiar sensation in his throat as he coughed. Blood sprayed from his mouth, over the phone and down his shirt front. Then Jake winced as a big surge of pain swept through his body. He struggled breathlessly to continue, sinking slowly to his knees as he spoke.

'I know I should have kept at it, but it seems such a waste of time to me. I've got better things to do with my money, thank you very much . . . I've worked hard all my life. I'm not going to throw it all away now. Good luck to you, that's what I say. Good luck to you . . .' Jake was whispering now, lying on the floor, his cheek against the carpet, the mouthpiece of the phone resting on the ground, next to his lips. The blood was seeping and oozing into a wide puddle all around him. He closed his eyes and listened to the thundering of hooves landing in turf, and tried to picture himself, arrow-punctured, fallen, captured, the three shafts pointing emphatically at him – *You are here! You are here! You are here!*

Pangaea Ultima

THE phone call came in the middle of the night, waking me but not my wife, as though it had been dialled directly to my head. I hurried downstairs and picked up the phone in the living room. It was Tara.

'I'm bleeding,' she said.

THE jack fell out of the wall, as it often does with that loose connection, and it took me a few moments groping about on the carpet to find it and plug it back in. Tara was still there.

'What do you mean,' I whispered, keeping an ear out for sound above me, watching the living room door in case my wife came down, 'bleeding?'

'I just woke up . . .' Tara went on, in between quickly stifled bursts of sobbing, 'and the sheets were covered in blood.'

I tried not to let on that I didn't understand. Had she cut

herself in her sleep? Had someone come in the window and attacked her? Then I realised, and felt stupid. The baby.

'How much?'

'I don't know,' she sobbed, as though the question had been ridiculously unfair. 'Even a drop of blood is a bad sign. There's more than a drop. Much more.'

'OK,' I said, realising I was expected to take charge of the situation, 'try and keep calm. What do you want me to do?'

'Martin, I need to go to the hospital. I'm in no state to drive; I don't want to go in an ambulance on my own . . .'

I looked down at the clock on the video, which was glowing in the darkened living room. It was three fifteen.

'OK,' I said, 'I'll be over. Wait for me.'

I didn't know if this was an emergency or not. If Tara was miscarrying, what could they do to save it anyway? What could they do at three fifteen that they couldn't do four hours later? In any event, they would probably just advise her to lie on her back and hope for the best. But I couldn't say this to Tara. Nor could I remind her of the difficult situation she had put me in. I had to think of something to tell Natasha, who was still asleep. I would have to wake her up and tell her. I got dressed and she still hadn't woken, and I still hadn't thought of an excuse. In the end I decided to leave her a note: *Have had to go out, slight emergency. Nothing to worry about. See you later.* Not very convincing but at least it would give me a few hours to think of something.

THE lane down from the village was teeming with sheep who'd strayed through an open gate on to the road, filling it. They looked oddly menacing in the headlights, their retinas reflecting the glare, each white head glowing with two green lamps. The sheep moved so in unison, flowing with each other; it was like steering a ship through ice floes.

It was only ten minutes to Tara's, but she seemed to think I'd been taking my time. She opened the front door for me without catching my eye. Her hair was wet and the sitting room smelt of marzipan. I put my arms around her, but hers hung loosely at her sides. Almost without speaking we walked together to my car. Just as we were about to get in, Tara went back to the house. I thought she must have forgotten something, but she was just checking the front door was locked. She made a very thorough job of checking, though. She tried the handle several times, and when that seemed OK, she pushed the door repeatedly with the flat of her hand, giving it all her weight, just to make sure.

It was twenty minutes to the hospital. We had to go to casualty. There were people in there sprawled across the chairs nursing bandaged limbs, weeping with pain. Tara thought her bleeding had stopped and I wondered if we were wasting the nurses' time. We may as well have come in the morning. But the nurses seemed concerned after all, and sent Tara to have an emergency scan.

In the small waiting room was one young woman with red eyes, drinking water and refilling her glass from a plastic jug.

We had to wait a long time. There were posters on the wall about violence against women, pictures of bruised wives and underneath, in big black lettering,

Remember your first date?
First kiss?
First fist in the face . . . ?

I glanced at Tara to see if she was looking at the posters. She wasn't. She looked very beautiful. She was wearing the white fur coat I had bought her in Rome, the first thing to hand when we had hurried out of her house. It would have seemed absurd for anyone but Tara to be wearing a fur coat in a hospital waiting room. I read another poster.

To love and to hold
To honour and obey
To be thrown down the stairs

Zero Tolerance of Violence against Women

There was an approving tick at the end of that last line. I felt embarrassed. I felt as though the walls were shouting at me. I wanted to put my arm around Tara but felt unable to. She had been frighteningly quiet all the while. When I caught sight of her face it seemed unbearably tragic. If an actor had made a face like that you would have said they were overdoing it. I noticed another poster.

15% of women miscarry due to injuries inflicted
by violent partners.

Zero Tolerance of Violence against Women.

Is this really the best place to be told these things? I wondered. And then I couldn't help thinking that if only the doctors would hurry up, I might get home again before Natasha woke up. She might notice nothing amiss.

We were ushered into a dimly lit room and Tara lay on a couch. Before we arrived, I had not been expecting that she would have to undergo a scan. I don't know what else I had been expecting. The gentle pummelling of Tara's tummy by expert hands, perhaps. The insertion of probing instruments. But not a scan. They were for happily married couples expecting their first child. They were for holding hands and squealing in delight at the wonders on the screen, the first sight of new life. If Tara had miscarried I didn't actually want to see it. And what should I expect to see? A tiny little body dissolving before our eyes, the limbs falling away like petals? Little fingers clutching at the dark straws of Tara's womb?

'I don't want to look,' said Tara, as the radiographer pulled Tara's blouse up to expose her slightly swollen midriff, and pushed the elastic of her chinos down to the fringe line of her pubic hair. Gel was squirted on to her belly with an undignified farting sound. 'I don't want to look,' she repeated, and took hold of my hand, but I was transfixed by the processes going on. My children had been born before the age of ultrasound and so I hadn't experienced this marvel before. It was as though the radiographer had shone a torch into Tara's body and lit up the dark caverns of her insides. The sweeping images seemed to show a map, like an aerial view of fields or gardens. I looked at Tara, who was holding her forearm across her eyes, and smiled, though she couldn't see. I couldn't help feeling thrilled by the power of this technology to render Tara so transparent. The radiographer named the different regions of Tara's interior for me in a dispassionate, mid-European accent, clicking his cursor on the different sections – *here is the pelvic bone, here is the bladder, here is the womb . . .*

I looked carefully at the womb. It was a small white circle.

'The foetus is still attached,' the radiographer said, quietly.

'Can you see it?' I asked.

'Not very well, but it is in place so that is good. I think it would be best if you drank some water and we try again in half an hour maybe.'

He was saying this to Tara who, on hearing that the foetus was still attached, had taken the arm away from her eyes and was doing her best to sit up. She wanted to see the screen.

The radiographer tried to show us but we couldn't see anything that looked remotely like a foetus. All we could see was the empty white circle of the womb. It looked like a cold, bleak place.

So we went back into the waiting room and the nurse provided a jug of water, and Tara drank glass after glass. Her spirits had lifted a little. There seemed to be some hope that the baby was still alive. I felt great relief that the scan hadn't shown macabre pictures of a dying foetus, that everything in there had seemed orderly and calm. But when Tara went to the bathroom to check if anything was coming out, she reported that there was still a dribble of blood.

'Those were amazing pictures,' I said, partly to distract her from her fretting, but also because I still couldn't quite believe what I had seen. 'It was like looking at a map or something.'

I now realised what the images of the scan had reminded me of. I once saw a TV programme on plate tectonics where there was this diagram that showed how the continents had all started as one solid land mass before breaking up and drifting apart. This original land mass was called Pangaea, and on the programme they demonstrated how it was formed of all the present-day continents slotted together like a jigsaw puzzle. That was what the scan had reminded me of. Continents squashed up against each other with no space in between – pelvic bone, bladder, womb . . .

Tara didn't say anything, but drank.

When she was scanned again the pictures were much clearer.

The womb had moved more fully into view. And this time, when the radiographer pointed out the foetus, we could see something. A small dark oval latched to the top of the womb, as though it was hanging from the ceiling. A tiny continent. 'This is the liquid in which the baby is living,' said the radiographer. He magnified the image. 'And there you can see the heart beating.' We both looked carefully, and there it was, a grainy throb at the centre of the dark oval, a flicker of rhythmic movement. Tara gasped, and clutched my hand.

There was no visible, limbed body within the dark oval, just a pulsing shadow.

'It's alive?' asked Tara.

'Yes,' said the radiographer cheerfully, 'everything is looking good. Still firmly attached to the womb lining. It is well situated, high up. Heart beating. Quite happy.'

'But then why am I still bleeding?'

We had to wait until the doctor arrived before that question could be addressed. He was a youngish, rather awkward man who took us into his consulting room.

'I would like to keep you in hospital for a while, Mrs D'Angelo,' he said. 'Although the foetus seems healthy, there is still this bleeding, and it would be best if we could monitor the situation for the next twenty-four hours or so. Get some sleep on a ward, then we'll scan you again later today. If everything is fine and the bleeding has stopped, you can go home. I'm afraid there's not much we can do to remedy the situation, but it would be better to have you settled and comfortable here, rather than ask you to go home and come in again for a scan.'

'What are its chances?' I said, seeing that Tara was struggling to phrase that question.

'There is no reason why this bleeding should not stop and

you go on to produce a perfectly healthy baby. On the other hand, the longer the bleeding goes on, the greater the chance that there is something more seriously wrong. We have to consider your age, Mrs D'Angelo. The risk increases significantly as you get older, so you must be prepared for that. But fingers crossed . . .' The doctor tried his best to end on a light note. I always felt humbled by the presence of doctors, especially young consultants like this. It seemed unfair that they should know so much.

The heart was still beating. That's what I kept saying to Tara. As long as the heart was still beating what was there to worry about?

I saw Tara up to her ward. By now it was around five thirty in the morning. Another hour or so and Natasha would begin waking up. I still had to think of a decent excuse for being out in the middle of the night. The best I had come up with so far was something wrong at the Portakabin. I could say I got a phone call reporting suspicious activity and that I'd had to go and check it out, perhaps kids were vandalising the cars. The trouble was I would need to enlist somebody else to back me up if Natasha decided to test my story. Who had phoned me? Brian? The police? I could get into deep water. Maybe I should say I thought I left the heaters on, though that seemed a bit lame.

But now Tara was asking me for more help. She wanted me to go back to her house and get her some overnight things: pyjamas, dressing gown, slippers, all that sort of stuff.

'Now?' I said. 'Right now?'

The errand would end any chance I had of getting back home undetected before Natasha woke up.

'I'm in hospital, Martin. I need my things. You know I haven't got anyone else.'

'Of course,' I said, quelling my anxiety, and giving her a rather too father-like kiss on the forehead.

So I drove back to Tara's house as fast as I could, and found myself alone in her bedroom for the first time in my life. It was a peculiar experience. Everything looked different. I rifled through her underwear drawer bringing out handfuls of silk panties and lacy bras. I couldn't help it, I had to hold the material to my face and enjoy its scent. I gathered it up in my two hands as though I was taking a drink from a pool. What a gorgeous sensation, even though they were fresh from the washing machine. I wasted many minutes like this. The trouble was, Tara possessed no clothes that were not erotically charged in some way, through their texture and smell. The only pyjamas she had were of black silk so fine that I could crush them to a ball in my fist.

When I got back to the hospital after another high-speed drive, I found Tara in a room by herself. She was lying on top of the bed, still clothed, with her head on the pillow and her eyes closed. Somewhere in the distance there was a sound of machinery, the rhythmic crashing of a production line, like a cotton mill, or a printing works. Odd, I thought. Only later did I realise it was an unborn baby's heartbeat, amplified by a microphone attached to the abdomen of another mother at risk. I carefully settled the carrier bag of things from Tara's house on to the armchair that was beside her bed, not wanting to wake her up.

'I'm not asleep,' she said, without opening her eyes, just as I was about to leave. I waited a while before saying anything.

'Are you still bleeding?'

Tara's reply was to take from her cabinet drawer a piece of white material and hand it to me, as though it was a letter that explained everything. But it was a sanitary towel. At its centre was a misty patch of red, like a lipstick kiss.

'She's leaking away,' said Tara, 'drop by drop. Her life's falling away.'

Tara's use of the gendered pronoun horrified me.

'I feel like an hourglass,' she continued, 'but with blood instead of sand. It's just a tiny amount but it's continuous, and it builds up minute by minute. Her life . . .'

'There's still a good chance,' I said, 'The scan was good.'

'If the bleeding doesn't stop by this afternoon I'll have lost her,' said Tara, 'that's what they were trying to say. I was speaking to a nurse . . .'

'I've brought your things,' I said, trying to take her mind off it, and lifting the carrier bag up for her to see. 'And look, something for you to read.'

I lifted out the new issue of *Cosmopolitan* I had seen on the coffee table on the way out of Tara's house. It still had a promotional tape around it, so I guessed it was unread. Tara gave a half-laugh and lifted a weak hand to receive the magazine. I removed the tape for her; glossy flyers and advertising junk flopped out and slithered over the bed.

'I'd better be getting back,' I said.

'Aren't you going to kiss me?'

'Of course.'

I lowered my head gingerly, feeling as though I was putting it into a trap. Just as our faces were about to touch Tara suddenly grabbed me by the shoulders, holding them firmly. She stared into my face.

'Natasha,' she said.

'What?'

'Natasha, your wife.'

'What about her?'

'Bring her here.'

'What for?'

'Isn't it obvious? I don't know why I didn't think of it before. Natasha is a healer. She could save my baby.'

Natasha was a healer. Well, anyone can call themselves a healer these days. And Natasha doesn't even go as far as that. A couple of things had happened in her life that had given her pause. One of our nieces had severe mumps when she was a child. The disease vanished shortly after Natasha travelled three hundred miles to visit and hold the baby. Another time, someone at work's husband was diagnosed with a brain tumour. Natasha went to visit and hey presto the tumour vanished. Both these things had happened years and years ago, but it was only recently that Natasha had started wondering about them, and what they might mean. Now that alternative healers were springing up all over the place it got her to thinking about these two occasions when people had undergone miraculous recoveries after a visit from her. In her mind, fortunate coincidences became possible evidence of psychic healing powers. Both times, Natasha was keen to point out, she had touched the patients. She had held the baby. She had patted the hand of the friend's husband. Perhaps she had some sort of power after all. Perhaps there was something special about her.

But that was as far as Natasha's career as a healer had got. Ruminations on past miracles. She had never advertised her services, or taken money in exchange for the channelling of healing energy. But she had thought about it. Perhaps she should start going to healing classes, discover if there was something special about her, and see if she could develop it. But she hadn't yet.

Tara had met Natasha just once, at a leaving do at the showroom when Tara was still with Jack. She made a beeline for us, although she'd promised to behave as discreetly as possible. She wanted to watch me squirm as the two halves of my life were brought together. Instead, she had fallen into deep conversation with Natasha about healing. That was when all the stuff about our niece and the friend with the brain tumour had come out. I listened in for a while, intrigued that they might be talking about me, and felt a little disappointed.

'Oh yes,' I heard Tara say, 'it can't be coincidence, you must have a special power. You're a natural et cetera . . .'

How different Tara seemed now. At the leaving do she was the centre of attention in an off-the-shoulder number, pearls, hair all brushed up and shiny. Ridiculously overdressed but somehow she could carry it off among all those pristine Novas and Vectras. No one minded. She had such confidence. That was the thing about her. You couldn't wear things like that without a couldn't-care-less deportment, swanning and lording it about the place like she did, yet somehow remaining utterly charming. The Tara I saw before me now was very different. There was no resemblance with the pale creature in the bed. The swagger had gone. The face itself seemed hollow and fallen. She was clinging to me as though to a shred of wreckage.

'Natasha isn't a healer,' I said, quietly.

'Yes she is, she's told me about it.'

'They were just coincidences. Good luck.'

'Coincidence is only another name for it. Why were there coincidences? Why did they happen at that moment?'

'Don't you think . . .'

'What?'

'I mean, to bring Natasha here – she would have to know everything.'

'What does that matter when we're talking about the life of a child?'

'But he's not even three months old.'

'It's still life, Martin. This might be my only chance. You

agreed you would do everything you could to support me. You gave me your word.'

'Yes, and I still mean it. But this isn't support, it's just fantasy land.'

'It would be support for me. You must tell Natasha and bring her here, right now.'

I looked at Tara, unable to know what to say.

'If you don't do this thing for me,' said Tara, 'then it's over between us.'

'But it'll be over between us anyway, if Natasha finds out.'

'If you don't, then I'll phone her now. From my bed, while you're driving home. So what do you want, Martin? Are you going to tell her or shall I?'

THE sheep were back in the fields by the time I drove back through the village. They were still awake, and watching me through the fence. White faces, extraordinarily clean in the moonlight.

I drove up to the house, freewheeling the last few yards to be as quiet as possible, crept indoors and up the stairs. Natasha was still asleep. I couldn't quite believe it. I had half expected her to have been woken by Tara telephoning from the hospital after all. I looked at her as she lay in bed trying to think of what ways she was different from Tara. She was still beautiful, especially since she'd had her teeth done. She was worried that they looked too perfect. Too white. But I thought they were great. Tara had called her an archetypal car dealer's wife, by which she meant, I suppose, blonde and busty and high maintenance. But Tara herself had been married to a car dealer. In some ways they were very similar. And now I faced the prospect of losing both of them and the baby into the bargain.

I took a shower, put on my dressing gown and spent some

time in my study, trying to think. There was no way I could afford to lose Natasha. And then I thought of Tara alone in the hospital, and that little beating heart alone in the womb, and me alone in my study looking at the shut-down computer.

Then Natasha appeared in the doorway, bleary and heavy with sleep. She leaned against the door frame while I switched on the computer. I listened to the hard disk building up to its thousands of revs per minute, then the fan came on with a gush.

'You're up early,' said Natasha.

'Yes,' I replied, in a tone that might as well have said 'What of it?'

Natasha shrugged and went off to have a shower.

'Natasha!' I suddenly called, not quite knowing why.

'What?' she replied lazily from the hall.

When I made no reply, she was curious enough to return to my study and look at me quizzically. Perhaps she had noticed something in my voice.

'I was just wondering,' I said, 'you know all that stuff about healing little Alice, and that chap with the brain tumour, Brenda's husband. You didn't really think it was supernatural powers or anything, did you?'

Natasha looked at me, blinking.

'What the fuck are you talking about that now for?'

'Oh, it's just – friend of a friend of a friend at work died of bowel cancer the other week. It's been preying on my mind, that perhaps I should have sent you round to see if you could work your magic on him.'

Natasha gave a baffled laugh.

'But you're the last person to believe any of that stuff.'

'I know but, if there's no option, perhaps you'll try anything. So if I'd have asked you, would you have gone round?'

'Maybe. Couldn't have done any harm.'

Natasha, who'd been lingering in the doorway, came further into the room.

'There's someone else, isn't there?'

'What?'

'Someone else who's ill. You're thinking of asking me to heal someone but you're too embarrassed to admit I might have powers.'

'Yes,' I said. I hadn't thought to say this at all. I didn't know what was happening. I had come home to forget about the whole episode in the hospital.

'Who is it?'

'A friend of a friend again.' I had found a way of talking about it. 'You met her once, at a leaving party. You told her about your healing abilities and she just phoned me to ask if you can help. She's pregnant and she's very close to miscarrying. She thought you might be able to save it.'

Natasha's eyes filled with tears as I spoke, evidence of that baffling woman-to-woman empathy I had occasionally witnessed in her.

'The poor girl,' she said. 'Of course I want to help. But it's only happened twice, she knows that, doesn't she? I can't guarantee anything.'

So Natasha agreed to heal Tara. I would drive her over to the hospital as soon as she was dressed. I thought, if I played it as carefully as possible, if Tara and I were on our best behaviour, we might just get away with it. We might just get through this whole grim process intact.

I felt wonderful. Truly, truly, wonderful. I sat before my computer and typed 'Pangaea' into the search engine. In a few seconds I was looking at a map of the primeval supercontinent, the original land mass. In the map I was looking at, the present-day continents nuzzled up against each other; North and South America, Africa, Europe, Asia – all tessellated together with hardly any space between. Like Tara's scan. The tightly fitting land masses with nothing between them.

I read on a little. The continents had started to drift apart over two hundred and twenty-five million years ago. First they'd broken into two halves – Gondwanaland and Laurasia – and then these had broken down even further. India was once an island, but had shunted into the underbelly of Asia and thrust up the Himalayas. Huge oceans had opened up between the other land masses. North and South America had somehow become joined by an umbilicus, the Isthmus of Panama. You could see, where one land mass had broken away from another, how the debris of that separation had left a trail of islands, like those that separate Sri Lanka from India, or Australia from South-East Asia. The Map of the World as we see it today is a shattered, fractured, ruined, chaotic thing. Pangaea, by comparison, was one pure and uninterrupted stretch of land. Simple. Uncomplicated. Undamaged.

As I read on I came across a theory that intrigued me. Some geologists, it seems, are wondering where the continents are heading next. Will they just go drifting on and on? Will South America simply get further and further away from Africa? Apparently so. But not for ever. One day it's going to go right round the back and crash into Africa again. And eventually all the continents will meet up on the other side of the world and form one big supercontinent again. Pangaea II, some people call it. Or Pangaea Ultima. All the splintered fragments of the original Pangaea crashing together again to form just a single place. I liked that whole idea. I found it strangely comforting.

Then Natasha called me from the hallway. She was ready.

Strawberries

Dr Newman, disgraced after an affair with a first-year undergraduate (the absurd details of which provided weeks of amusement for his colleagues when they were meticulously recounted in court), seemed to find no humiliation in taking employment at the same university in which he'd once lectured on Industrial Economics, this time as a kitchen porter.

Among the staff of the subterranean kitchens, he was regarded with indifference. To his surprise they didn't even know who he was. But then, the reverse was true. For fifteen years he had taken his meals in the third-floor refectory, the food delivered to his table by an acned teenager, usually, in the ill-fitting uniform of the university caterers, but he'd had no idea (not that the question had ever much bothered him) where the food had come from.

Well, now he knew. Four floors down from the staff refectory, in the vast below-ground kitchens, gloomy with cracked tiles and wobbly stainless-steel prep tables, where half a dozen ovens blazed all morning with roasts, and rice was boiled hourly in simmering tureens, where everything seemed to be made for giants (sieves the size of tennis rackets, ladles as big as buckets), where a tinny tannoy shrieked continually with such amplification it made a shy waitress on the first floor asking for more chicken drumsticks sound like the voice of a tyrant god: this was where it had come from. And now he knew how all those beef Wellingtons and salmon terrines had been made: by an angry, ladle-banging, racist, ex-army Welshman, it seemed, who loved to shout accounts of his weekend thuggery across the kitchens while he cooked (and yet the food, when it had arrived at Dr Newman's table, he remembered, had always seemed so tepid, so soft-edged and limp).

He worried at first how he would fit in, in the kitchens, and wondered if he should adapt his manner and tone of voice so that he wouldn't stand out. He tried toning down what one supervisor had called his 'hi-tech language', and even had a go at swearing. But whereas the cooks' and pot-washers' expletives went almost unnoticed, his 'fucks' and 'shits' drew looks of astonishment from those who used such words routinely. And he once (only once) tried mimicking the porter he was replacing by jibing at a colleague for taking a cigarette break in the loading bay – 'Get on and do some work now, you lazy sod.' When Ernie had said that, it had drawn a jeeringly good-natured response, but when Dr Newman tried it, using exactly the same words and tone of voice, there came that look of shocked astonishment again. And later, at his locker, putting his overalls away, he overheard the porter muttering to a friend, 'Did you hear what he said to me, said I wasn't doing any work. Who does he think he is?'

Dr Newman didn't need to worry about fitting in, because there wasn't really anything to fit into. Beyond the yelling of cooks and the banging of saucepans, the wailing of the tannoy and the hollering of delivery men, there seemed to be no real community in the kitchens. People wiped grease out of the runnels, or stirred their vats of pasta with spoons from the giants' table, but mostly they kept to themselves. An anecdote might suddenly burst forth from one of them, or the recounting of something seen on TV. There was a cutter-up who loved to talk about football, and assumed everyone shared his interest, and there was an old crone of a pot-washer who'd tell him, in a heavy Irish accent, that he was a 'darling boy', but there were no conversations. After a lifetime in academia, with its endlessly competitive discourse, whose jabbering sophistry would penetrate, sometimes, even into his remotest dreams, Dr Newman found this something of a relief.

Ernie, the porter he replaced, had taught him everything he needed to know in a single day, though Dr Newman had to shadow him for a week. Ernie had an 'office', a dank space furnished with rat traps behind the lift. There was a chair and a desk, but no phone. It had a broom, and some big, bulging, half-torn cardboard boxes stuffed with things nobody wanted – leaflets advertising giveaway offers long past their closing dates; a nest of plastic teaspoons, redundant since the new catering manager had insisted on metal cutlery. There was also a pile of junk Ernie had salvaged from the skips, most of which seemed to have nothing to do with food. A battered old video player. Brackets. Piping. Sheets of Perspex. Coils of cable. Ernie had pointed out the video player. 'I can take the motor out of that, use it to power one of my merry-go-rounds.'

Ernie was a model-maker in his spare time, fashioning little carousels out of odds and ends for the entertainment of his grandchildren. Dr Newman doubted that these models were up to much, or that Ernie's grandchildren were particularly impressed by them. He just didn't strike Dr Newman as a craftsman, of even the most basic kind. And from what Ernie had told him about his family, how he'd ditched his children when they were young, and how they all subsequently embarked on lives of crime, abandoning their own children to what looked like a similar fate, he didn't think the kids would be likely to care much for rotating pageantry, not when they had cars to steal, and housing estates to wreck.

In a week Dr Newman learned far more about Ernie than he wanted to know. About how his mother had rejected him in favour of his brothers: 'She'd never say anything nice to the kids, but was all over my brothers' kids. "Why don't you ever visit us?" I said. She said she couldn't afford the bus fare. It costs 10p for pensioners. She said she didn't write because she couldn't afford the stamp. So I went round there and I gave her a fucking stamp and fucking 10p. Still nothing. So I said, "This is the last time you'll fucking see me. If you drop dead tomorrow I won't walk behind your funeral."' And he didn't when she did die, shortly afterwards. 'After all I done for her, fixed her fucking washing machine, her Hoover . . .' Ernie punctuated these remarks with toothless grins and a hopeless shaking of the head. Dr Newman wasn't sure how to respond, but decided shaking his own head was probably the safest bet. He wasn't sure about the grinning.

Ernie seemed to have spent his career among the detritus of modern life, repairing washing machines ('until they went fucking computerised'), scouring salvage yards and rubbish tips for scraps. He had spent most of his early working years on the fairgrounds, and the itinerant, casual nature of that trade seemed to have marked his whole life. He was continually pestered by ex-wives, in-laws and his eight children, one of whom had only been out of prison for two weeks. He spent his evenings at home in his council house in front of the telly with headphones on and curtains drawn. He could hear people knocking on the door and banging on the windows but he ignored them. He just wanted a quiet life now, he said. He'd never been to prison but he'd been hounded by the police all his life. He was once done for pushing a pram without headlights. The magistrates told the police off for wasting their time. There was this one particular policeman who had it in for Ernie and would come up with these ridiculous charges. They'd played cat and mouse like this for thirty years. 'He's never caught me. I'm too fly.' Later the policeman chased Ernie's children instead, arrested one of them on the trumped-up charge of attempted theft of a car, when the car in question was an old wreck with no wheels and no engine. When his son was in court Ernie spoke up for him. 'I said, "Madam, the law is an ass! The car's got no fucking engine." He was done though. Got two months in borstal.'

The policeman was retired now, but they carried on their games of petty vengeance. 'I send the lads round to slash his tyres every now and then. He tries to get the new lot to come round and bother me, but he doesn't hold the sway he once had. He's just an old man now, like me, growing rhubarb. (Not that I grow anything, apart from old.)'

That toothless grin again, the wag of the head, as though he was speaking for Dr Newman as well, as though we all end up like Ernie, under siege in a council house, making merry-go-rounds out of old soup tins. But Ernie could see Dr Newman was different.

'I don't suppose you've had many brushes with the law, eh? Just a speeding ticket now and then?'

Dr Newman shook his head.

'I don't drive.'

That took the grin off Ernie's face. That was a real shock.

IT turned out that the bangings on the doors and windows that Ernie tried to shut out with his headphones every night were not the persistent badgerings of his children and ex-wives, but local estate youths who had decided to pick on Ernie for sport. A scaffolding pole through his front window was the last straw. Had Ernie been sitting in his usual chair it would have gone right through his chest. The thought so shocked Dr Newman that he felt an embarrassing urge to reach out and offer Ernie a comforting pat on the arm when he told him about it. It was his last day before Dr Newman took over, and he didn't have a home to go to.

Ernie didn't seem that bothered. The old fairground roustabout was used to kipping down wherever he could. He was going to sleep at the railway station for the weekend, then get social services to sort things out for him on Monday. He was entitled to a flat, he told Dr Newman. That was how Ernie put it: 'I'm entitled.'

And so Dr Newman was left in charge of the kitchen rubbish. The waste disposal. A kitchen and four restaurants generated enough trash to keep him busy nearly all day. By the time he'd done one round, starting on the top floor and finishing in the kitchen itself, dumping the rubbish into a wheelie bin, to be taken down in the service lift with its bell and its trellis doors, and pushing the wheelie bin all the way down the long, narrow corridor that led to the loading bay with its dumpers, compactor and skip, it was almost time to start again. Then there was the swill to deal with. A couple of men turned up once a week in an unmarked van to take that, slopping the tall blue bins of swill into their vats in the back of the van, a task they performed with a certain air of discretion: rather like undertakers, they were careful not to let anyone see the matter they dealt with.

A day could pass quickly in this way. There was little time to ponder and dwell on things, though occasionally Dr Newman would pause in the kitchen longer than he needed to as he taped up the neck of a black bag, his attention caught by beef Wellingtons taking shape on a table, the angry Welsh chef clattering and banging about as he prepared them plate by plate. In a few minutes they would go over to the dumb waiter to be sent up to the third floor, and there his former colleagues would devour them while talking their usual talk – the funding crisis in higher education, the state of British car manufacturing, the best time of year to plant rhubarb. He wondered if they still sniggered over the details of their former colleague's court case. How they must have pored over the newspaper reports, they who couldn't between them muster a single witness to speak for his good character.

The plaintiff claimed that Dr Newman had placed his hand on her left buttock. Mr Turner (prosecuting) asked her how long Dr Newman's hand had remained on her buttock. 'About ten seconds,' the plaintiff replied. 'And during that time,' Mr Turner went on, 'did Dr Newman's hand remain still, or did it move?' 'It moved,' the plaintiff replied. When asked what sort of movement, the plaintiff said that Dr Newman had squeezed her buttock. 'And so this movement in no way could be described as what we have come to know as "an affectionate and playful pat"? The plaintiff said that she did not think the movement could be described that way.

Not quite the hero, Dr Newman had to concede. Having begun the trial quite certain of his acquittal, instead he found his reputation shorn and shredded. The case had always been likely to turn on the personalities of the defendant and the plaintiff, but even so Dr Newman had not expected it to get quite so personal. 'I ask you,' the prosecuting lawyer had said to the jury at one point, 'are we seriously expected to believe that a young woman of twenty-four is likely to choose as the object of her sexual attentions a sixty-year-old, pipe-smoking man with a ginger beard?' Dr Newman had looked desperately at his own lawyer for an objection, but even he seemed to think a fair point had been made. So the law was expected to turn on the aesthetic value of facial hair? It got worse.

The plaintiff was asked if the use of an armlock was an over-reaction to Dr Newman's buttock-squeeze. She replied that it was after the buttock-squeeze, when Dr Newman had tried to kiss her, that she used the armlock. When asked why, the plaintiff had said that she was frightened. They were alone in his office, he had made an advance at her and was trying to kiss her neck. She felt trapped in a corner of the office. Her only option was to use force. She employed techniques recently learned at self-defence classes. 'Did Dr Newman say anything during this struggle?' Mr Turner asked. The plaintiff replied that Dr Newman had said 'something like, "Please let go of my head, I can't breathe," but it was difficult to make out the exact words . . .'

Some of the tabloids had provided crude artists' impressions, both of the court case and of the events under examination. The discrepancies in representation had been revealing. In the courtroom scenes he was pastelled in as a sallow, sagging figure hunched in the dock, while in the depictions of his alleged crime he was vigorously crayoned as a towering, pointy-bearded demon, fingers outstretched (they may as well have had talons on the end), groping for the frightened female figure that shrank before him. She, of course, remained dignified and chaste throughout the whole proceedings. How hard it would have been for the jury to see the flirtatious woman he'd known, who talked all through her tutorials about the feebleness of her boyfriends while asking him if he liked her new top. A mature student, twenty-four years old: old enough to be married with children, yet suddenly to everyone, it seemed, as frail and as vulnerable as a child. It was when he saw himself the subject of a crude satirical sketch on television one night that he knew his career would never survive.

His only character testimony had come from his psychiatrist. Dr Newman had been seeing a psychiatrist since his suicide attempt four years ago. The case had all gone horribly wrong. The psychiatrist's testimony was seen as a crude attempt to elicit sympathy and excuse his actions. He should never have mentioned the death of his daughter, Megan, who fell victim to a voracious streptococcal virus at the age of four. Yes, the event had shaken him to the depths of his being, and his own wife's departure shortly afterwards hardly helped. Yes, it had driven him to make an attempt on his own life, spending three hours on the parapet of the suspension bridge hanging on to the supports in a freezing breeze while a terrified policeman told him not to think about the future, not to think about the past, just to think about the now. But he had never wanted to be thought of as weak. Not weak.

Megan had died like a house dies – the organs and systems failing one by one, like the lights being turned off in all the rooms. In the end she was just a crackle of electrical activity in the nervous system, until that, too, was shut down.

Now he relished the physical work of the kitchens. At sixty years old, he was lean and supple, apart from an occasional stiffness in his Achilles tendons, which was surprising considering how little exercise he'd taken in his life. For the most part, the hardest physical exertion he'd experienced previously was standing up for an hour while lecturing on the movement of industrial capital. Upstairs, on the third floor, the professors sat at their usual tables growing fat on beef en croute with buttered asparagus and glasses of claret.

'To kill or not to kill?' These were the words, spoken with a mock-humble, questioning lilt, the man from Rentokil used to introduce himself when he appeared at the office door one day. Dr Newman was having a rare sit-down and felt a little embarrassed, as though he'd been caught skiving. One of Ernie's duties, it seemed, had been to spend an hour or two gossiping with this man, following him around while he inspected and replaced (if necessary) all the rat traps in the establishment, and he was clearly expected to do the same. Dr Newman obliged, as far as he could without letting the bins go unemptied for too long. He was fascinated by the tour of the traps he was given, and by the Rentokil man's odd and faintly charming disposition. The traps themselves, white plastic tubes containing small but high concentrations of alluring poison, could only be picked up using a metal rod with a small hook on the end. With this, the man would examine the traps one by one, taking a quick peep inside to see if they housed any corpses, then a quick sniff to see if the chemicals were still active, then putting them down again.

'Do they ever catch anything?' Dr Newman asked.

'Oh yes. When we first took over the contract, these traps would fill up every week. But I haven't seen a mouse down here for three years now. We call them rat traps but they're for mice really. Rats need something a bit more heavy-duty.' The man gave Dr Newman a faintly horrified look – a look that said: Now you know the terrible kind of life I lead, but I love it really.

'And how do they work – poison, is it?'

The man spoke as someone never before asked this question, a surprise that knocked the certainty out of his answer.

'Yes. I suppose it's just a bit of poison. That's what it is. But the mice love it.'

The traps were in all sorts of hidden-away places. Dr Newman and the Rentokil man would get down on all fours and peer under storage units. Then the man would reach in with his hook and pull out another empty trap. There were even traps in the lift void at the bottom of the shaft, reached with difficulty down a set of dusty rungs. And there were traps in the serveries upstairs. There must have been thirty or more traps in total (Dr Newman lost count), all of them empty.

'Have you had your health and safety training thing yet?' the man asked as Dr Newman followed him out to his little van which was parked in the loading bay.

'No,' said Dr Newman, 'not yet.'

'Well, when you do,' said the man pushing his hands into the small of his back, as if the better, so Dr Newman thought, to display his pot belly, 'they'll tell you not to touch the traps. That's my job. In a food establishment you leave the rat traps to the professionals. If you got any of that stuff on your hands, just a smear of it, and it got on to the food, you could have a crisis here. So be warned. Here. Do you want a dog?'

'A dog?'

'Yeah. I got six dogs, the council's just told me to get rid of them. Neighbours complaining about the noise, RSPCA saying I don't look after them properly. I do, it's just that I haven't got a decent garden and I haven't got time to take them out for walks. The council will put them down if I can't find homes for them. Interested?'

'Not really,' said Dr Newman. The Rentokil man shrugged, as though he'd always thought it a long shot, and got into his van. Dr Newman noticed two books lying on the passenger seat. *The Encyclopedia of Patience*, and *Who's Who in Shakespeare.*

OUT of the blue Dr Newman's wife would phone, usually very late at night, just as he was getting his head clear, with the help of a few shots of single malt, of the clangings and pointless hollerings of the kitchens.

'Hello, it's me. I've just found something with six legs and a pointed sort of nose crawling up my bedroom wall. What do you think I should do?'

'Come back and live with me.'

'You know I can't do that, dear.'

'Have you got someone else?'

'No, I haven't.'

'Then why don't you come back?'

'Because I just can't. It just wouldn't be right.'

'It's because you've got someone, isn't it?'

'Don't you think if I had someone they'd be dealing with the six-legged thing with the long nose? Why do you think I'm calling you?'

'Is that all you think of me? Something to deal with insects?'

'OK, I suppose I'll just have to deal with it myself . . .'

'No, don't, I didn't mean –'

But she would hang up. Dr Newman knew there was no point in phoning back. It would be off the hook.

They had already been separated for four years by the time of the trial. Halfway through the court case he was at home one evening when he got a phone call. It was a woman's voice and said just two words, 'You beast!', before hanging up. Dr Newman never knew who the call came from: it was too brief, and the voice too full of anger to be easily recognisable. But he wondered if it had been his wife. He didn't ask her, and she'd never given any clue that it could have been; in her calls since, she'd seemed perfectly amiable, if remote. But it was just the sort of phrase she would use, and there weren't many other women who knew his home phone number.

DR Newman picked up one of the rat traps in his office and examined it. A square tube of white plastic, open at one end, closed at the other. The closed end came away, and Dr Newman could see that there was a wad of material inside. The seat of the poison. A soaked pad of cotton, felt, or some other absorbent substance. It was damp enough for beads of liquid to appear when he pressed it with the tip of his finger. Little droplets of poison, so powerful that a mouse would die instantly on sniffing it. That was why there was no door on the open end of the traps. There didn't need to be. Once a mouse went in, it wouldn't be coming out again. Dr Newman brought his dampened finger to his own nose, and sniffed, tentatively. He could smell only the faintest hint of something fruity and sweet. He thought about tasting it. Decided not to. Instead he went out into the kitchen and washed his hands at one of the wall-mounted sanitisers that were posted at all the entry points into the kitchens, and were supposed to be used by everyone when they came in, but weren't.

THEN the strawberries arrived. Dr Newman had been working in the kitchens for about three months. In this time he had settled into a grinding routine of manual work, of lifting and wheeling, throwing and emptying. His understanding of the geography of the kitchens and the four restaurants they served had become so detailed that, had they been destroyed in some freak cataclysm, he could have reconstructed them perfectly from memory. He journeyed back and forth through this landscape along such clearly defined routes, he was almost surprised he hadn't worn footprints into the stone floors. He chatted occasionally with workmates. Unquestioningly they recognised him as an educated man, and he was often called upon to settle disputes over trivial matters of fact, answer tricky clues in quick crosswords, or help fill in a prepper's word-search. When one of the supermarkets started giving away scratchcards with general knowledge questions, there was an almost constant queue of hopeless cooks at his office door, wanting to know the capital of Kazakhstan or Michelangelo's second name.

But most of the time, he carried out his work with such energy and at such a pace, building up a sweat as he hoisted black sacks from their bins, wrenching open the lift doors and pulling out the rumbling barrow, hurtling through the kitchens so that tray-carrying cooks had to hop out of his way, that people could not keep up with him enough to engage in conversation.

Sometimes he would be caught in the loading bay where a hapless delivery driver might be wandering, lost with a pink invoice in his hand, looking for someone to sign it (Dr Newman usually did, whatever it was), and he might find himself lumbered with a pallet-full of napkins, or paper cups, or five-gallon drums of vegetable oil to wheel away somewhere. And that was how he first came across the strawberries.

They were delivered by two muscly, brutish men with pregnant bellies and old-style tattoos on their forearms (pierced hearts gone out of focus with age). They handled the strawberries with great care, carrying the punnets in their hairy hands as though they were lifting babies out of their cots, and placing them gently into a high-sided cage.

Fifty punnets of strawberries. Dr Newman signed the delivery note and the men waddled back to their lorry with a curious air of shamefulness about them, almost as though they had stolen something.

There was something different about the day, Dr Newman could tell. The delivery of strawberries itself was unusual, but other food he saw in the kitchens surprised him. The ovens were roasting more than their usual number of chickens. There were sides of beef on a slow heat, crown roasts, racks of lamb. Commis chefs and sous-chefs worked in silent concentration. The angry Welsh cook had become patient and thoughtful.

In one of the storerooms, he came across Kay, the catering manager, clipping the stems from big bunches of decorative foliage and fiddling with corkscrews of driftwood. Evergreen leaves were scattered around her on the floor. It shocked Dr Newman to find Kay engaged in as delicate and sensistive a pastime as flower arranging. He'd always thought of her as a rather savage woman before. She was enormous in stature, morbidly obese, and she lumbered about the kitchens with a menacing deportment, so that the ground seemed to shake beneath her. Moreover, flower arranging seemed to give her no pleasure. She frowned over her sprays of thrift and honesty, as one might over a fiendish oriental puzzle, her heavy brow sweating, as it nearly always did, and she muttered to herself impatiently. She gave no sign that she was gratified by Dr Newman's interest, and even seemed a little suspicious of it.

'What's it to you?' she said, only half jokingly, when he asked her about it.

'I just never knew you did flower arrangements . . .'

'It's me hobby . . .' she said without looking up from some

stalks she'd just scissored through, adding, in a grumbly undertone, '. . . or one of them.'

As though she thought he should know that she was a woman with more than one hobby.

'Is it a special occasion?'

Kay looked at him as though he was making a poor joke. She poked a sprig of laurel into an oasis.

'These have got to be in the hall in half an hour's time.'

Dr Newman left the cage of strawberries outside the chef's office and went on with his work. But the strawberries punctuated the rest of his morning, dazzling him from unexpected corners of the kitchen. Later, rounding a prep table, he came across an unusually touching scene: the angry Welsh chef and two others, all in their whites, busily engaged in the laborious task of destalking the fruit. They were performing the task with the quiet devotion of bomb disposal experts, each strawberry yielding its green fuse to their expert touch. A heap of spent stalks filled one of the punnets, and looked pathetic. Then, still later, wheeling his barrow out of the lift, the strawberries again surprised him, filling a huge stainless-steel colander, almost as big as a bath. They were so brilliantly red, astonishingly red in those gloomy kitchens, it was as though they had jumped out at him from behind a pillar to shout 'We Are Here!' And they were on their own. Plucked and rinsed, they were waiting for the next stage of their journey through the kitchens. He felt rather protective of them. He felt like turning to the cooks and saying, 'So you're just going to leave them, are you? All on their own?' He had, after all, been present at their arrival. He had been the first to handle them.

But the kitchens were emptying now. Lunch was over, and the staff had drifted off having finished their morning shifts. It was the usual early-afternoon lull before the evening shifts began. Soon there were just two or three people left in the kitchens. A pot-washer was lifting the last few crates of crockery off the runners. Someone in a far corner was whistling.

Dr Newman returned to his office, slumped into the dusty armchair that Ernie had salvaged from one of the skips, and picked up his bottle of poison. It had taken him a long time to accumulate, squeezing the few drops out of each rat trap in turn. His harvest hardly amounted to more than a teaspoonful, but it half filled the tiny scent bottle he'd found one day near one of the bins. He held the bottle so that it formed a vertical between his thumb and index finger. The liquid danced in its tiny glass space. He held it close to his eyes so that he could examine it. Almost colourless. Perhaps the faintest tinge of yellow, like watered-down Chardonnay. There was no more poison to steal. Not until the traps were changed. Dr Newman unscrewed the tight black stopper and sniffed at the open neck. Something sweet. Almonds.

There was a crash and a female scream from the kitchens. Something metal had been dropped. Such accidents were usually greeted by groaning, ironic cheers, but the kitchens were so empty that the crash and squeal simply expanded into an all-surrounding sea of indifference. Dr Newman quickly stoppered the bottle and put it away, then left the office. He saw immediately what had happened. There on the floor, not twenty feet away, a prep girl in a white overall and white cap was kneeling beside the tray she had dropped. The tray had evidently been loaded with strawberry tarts, for these were scattered across the tiles beside her. It looked like the scene of a violent crime. Red was smeared across the floor in big, luscious stains. In her confusion, the girl had stepped in some of the tarts she had spilt, and red matter clung to her shoes, and stained her white overall. As Dr Newman neared, watching the girl as she desperately tried to decide what to do – whether to rescue some of the less damaged tarts, how to clean up the mess – he saw that she was crying.

He had noticed this girl many times, but he had hardly spoken to her. She was always busy at her table – chopping, slicing and peeling things. She walked with a fast-paced purposefulness that had occasionally brought her into near-collision with Dr Newman's barrow. But she had always smiled at him when they passed each other, and he had found himself valuing that smile very much. One of the things he had first noticed about the kitchens was that it was a place where smiles were rarely given, and rarely returned. They were associated with the false values and hypocrisies of management, or the frozen, switch-on-switch-off smile of public relations. Managers and PR people smiled. Not cooks and porters.

Looking across to the other table, Dr Newman could see an array of strawberry tarts set out, a glossy regiment. There must have been hundreds.

'Two hundred strawberry tarts,' the girl said, still crouching down. 'I'm supposed to do them by three o'clock and I'm on my own.'

By now, Dr Newman had had his health and safety training. He recalled that any spillages had to be cleared away before further cooking or food preparation could take place. The girl would have to spend several minutes scooping away the wounded tarts, searching for a mop and bucket, wiping up every last smear of juice, arranging the 'Caution – Slippery Surface!' signs.

As Dr Newman knelt down beside the girl, sweet in her whites, her dark hair folded away into a net at the back of her hat, he couldn't help picturing that artist's impression the tabloid newspaper had thought it necessary to publish. Him with his goat-beard and talons bearing down upon a frightened, fragile female. It made him hesitate. He didn't want to frighten her. But he felt compelled to help.

He picked up the tray for her.

'You take these back and I'll clear up this mess. You carry on with your tarts.'

It wasn't his job. He wasn't a cleaner. But it was a favour. The girl gave him a grateful smile through tear-stained eyes.

'They've called me in specially to do this. It's my day off. And then they just leave me to it.'

Dr Newman found a mop and bucket and began wiping out the strawberry mess. A few yards away the girl worked silently. Dr Newman moved the mop gently back and forth. The stain gradually disappeared. Glancing down the corridor, he saw Kay lumbering off with wilted flowers in her hands. When he'd finished (the 'Slippery Surface' sign in place with its pictogram of a figure falling backwards), he lingered about for a while, watching the girl. Her long table was crowded with materials – pastry cases, strawberries, buckets of custard, and a substance he'd seen used before, Merjel, for glazing the tarts. She was standing there, head down, intently working these materials, but at such a speed things were getting spilt, or dropped. On an impulse, he went over.

'Do you need a hand?'

The girl looked up at him. Dr Newman instantly regretted his move. The eyes showed shock, dismay, as much as if he'd asked her to marry him. But then it had been something of an outrageous suggestion. He'd already noticed how rigidly the kitchen staff kept to their own patch. For the non-food handlers – the washers-up, cleaners and porters – an even bigger boundary was in place. But there was no one else around.

This girl (Kirsty, her name badge said, which Dr Newman was now close enough to read) was on her own. Two hundred tarts to make by three o'clock. She was running out of time. Somewhere upstairs people were getting hungry for strawberries. Two hundred people.

'You'll need to do your hands,' she said, nodding towards the hand sanitiser on the wall nearby. She said the words carefully, delicately, for fear of offending Dr Newman and losing his offer of help. Obediently he went over to the machine and washed his hands, smearing them with the cold grease that it dispensed. Walking back to the table, still wringing his hands, which now felt clumsily slippery, he listened to Kirsty's quick, hushed instructions. She showed him to the plastic tub that was filled with the ready-made custard, a yellow gloopy mess, like impossibly thick emulsion paint. She told him to spoon a little of this substance into each of the pastry cases. She supervised him as he did the first few. It wasn't easy with his slippery hands, which were shaking slightly. The custard was thick and sticky. He wasn't sure how to get it off the spoon and into the cases. If left to himself he would have used his fingers but realised this wouldn't do. He tried shaking it off the spoon into the case but this was unreliable. Some custard splattered on to the table. Kirsty showed him how to use a second spoon to ease the custard into the case.

'Very good, but that's too much,' she said of his first attempt. His next had too little. Eventually he found a median amount, and fell into a rhythmic filling of cases, which Kirsty would take, building little tumuli of strawberries on his firm custard foundations and then glazing them with Merjel.

'This must be a special day,' said Dr Newman, after they had been working together silently for ten minutes.

'Graduation,' said Kirsty, quietly. 'That's why there's no one here. Everyone's helping out upstairs.'

Dr Newman carried a tray of finished tarts over to the dumb waiter. A miniature lift without doors. He pressed a button (which automatically rang a bell on the destination floor), and watched his strawberries ascend into the darkness.

Graduation. It had never crossed his mind. Normally he would be in his gown, walking solemnly to Handel as part of the academic procession. Congratulations and handshakes, photographs, formal and informal, meetings with parents dressed up as if for a wedding. His colleagues would be there now, about to sit down to the great banquet in the main refectory, which would be blue-carpeted and bedecked with grand flower arrangements (though they would never have seen them in preparation, as he had), with strawberry tarts to arrive for the final course.

He rushed back to the table, joining Kirsty, and they worked side by side. She gave him a little, grateful glance every now and then.

As they worked Dr Newman found himself thinking about Megan again. He remembered the first time she ever saw an apple. She thought it was something fantastic. Shiny, red and round, like a ball, but sweet-smelling. She played with the apple as though it was a toy. To show her what to do with it, Dr Newman had taken a bite out of his own apple. Megan copied, but had got it very wrong, trying to eat the stalk first. Dr Newman had demonstrated how to take a bite from the side. And she eagerly attempted, opening her little mouth, with its tiny teeth, as wide as she could, so wide that her eyes were pulled downwards, giving her a sad expression. But then she triumphantly bit, and showed her father the proof – an apple with a tiny scar of white in its skin.

* * *

AN hour later, the strawberry tarts finished and Kirsty gone, Dr Newman put away his overalls and clocked off. The evening shift was shuffling in. The deep-fat fryers were heating up for fish and chips. As he made his way upstairs and out through the main entrance, he found himself in a forest of families. The new graduates and their parents jostled about on the pavement, photographing each other with little silver cameras – proud, bearded dads with their arms around their robed daughters' shoulders; weepy mums in modest jewellery; embarrassed and slightly jealous brothers and sisters. They filled the pavement and the closed road beside it. And Dr Newman had to weave in and out of them, being photographed in the background of countless proud moments. He felt like turning and running back to the kitchens. But then he smelt something sweet. A wafting drift of perfume from somewhere. And he remembered the strawberries, and how they had so recently been digested by these people that they still came on their breath. Or perhaps it was the scent of the fruit still on his hands, though he'd touched very few strawberries. When he smelt his fingertips they smelt sweet. Sanitised.

Paradise

THE ant colony hadn't been a success.

'They're all dead,' said Matthew in a flat little voice.

'No,' said his mother, 'I can see one moving. There's one that's still alive.'

ANT World had been a Christmas present from Matthew's grandparents. It was a little plastic kit which, when assembled, sandwiched layers of soil and sand between two Perspex sheets, so that the tunnelling activities of ants could be observed. Of course, they had to wait until the summer before some ants could be found to put into Ant World, but as soon as the ant season started, Matthew had been out in the garden, catching them and putting them into his formicarium (a word he brandished at every opportunity). It had been a fraught task, finding and catching the ants. The eye-dropper device provided with the kit was useless. In the end Matthew resorted to picking up the ants between finger and thumb. 'You'll squash them,' his mother had protested. But she had to admit that, once they were in Ant World, the ants looked quite intact and undamaged. Matthew had followed the instructions that came with the kit very carefully (he was a good reader for his age). He had been careful to select ants from the same nest 'otherwise they might go to war!' And he had given them a pinhead of apple to eat. That would be enough, so the instructions said, to feed a colony of thirty ants for a week.

But the ants hadn't taken to Ant World. At first they seemed full of energy, excitedly exploring every millimetre of their new home (either that, thought Matthew's mother, or they were desperately looking for a way out). They walked upside down on Ant World's ceiling, or scuttled along the plastic tube that led to the circular observation chamber (with magnifying lens set into the roof), a structure that to the ants must have seemed like the rotunda of a small cathedral. If they met another ant, there would be a brief touching of feelers before both moved on. According to Matthew, they were tasting each other, which was their way of communicating. Chemicals around the mouth parts did more or less the same job as words, he said. (His mother wasn't sure whether to believe him.) But after a while, the ants began to slow down and gather, as though for a very important meeting, on top of their thin layer of soil. If one observed closely (face a few inches from the Perspex) one could see them congregated at one end of the soil, and Matthew's mother was sure that their heads were lowered, hung in despondency, like a gang of unemployed teenagers.

Matthew's mother wondered what else the ants were supposed to do. Matthew said they should be busy making tunnels. That was the point of Ant World: you could see the tunnels they made. The picture on the box showed a network of tunnels like the map of the London Underground. Matthew's ants did have a go at making a tunnel, but it was a bit disappointing. The tunnel went down for about a centimetre, then came back up again, forming a little U-bend. And that was as far as they got.

Matthew went on adding ants. He thought that perhaps the balance of the population wasn't right. There weren't enough of them. There probably needed to be a certain number before the ants could feel like there was a society that needed organising. Too few and they were nothing more than a collection of individuals. Every now and then, Matthew added more, running into the house with an ant between his finger and thumb after a long and patient hunt on the patio. It was difficult to keep count but Matthew thought that he'd got the population of Ant World up to fifty. The pattern was always the same: the new ants would explore their home in a state of frantic excitement, exchanging chemical words with all the other ants, until they, like their predecessors, seemed gradually to relinquish hope, ending up in a corner with all the other ants, motionless, heads hanging down.

Matthew wondered if it was the food. Perhaps the pinhead of apple wasn't enough after all. He put in a bigger piece, more like the size of a pea. But the ants didn't seem hungry.

And then they started dying. The instructions said that ants should live for at least a month in Ant World, and possibly a lot longer. But the ants started dying within days. The instructions said that ants would often carry their dead to a place separate from the colony, like a little cemetery. But the ants in Matthew's colony left their dead where they were – among the living. In this way it was difficult to tell the dead ants from the live ones at first, though after a while the dead ones seemed to shrivel a little bit.

MATTHEW'S mother was going to the supermarket for the usual Saturday-morning shop. Matthew asked her if he could stay at home this time. It was the first time he had asked to stay at home by himself and Matthew's mother was rather surprised. She had to give it a few moments' thought. For one thing, she wasn't sure if, legally, she was allowed to leave Matthew in the house on his own. But then, he was very mature for his age. A very sensible boy. Although, he could seem rather naive. He still believed in the tooth fairy and Father Christmas, for instance, (or it seemed that he did) and she thought he might get frightened if he was all by himself, even in the daytime. She remembered those nights, only a year or so ago, when he'd been unable to sleep and had to come into her bed, which he hadn't done since he was three. It was very soon after his father had moved out. Apart from that, he'd adapted very well to his father's absence.

'Are you sure you'll be all right?' his mother asked.

Matthew was peering closely at Ant World's devastated population.

'Yes,' said Matthew.

It was very tempting. Shopping with Matthew was difficult because he was so interested in all the products on the shelves, even the cleaning things, and was always trying to persuade his mother to buy stuff she didn't want. Without Matthew she could do the shopping in half the time.

'Do you promise to be good?'

'Yes.'

'If there are any phone calls, just ask to take a message.'

'It's all right, I won't answer the phone.'

'No, you'll need to answer the phone in case it's me – if there's an emergency or something – which there won't be, but you never know.'

'Should I answer the door?'

Matthew's mother thought for a moment.

'Not if it's a stranger. Take a look through the window, but don't answer the door unless it's someone you know.'

'What if it's a policeman?'

'Yes, but ask for identification first.'

'Postman?'

'Yes, that's OK.'

'A man in a really smart-looking suit with a clipboard?'

'No. Leave the door if it's someone like that, even if they do look smart.'

'What if it's Dad?'

'Why should it be Dad? You know it's not Dad's day.'

'But what if it is?'

Matthew's mum hesitated again, wondering why Matthew had asked the question. Did he mean anything by it, or was he just playing a game?

'Of course you can answer the door to Dad.'

'But should I let him in?'

'Matthew, Dad won't call round. Now just leave it, or I'll make you come with me to the supermarket.'

Eventually Matthew's mother left to do her shopping. Matthew, she could see, was very excited about the prospect of being on his own in the house. He saw her off the premises, coming all the way down to the front gate, then racing back to the house as soon as she was out on to the street.

She couldn't stop thinking about Matthew alone in the house all the time she was shopping. She wondered what he was doing. What if he got frightened? It could only take an unexpected creak upstairs to set his mind racing. Supposing a door slammed, like they do in nearly empty houses, for no obvious reason? That might trigger all sorts of painful memories for him, and frightening memories too. That led her to thinking about Matthew's father. Supposing he did call round. It was a thousand-to-one chance, but supposing he did. What would he do if he discovered Matthew had been left on his own, at the age of eleven? Had she done something against the law? Would Matthew's father realise this, and perhaps use it against her? There could be all sorts of legal complications.

Matthew's mother raced round the supermarket as these thoughts took hold, bumping her trolley into shelves, clashing with other trolleys. She thought of phoning Matthew to make sure everything was OK, but then she thought of the time she would waste postponing her shopping and looking for a phone. She had been meaning to get a mobile phone for a long time – she needed to overcome the aversion she felt towards the things. They sold mobile phones in the supermarket. Perhaps she could buy one there and then and use it straight away to phone Matthew. She saw a little display of phones in a glass case, like jewels, all shiny and faceted. But then she told herself off for being ridiculous. She got on with the rest of the shopping, calming herself down with deep breathing as she did so, worked her laborious way through the checkout and drove home.

As she pulled up outside the house, she was startled to see two people emerging from the gate on to the street. There had been visitors to the house after all. A middle-aged man and a woman, very smartly dressed; the man was carrying a small leather case, not quite an attaché case, not quite a shoulder bag. Matthew's mother watched them from the car, relieved to see that they were on their way to next door. They were doing something door-to-door, and hadn't called specifically to see her. Matthew, she hoped, had kept to his word and ignored them.

When Matthew's mother entered the house she found Matthew in the living room, sitting quite happily next to Ant World, so absorbed in reading something that he hardly noticed her come in. He got up, though, when she closed the front door.

'Everything all right?' she asked, as she placed her shopping on the kitchen table.

Matthew nodded. He didn't say anything about the smartly dressed visitors.

Silently, he helped her get the rest of the shopping from the car. Once everything was inside, he went back to the living room and carried on reading whatever it was he'd been reading.

Matthew's mother busied herself with the stowing away of her shopping.

'So nothing happened while I was away?' she called to him.

Matthew didn't reply, he was too absorbed in his reading. She had to call again.

'So nothing happened while I was out?'

'No,' said Matthew, distractedly.

'No phone calls? No one knocking?'

'No. Apart from two people.'

'Oh?'

'But I didn't answer the door.'

Strangely, Matthew's mother felt disappointed. She would have liked to know what that smartly dressed couple were selling.

'I hid at the end of the hall. They didn't see me.'

'Good boy.'

'They put something through the door and went away.'

'What was it?'

'I'm reading it now.'

Matthew's mother paused in her sorting of the shopping and leaned her head through the kitchen door so that she could see Matthew in the living room. He was sitting next to Ant World, just as he had been when she arrived. In his hands was a small leaflet.

She walked over so that she could read what was written on the front.

There was a picture of two black people sitting in a meadow. In front of them was an array of fruit and vegetables (mostly pumpkins) and behind them was an enormous moose, or elk, or something with antlers. In the distance, a white woman with blonde hair was riding a grey horse. In the further distance were a log cabin, pine trees and snowy-peaked mountains. The black people were dressed in smart casual clothes and were smiling broadly. Across the top of this picture the caption proclaimed in big black letters:

All Suffering
SOON TO END!

'They left this little leaflet,' said Matthew. 'Do you like the picture?'

'Hmm,' said Matthew's mother, not wanting to commit herself.

'It's pretty,' said Matthew.

He spent a good two hours reading the leaflet. While Matthew's mother continued working in the kitchen, putting the washing machine on, getting lunch ready, washing up, Matthew studied the small print. Every now and then he would read something aloud to her, shouting it from the living room so that he could be heard over the noise of the washing machine.

'The wicked ones will be no more . . . but the meek ones themselves will possess the earth.'

'What's that, Matthew?'

'It says here, "The wicked ones will be no more . . . but the meek ones themselves will possess the earth." What does that mean, Mum?'

'I'm not sure, Matthew. Now, I want to do the hoovering in here, you'll have to move.'

Matthew shifted a little as his mother brought over the Hoover and plugged it in.

'"The righteous will possess the earth and they will reside for ever upon it."'

'Could you lift your feet up?'

A little while later, Matthew's mother came in to dust the living room.

'"God will wipe out every tear from their eyes, and death will be no more, neither will mourning, nor outcry, nor pain be any more."'

'Matthew, what shall we do with the ant colony?'

Matthew's mother had dusted the sideboard up as far as Ant World.

'I don't know,' said Matthew, still reading.

'Are there actually any ants alive in there?' Matthew's mother was bending down to peer inside the Perspex box.

'"The God of Heaven will set up a Kingdom that will never be brought to ruin . . ."'

Matthew's mother wondered if he just liked the sound of the words.

'I think they're all dead.'

'I think there's one alive . . .'

'I tell you what, Matthew. Why don't we throw these ants away, and start afresh with a new lot? Shall I take them outside now? Will that be all right?'

Matthew nodded slowly. As she picked up Ant World and took it outside, she could hear him reading to her.

'"In that new world, even dead ones will be brought back to life to share in those blessings. There is going to be a resurrection of both the righteous and the unrighteous. That is why Jesus Christ could tell a repentant evil-doer who expressed faith in him: 'You will be with me in Paradise.'"'

The Hat

THIS guy arrived at the garden party wearing a hat. A straw thing, clamped to his head, or sometimes set back. It had a wide brim and a kind of leather strap with a bead at the end, which could be drawn up and down to vary the strap's tightness. That was what it looked like anyway. He said he couldn't go out in this sun without protection. One of the History women made a joke about condoms, and he told her off for being obvious.

There was no reason why he shouldn't have worn the hat, but there was something about it that drew comment and observation. It was as though he had done something irredeemably foolish or sentimental. Some thought it an outrageous token of his vanity, or of his need to draw attention to himself. But people were good-natured about it at first, even if, despite themselves, they were unable to withhold their comments and remarks. On meeting him, their eyes would gravitate towards his hat, then look away sharply again, as though they had just looked at the sun. 'That's a nice hat,' someone would observe. Others would just smile or say something pointless, such as, 'You are wearing a hat.' They would ask questions about where he'd got it, and he would answer with blunt parochialness. He had bought it in a local department store. Questioners would be unable to conceal their disappointment. 'I thought you were going to say you bought it on a Greek island or something.' Still, the compliments came. 'I like your hat' – although this seemed rarely to express an opinion, it was more a way of saying, 'I have noticed your hat.' Some of us did think it looked good, as I recall, but those of us who thought it didn't kept quiet about it.

About halfway through the party I noticed that people's attitudes towards the hat were beginning to change. It was as though they were growing tired of looking at it. The hat wasn't anything exceptional, just a regular straw sun hat with a long strap. But I sensed people were beginning to feel it was somehow intrusive. That it interrupted conversations. Now the remarks that were made about the hat were along the lines of 'Where the hell did you get that thing?', 'Why have you still got that on? The sun's gone in.' I began to notice whisperings, low, discontented murmurs. 'Who does he think he is in that hat?' I heard someone say. 'David Livingstone or something?'

I didn't know the guy in the hat at all. Someone said he worked in the Religious Studies Department. They said it as though it explained the hat. I wasn't sure about that, but there was something priestly about it. Perhaps not priestly exactly – ceremonial. Crowns, mitres, mortar boards. It was headgear of that ilk. And perhaps that was why people were getting upset about it. Why couldn't he just wear an honest baseball cap? Anything but that ostentatiously brimmed and strapped thing.

I heard one woman come out with a curt remark.

'That hat just doesn't suit you.'

I felt that was going too far, to say it to his face. The guy seemed unperturbed however; he even laughed.

'Why don't you ever take it off?' I heard another woman say. I couldn't hear the man's reply, as they were a few yards away and there were several chattering people in between, but he seemed to be in an intense conversation with her about the hat.

PERHAPS it was the wine going to people's heads, but the next time I noticed the guy in the hat, someone had thrown a glass of Chardonnay in his face. The hat was still in place, albeit knocked back slightly. Since it was white wine, there wasn't much of a stain, but the man's face was screwed up to keep the drips out of his eyes, and then he blinked and gaped like a fish while someone procured a tissue for him to dry his face with.

'Was that about the hat?' I asked my companion.

'Don't be silly,' she said, 'why would anyone get that worked up about a hat?'

But people were getting worked up about it. I heard someone saying, 'I can't talk to him. I know it sounds stupid but I feel as though his hat is laughing at me.' I heard similar comments from others. 'I don't know what to say to his hat, what can you say to a hat?'

Like I said, perhaps it was the wine going to people's heads. That, in combination with the hot weather. I went and stood near the fountain, and I didn't notice the man in the hat for some time. Then an old friend and colleague, someone I've known and trusted to be of perfectly sound mind for twenty years, came over to me almost in tears.

'That man over there, the one in the . . . the . . .'

'In the hat?'

She seemed pained by the word.

'It just insulted me.'

'What did he say?'

'Not the man; the hat.'

'The hat just insulted you?'

'Yes . . . It insinuated . . .' my friend had a great deal of trouble controlling her voice, '. . . it insinuated that I had had too much to drink. It also made remarks about my figure. Derogatory remarks.'

By this point, my friend was weeping and I put an arm around her.

'Would you go and have a word?' she said suddenly. 'It's not just me. It has insulted several people. Someone needs to do something. This is meant to be a happy occasion.'

I tried being as blunt as I could with my friend.

'Hats can't talk,' I said.

'I know,' she replied, 'that's what makes it so upsetting.'

I was going to suggest that maybe she had actually had too much to drink, but the truth was that I could see she simply hadn't. She wasn't the type to drink too much. She was sober and she was upset, and she believed that a hat was talking to her.

Others were showing symptoms of the same kind of madness. Moderate, responsible people were talking about the rudeness of the man's hat – how it made taunting remarks about wives to their husbands. Someone even claimed that the hat had thrown a glass of wine in their face. In a peculiar way it made me feel afraid. I didn't want to go up to the man in the hat in case I too should be subjected to the same kind of delusions. As though the hat cast a penumbra of dementedness. It was just a straw hat with a strap, but there was a bad atmosphere developing, I could sense it.

I was crossing the lawn towards the man when I heard a voice, a dry, reedy voice that I hadn't heard before, saying, 'Surely you are not suggesting a university isn't the proper place for such a debate? Let me put it another way. Your arse stinks.'

This appeared to be directed towards the deputy vice chancellor, but he was not the sort of man to be shaken by such remarks. He absorbed the insult with a bemused smile and a sip of wine. I was distracted at this point by the attention of another old friend, a former student of mine, and after our brief chat I couldn't see the man in the hat. It appeared that he had made a hasty exit, which was just as well, I thought.

It was remarkable how quickly the atmosphere reverted to its former conviviality in his absence. He had done the very opposite of making a lasting impression. In fact, he had made no impression at all. He was a footstep on polished marble. We passed the rest of the afternoon pleasantly by the fountain or beside the herbaceous border which was magnificent with delphiniums. The gardeners had really done us proud. Towers of clustered bells and trumpets in pink and blue filled the flower beds, worshipped by the bees. And that old efflorescent wall behind them. You could hardly ask for more.

I remember talking with a colleague from the Psychology Department who told me about one of Freud's case studies. Madame S, I think it was. She was under the delusion that her turds were spelling out messages. Just one or two letters at a time. She would look down into the lavatory pan and see her shit coiled and looped like an alphabet, and over the weeks words were formed, turd by turd. One such message was something like, 'Can God spread a table in the wilderness?' Which comes from the Bible.

Apples, Oranges

AT the age of ten, I was given the job of walking the greengrocer's daughter to school.

If I wondered why her parents had chosen me as their precious child's escort, I supposed that they must have seen me walk past the front of their little shop every morning (slumped, slow, dragging my feet), and in the evening on my way back (twirling my kitbag, pirouetting round lamp posts), and they must have looked upon me as a solution to a long-perplexing problem. I'd thought no one ever saw me during that mile-long walk, down three alleyways, past two other schools, through a park, across two busy roads and eight minor ones. But all the time I had been observed by the greengrocer and his wife, who'd looked up from their weighing of potatoes and onions, or from the tipping of their veg into the held-open shopping bags of housewives, and noticed me.

And then they must have made the connection with the

tall middle-aged woman who bought King Edwards and aubergines and globe artichokes on Saturday mornings, the woman with the melon-seed necklace and the sapphire bracelets and the Dunhill Kingsize on fire between her lips. They must have seen me loitering outside when my mother got her week's vegetables, lording it in the greengrocers' as they filled her bag (alternating layers of newspaper laid down like a damp course) to its brim. Suddenly the troubling question of how to get their daughter to school when mother and father were both tied up with greengrocery (and Jesus there must have been a lot of preparation to do: slashing open those sacks of carrots and Brussels sprouts, building those wonderful apple cliffs and cauliflower pyramids, arranging those AstroTurf draperies, writing those poorly apostrophised signs) was answered.

And a little conversation must have taken place, as it so often did when my mother went shopping. I might even have been watching through the glass at the time, not thinking of lip-reading, though I might have wondered what all those nods in my direction were about. A little chat, which had elicited the vital information: our children go to the same school – we have trouble getting her there in the morning – bringing her back in the evening – what with the shop and the hours and the early morning forays to Covent Garden (or wherever they had to go). Could your son (standing on the pavement kicking at the grey stem of a road sign) possibly? More nods in my direction.

And I can remember my mother breaking the news to me, giving me the illusion of a choice – 'You don't mind, do you?' – having first plied me with treats (a *Beano* and a Jamboree Bag), so that, throned in the best armchair with comic in one hand, fizzy drink in the other and the stalk of a lollipop sticking out of my mouth, to have objected would have seemed like the peak of selfishness.

PERHAPS the greengrocers didn't know many people. They were from another country, I wasn't sure which one. I could tell by the blackness of their hair, and their slightly husky voices, the way they hammered out their consonants like some echoey clog dance. Perhaps the residents of this well-to-do corner of London were being slow to accept them. Whatever the case, when I reluctantly presented myself at the shop on the Monday morning, I felt as if I was stepping on to an island of loneliness and plenty.

The shop was empty but for stacks of fruit and veg, and the two parents whose daughter I was to escort to school. They stood in the centre of their muddy floor looking nervous, and I sensed that their nervousness was to do with meeting me. They seemed very anxious to please me. They were frightened that I might not like them. It was perhaps the first time in my life that I'd felt powerful.

The mother wore a pink pinafore dress with bare legs, brown sandals and green socks. She held her hands together before her, resting just below her tummy, in the manner of a ballet dancer about to go up on her toes. The feet were even slightly turned out. The man was her more outgoing counterpart, whiskery, growly, a little frightening, with big pawlike hands, which he used a lot when talking. I understood little of what they said, not because what they were saying was difficult to understand, I just couldn't bring myself to listen to them properly. But I got the gist of it. My name was said several times, each time with increasingly accurate pronunciation. There was embarrassed laughter. The man's hand approached the top of my head, as if about to rummage in my hair, but was withdrawn at the last moment. And then the daughter was revealed, brought out from the room that lay hidden behind a strip-curtain like an undone maypole, where she must have been sitting, or lingering, among sacks of root vegetables.

I didn't like the look of her. I couldn't understand why everyone said she was so pretty. Not at the time, at least. Enormous catlike eyes, black and sparkling; dark, bruise-coloured lips that curled downwards slightly, as though an hour ago she had tasted something sour; ounces of dark hair that tumbled all around her face, and downy dark hair on the face itself, thickening above the top lip. She was wearing the school uniform (optional in those days, very few children wore it) – a green tunic and blazer trimmed with gold. Skinny legs protruded from beneath, also slightly dark with hair, and bulging inwards at the knee. We didn't exchange any words, nor hardly looked at each other. We were gently pushed and prodded together. Reassurances were muttered to the little girl by her mother, who bent down to whisper at ear level. The girl shook her head in that way children have when they know they are utterly powerless – slowly and mechanically, unemphatically. I was being presented to her as something safe and reassuring – the father referred to how tall and grown up I was, 'a big, sensible boy', almost as good as an adult. I would see her safely over the roads and protect her from any bullies she was likely to meet. Seeing the hopelessness of the situation, she eventually dragged her feet towards me and together we made our way out of the shop, watched over by the mother and father. They seemed to be peeping over a wall of carrots and swedes to wave at us as we left.

Almost immediately we had to tackle the main road. There was no crossing point. We just had to take our chances with the traffic. I turned reluctantly to the little girl, who I was told was called Melanie, and informed her that she would have to hold my hand (having first checked that there were no other children around to witness this event). Melanie held out a small, damp palm and I took hold of it. It felt repulsive, as though I'd picked up the body of a small, hairless rat. I yearned for a gap in the traffic to open up as quickly as possible so that I could release this thing, but the flow was thick, thunderous and constant. It seemed like hours before a crossing opportunity arose, and when one came we charged across the carriageways, both as eager as each other to get across and break our connection, which we did as soon as the opposite pavement was reached.

But then I realised I rather enjoyed this power I had over the girl. I could command her to hold my hand, and she would do so, even though it was something repugnant to her. I made her hold my hand ten times that first morning. By the tenth time I had no need to say anything, I only had to extend my hand and she would obediently take it.

In between road-crossing we walked in silence along pavements and alleyways. Melanie would hang back, dragging her feet, swinging her satchel in a pathetically defiant way. When I stopped to wait for her she slowed even more, and would talk to an imaginary friend, though the conversation didn't seem a particularly friendly one. She would quietly scold her invisible companion, whispering admonitions and offering sulky *I don't cares* in response to some criticism. I tried my luck with more commands, saying 'Come on' and 'Hurry up' a few times. Melanie obeyed at first, but towards the end of our journey would only give me a scowl in return.

When we arrived at school we separated silently having already drifted apart by several yards as we approached the gates, so that no one would spot us together. During the day we saw nothing of each other. Melanie was three years below me, somewhere in the distant corridors of the infant school with its plasticine and powder paint. The infants had a separate playground from the juniors, hidden away at the back of the school, though you could still hear all its squealing and shrieking. The school was laid out in such a way that pupils, as they grew older, went on a journey from one end to the other. The infants began their education at one end of a long annexe, moved up a classroom each year until, at the halfway point, they reached the dining room. Then, crossing the dining room, they arrived at the junior annexe, which ended in the only two-storey building in the school, the top floor of which was the classroom for the oldest pupils. When I had been an infant I had regarded the occupants of those classes as adults. I couldn't see any difference. Now that I was an occupant myself, I regarded those in the infant wing as babies, to be avoided at all costs. To have to associate with them would have been an unspeakable humiliation.

THE return journey was conducted in the same spirit of silent reluctance as the morning one. Melanie was waiting for me by the infant-school entrance, and without exchanging a single word we began our long, perilous walk.

Already, on that first journey home, I felt my authority begin to fade. A niggling refusal by Melanie to take my hand for the crossing of the minor roads. It began at Cavendish Avenue, where she refused to yield her damp little hand. She pretended to have forgotten, not to have noticed my waiting palm. When I sharply reminded her, the hand was offered and I thought nothing more of it. But when, at Hamilton Crescent, the hand was again withheld, I felt that first sapping of my power. This time she didn't even respond to my spoken command, but started walking out into the road.

'There's nothing coming,' she said, the first words she had spoken to me all day, and I had no choice but to follow. When we reached the other side, I had a go at sternly telling her off.

'You've got to hold my hand . . .'

But she was skipping ahead, chasing leaves, chatting to her own Miss Nobody.

Although she agreed to take my hand for the final road, which was still heavy with juggernauts, I felt disappointed with myself when I delivered Melanie back to her realm of fruit and vegetables. The shop was again empty of customers and both parents were standing at the entrance peering anxiously in our direction. I sensed they had been doing this for some time. We were welcomed into the shop like a victorious expeditionary force. Both parents poured over Melanie, and she ran to her mother, hugging her waist. Her father bent down to kiss and hug her, then quickly took her away to the spaces beyond the strip-curtain. I was about to leave when the mother stopped me.

Then, as though it had been an agreed part of the deal all along, she took a large brown paper bag from a bunch that were hanging on a loop of white string, fluffed it open with her hand while holding it in the palm of the other, so that it gaped in readiness of being filled, and said to me, with a slight sense of urgency:

'Apples or oranges?'

There they were, behind her as she spoke, a great heap of each fruit, side by side, a label on each showing the price in extravagantly serifed marker pen. I had not expected payment, or reward of any kind, and the offer of fruit came as a delightful shock. I didn't need to hesitate before making my choice, but I did, because it would have seemed somehow disrespectful to the greengrocers' apples to have said 'oranges' instantly. The mother deftly picked up four oranges in one hand, bagged them and swung the bag to seal it, giving it earlike twists at each end. And then they were in my hands and I was on my way home, another ten minutes of walking, and the oranges were quite difficult to carry.

When I arrived home, I was a little disappointed that my family didn't appreciate the oranges as much as I did. I plonked them on the kitchen table as if to say, 'There, look what I've brought home for you', and expected gasps of delight in return. But my mother was more interested to hear of my experiences with Melanie. How was the journey to school? she wanted to know. She was keen for me to say that it wasn't as bad as I'd thought it was going to be. But I wanted her to see the oranges. I peeled open the brown paper bag for her. 'Yes, that's nice. Some oranges,' was all she could say. My father was a little more appreciative when he arrived home from work an hour later. By then I had persuaded my mother to hunt out a fruit bowl, which she did, rummaging at the back of a difficult-to-reach cupboard under the picture window, and bringing out a ceramic bowl with a Chinese design, which she rinsed under the tap, dried, and placed on the table. It was not that we never had fruit at our house. My mother usually bought some at the weekend, but it was all gone by Tuesday. When it was in the house it sat in a bag on the kitchen worktop, or in a cupboard. It was never displayed like these oranges were now displayed. And I was convinced that I'd been given the best oranges, the ones that my mother never bought, budgeting instead for the hard, dry little things with scratchy skins and flesh clogged with pips that I would only eat when desperately hungry. My oranges were fat and glossy, a big powerful weight in the hand. Though I hadn't eaten one yet I imagined the skin as thick and pithy, easy to peel, and the segments beneath full of sweet, juicy, unpunctuated flesh. My father noticed them as soon as he entered the kitchen, even before I pointed them out and explained that I'd been given them free. He picked one up, felt its weight, sniffed it. 'Good oranges,' he said. 'It's nice to see oranges in the house.'

The oranges sat in their fruit bowl for the whole evening. No one ate any. They looked so perfect, such a prize in their Chinese bowl, that it didn't seem right to interfere with them. But shortly before bedtime I couldn't resist. I picked one up and took my mother's best carving knife. I was not very good at peeling oranges, and whenever I had to deal with one on my own I would cut it up rather than peel it. And that's what I did that evening. I cut it into quarters and ate each quarter, one by one, as you might eat a slice of melon.

MY experience at the greengrocers' the next day was very different. There were customers – a couple of elderly ladies in plush, buttoned-up coats and headscarves, chatting happily with the greengrocer's wife. The father swaggered merrily through the shop with a sack of carrots on his shoulder. Melanie herself was skipping about and ducking out of people's way, playing some cheerful little game.

'He's here,' she called to her mother as I came in, and then skipped over to me, grinning. The mother took a few moments away from serving one of the elderly ladies to give her daughter a kiss and me a gentle pat on the head. We still said little during the walk to school, but the atmosphere between us had lightened. The conversations with her imaginary friend were more affable, and Melanie generally did as she was told, although we reached an unspoken agreement that we would not hold hands except for the busiest roads.

That evening I was again paid in oranges, which I added to the fruit bowl when I got home.

'We'd better start eating some of these,' my mother said, seeing how the oranges now filled the bowl to capacity, 'or there won't be room for them in the house, not if you bring home four every day.'

And I did bring four home every day. Although, after the third day, I thought it might do to switch to apples. I wondered if I would be offered other fruit in future. Some pears, perhaps, or grapes, or bananas? But I never was.

The September of the new school year quickly grew into a solid, steady, very dry autumn. Low sunlight made the suburban roads into shadowy canyons beneath dazzling skies. The plane trees that lined nearly all the streets dropped big, clumsy, Manila-coloured leaves that would land with a clatter on the pavements. One of our many games on the walk to school involved races to be the first to trample on a particular leaf. If we spotted one recently fallen, lying seductively curled on the pavement, we would run, a mini stampede of sensible shoes, and whoever was first to the leaf would stamp on it, and enjoy the crackling crumpling sound of its disintegration. Of course, having longer legs than Melanie, I nearly always won these races. Sometimes I surprised myself by allowing Melanie to win, deliberately running slower than normal, though I usually explained to her afterwards that I'd done it on purpose. She would pretend to disbelieve me. One of our favourite varieties of this game was when I would be first to the leaf, and then teasingly hold my foot poised over it, ready to stamp, but allowing Melanie to think she had a chance of getting in first. She would run breathlessly up, and just as she was within inches of stamping on the leaf, I would allow my own foot to fall, denying her the pleasure. She found this really funny.

Another game we called 'Secret Agents'. I would walk along ahead, and Melanie had to follow me without being seen. Every few paces I would turn round, and if I could see her, I had to pretend to shoot her. I nearly always could see her, just as she darted behind a gatepost or into an alleyway entrance, or behind a lamp post. Usually I allowed her these little glimpses, even when I spotted the green tail of her blazer wavering (as she suppressed her giggling) behind a pillar box. Only if I saw her whole and complete did I fire my invisible gun. Melanie always wanted us to change roles and for me to do the hiding, but I thought this was taking things too far, believing myself much too grown up for such silliness. But I was enjoying our walks to school now, in a way that I never believed I could. We even had conversations, though they were almost entirely limited to the discussion of things we'd seen on the TV or at the pictures, and did little more than illustrate the gulf that separated our tastes. Melanie would enthuse about *Bedknobs and Broomsticks* while I recounted the shoot-ups and car chases of *Live and Let Die*. She even began to see me as a source of knowledge, asking me questions that I tried to answer, although usually they were unanswerable – 'Why does the sun have to be so big?' she asked once, and another time, out of the blue, she came up with 'Can geese burp?'

It was impossible to keep our partnership secret from my friends, but, to my surprise, they seemed indifferent to it. My friend Mark saw me from his parents' car as he was driven to school, and even seemed rather impressed when I explained our relationship to him.

'I'm in charge of her,' I said casually. 'Her mum pays me.'

'How much?' said Mark, his eyes wide with amazement. Money, and how little of it we had, was something we talked about a lot.

'Four . . .' and I nearly said 'oranges', but stopped myself at the last moment. Instead I said, '. . . pounds.'

'Four pounds?' A lot of money in those days. My older brother got fifty pence pocket money. 'A week? I don't believe you.'

'It's four pounds a day, actually.'

Eventually, after a long argument, Mark got it down to four pounds a month, which was a little more believable. To my surprise I found that I was envied by my friends. They began to wish they too had a little girl to shepherd back and forth from school, and to be paid for it.

IT was a while before I realised that we passed the greengrocers' home on the walk to school. Cavendish Avenue was where Melanie and her parents lived. If, on the journey home, we had turned left when we emerged from the alleyway on to the avenue, Melanie could have reached her house in a matter of seconds.

'Isn't it silly?' she said. 'I live just up there, but I've got to go all the way to the shop.'

I didn't believe her at first. Melanie was always exaggerating, or telling downright lies. Her father, for instance, owned a helicopter, which he kept at a special site near Stonehenge. She had a cousin who possessed a doll's house so huge a human family could live in it. We had many *yes I do, no you don't* conversations about these and other subjects, which sometimes could last the whole journey. It took her a long time to convince me that she lived in one of the houses in Cavendish Avenue.

They were rather grand houses for a greengrocer, I thought, terraced but of extravagant, Edwardian proportions. I was only convinced when she took me on the short detour to look at the house itself. She showed me where the key to the front door was kept, beneath a stone shaped like a wellington boot. The house had a glossy, green front door with a stained-glass window and blazing brasswork. She wanted to take me inside and show me her toys, but I refused, saying we were already late. What convinced me most of all that this was Melanie's house was what I could see sitting in the bay window, between the partly open curtains. A bowl of oranges.

I was young. In the eyes of Melanie's parents, the greengrocer and his wife, I was a child. In Melanie's eyes, however, I was a grown-up. An adult. To bolster this perception, her parents treated me as an adult. They were always talking about how tall I was, how manly and sensible. Her father sometimes shook my hand, as though sealing a business deal. As though, almost, I was co-father, *in loco parentis*, of this dizzy, dreaming girl. I was paid a wage. Oranges.

But I was young. I was something out of focus in the gaze of two opposing viewpoints, the parents' and their child's. I could materialise as a man in one lens, as a boy in the other. So when it came to making my first independent decision, I could have made the choice as either a child or an adult. It took me a long time to realise I had made a child's decision.

Melanie started pestering me to drop her off at her house in Cavendish Avenue, rather than taking her all the way to the shop. I always refused, saying her parents would be worried if I turned up at the shop without her. She wanted to go home because there was a cartoon she liked to watch – *Wacky Races*

– that was just starting as we crossed her road. In the normal course of events, having to wait while her parents shut up the shop, she didn't get home for another hour and a half, when all the children's programmes were over. She might just catch the end of *The Magic Roundabout* if she was lucky.

Then one day she changed her tactic. Instead of pleading with me and begging me to let her go home in her whiny, often nearly tearful way, she simply announced, in a very matter-of-fact voice:

'Mum said I have to go home today. I've got to go to the dentist, and Mum is going to meet me at home and take me straight there.'

'Why can't she take you from the shop?'

'Because she has to get changed of course, and wash. She can't go to the dentist's in her shop clothes. And there isn't time. I have to be there at quarter past four . . .'

Neither of us had watches or much of a sense of time.

I believed Melanie. I extracted many promises and cross-your-hearts from her. I let her skip off towards her house with its key under the stone wellington boot and its bowl of oranges in the window, rather proud of myself for having authorised something so important. Even if it did turn out that Melanie was lying, I thought, it didn't matter that much. She would be quite safe at home watching *Wacky Races.*

That's not how the greengrocer and his wife saw it. My solo entrance into the shop brought looks of shock and fear to their faces. I was urgently interrogated. Where was Melanie? She's gone home, I said, and wanted to explain about the dental appointment, but my voice was drowned out in the subsequent exchanges – *You'll have to go. But Derek's got the van. Take his car. Where are the keys? Terry will give you a lift. I could run there in ten minutes. Let me deal with this customer. Hurry!* The greengrocer rushed out of the shop still in his beige coat, slipping on a pinstriped jacket over the top, rattling a bunch of keys as he went, a haunted, frightened look on his face.

It was a while before the greengrocer's wife, having a customer to deal with, could turn her attention to me. I was hanging around, waiting for my payment. She was very nice to me. Don't worry, she said, we'll take Melanie to school from now on. We thought she might try something like this. She does love her cartoons. Thank you.

Realising that the payment wasn't going to be made, that no brown paper bag was to be held open and no choice of fruits offered, I slowly made my way out of the shop. I paused in the doorway, feeling that something else should be said. Some confirmation that I would not be needed again. But Melanie's mother was busy doing something at the till, and then another housewife breezed in, seeking beetroot.

The autumn had finished and somehow those great, crunching leaves had all disappeared. The pavements had been swept and the trees were bare, flexing their muscles. I walked home empty-handed.

Bike

ONE Saturday morning, the first Saturday morning of his retirement, and before anyone could stop him, Des went out and bought a bike.

It had been a startlingly simple transaction. He went into the cycle shop he'd been walking past (without ever entering) for forty years, saw the bike he wanted, and bought it. As someone who in his lifetime must have bought half a dozen cars, Des was expecting forms to fill, agreements to sign, contracts to negotiate. But the purchase of a bicycle turned out to be no more arduous than the buying of a pair of shoes, and Des was cycling shakily home that same morning.

His wife, Yvette, came cautiously out of the house to meet him as he wheeled the machine up the back garden path.

'What the hell have you gone and done?' she said, half amused, half frightened. It wasn't characteristic of Des to disappear on Saturday mornings. 'You've . . . is that yours?'

'I've bought a bike,' said Des, propping it against the dark brown bricks of the house. It was an Arden-blue roadster with sit-up-and-beg handlebars and eighteen gears.

'You've paid for it? With money?'

'It's got tyres made of the same stuff bulletproof vests are made from. It can't get punctures.'

DES had no reason to buy the bike. He had nowhere to cycle to. Having retired, he had little need of transport except for the weekly shop, when he took the car. If he wanted to get a paper or some milk from the corner store, it took longer to get the bike out of the shed, unlock the back gate and put his cycle clips on than it did just to walk to the shop and back.

But Des wanted to cycle. He lived in the suburbs, halfway between the city centre and the countryside. In whichever direction he cycled, there was more city. But it was surprisingly quiet. Away from the arterial roads, the city streets were as peaceful as country lanes.

He had thought he knew the city pretty well, having lived in it all his life, but in certain directions, twenty minutes' cycling, just twenty minutes, would bring him to an area totally unfamiliar to him. If he didn't take an *A–Z*, he could have trouble finding his way home.

He decided to set himself the task of exploring these hitherto unexplored regions on a daily basis, and in as much detail as he could. He intended to be as systematic as possible. Each day he selected a different point of the compass and set off in that direction. He noted his progress on a map so that he could remember where he had been and didn't end up going over the same ground too often. He pinned the map to his study wall and marked his journeys in red. Slowly a crimson spider appeared on the map, its crooked, frail legs growing longer each day, until it was not so much a spider as an anemone with dozens of radial fronds following the lines of the city streets.

He was delighted by the near-to-home surprises the early days of his cycling yielded. Who would have thought there was a golf course just a few streets away? He'd always been vaguely aware of an open space beyond the houses, but now here he was, amid greens and fairways, following the course of the little brook that he presumed finished its days as a sewer beneath his own district. And beyond the golf course were great towering mills, converted now into apartments, and a whole area that had been built as a model community, a century earlier, by a philanthropic capitalist.

Nearly every day he came across a primary school he'd never seen before. Mostly they were Victorian redbrick – squat little fortresses with high windows and spiked railings. There was one that delighted Des because the school uniform – bright pillar-box red – exactly matched the colour of the school's guttering and drainage, so that at playtime the place was a crazy tangle of gutters, drains and children.

Then there were the canals with their lonely, ill-equipped fishermen, the little metal-walled factories that had sprung up around the wharfs and produced little puffs of white steam from thin, steel chimneys. One he passed gave off a strong smell that it took him a long time to identify – turpentine. And the pubs, more pubs than schools or churches, old-fashioned, like the pubs of his youth – the domains almost entirely of elderly men who drank red beer from jugs.

DES was recognised on his bike. Now and then he'd pass someone with a familiar face, who would wave or call out or, more often, just stand there open-mouthed on the pavement, their eyes following Des as he rolled past. It became a topic of conversation whenever he met an old friend.

'You've got a bike,' they'd say, or, 'I saw you on your bike last week.'

It was usually said in a tone of mild shock, or sometimes amusement. One of his wife's friends could hardly contain her laughter when she said, 'I hear you're a cyclist these days.'

What did she think was so funny? Her mouth was crumpled with the effort of stemming laughter, her big permed head shaking with energy. Eventually she burst out with, 'You on a bike! I'd have to see it!'

ONE day Des found himself by chance in the vicinity of Norman's bungalow, and he decided to pay him a visit. Norman was Des's older brother. Ten years older. He'd spent most of his working life manning the presses at the canalside printworks which, Des had recently discovered, was being converted into flats. Des hadn't seen his brother for three years, even though he only lived three miles away. A mile for every year, thought Des as he cycled up Norman's cul-de-sac.

'You've got a bike,' said Norman croakily.

'You've got an earring,' said Des. 'What have you got an earring for?'

A little silver heart-shaped, diamond-encrusted stud in the lobe of his left ear.

'What have you gone and bought a bike for at your age?' said Norman, ignoring Des's question, and Des never did find out why Norman had had his ear pierced. It looked ridiculous.

'It gets me out of the house,' said Des.

They were both on the cement outside Norman's bungalow

looking at the new bike which Des had propped against the brickwork.

'Looks like a good model,' said Norman, with grudging approval, 'properly made, not like some bikes you see these days.'

'It's very solid,' said Des, trying to talk to Norman on his level, 'very solid, but light at the same time.'

'That's the trick with bikes,' said Norman, 'they've got to be solid and light at the same time. I rode a bike once. Someone at the works gave me theirs when they fell ill, said I should use it to get in for my shift. I tried cycling in one morning but after ten minutes I thought bollocks to this – and I never rode it again.'

'It was probably made of steel,' said Des, 'this one's made of amalgam. That's the same stuff they fill your teeth with.'

Des and Norman looked at each other, neither of them quite sure whether they should have been impressed by this last fact.

'So where have you been cycling to?'

'Just round and about. Here and there. Nowhere really. Like I said, it gets me out of the house.'

'Funny,' said Norman, chuckling to himself in a dark, hopeless sort of way, 'I'd do anything these days to stay indoors, but all the time there's these things I've got to do – go to the post office, go to the doctor's, go the shop. Sometimes I wonder whether I'd rather have the pain than have to struggle down to the surgery every week to pick up me prescription.'

A thought occurred to Des.

'Why don't I do it for you? On my bike.'

AND so Des found a use for his bike – picking up Norman's prescriptions every week. Des enjoyed it very much. It meant he saw much more of his brother. Each week he'd cycle over to the barricaded, razor-wired surgery and pick up Norman's repeat prescription which, Des discovered, was not for a single medicine but for a whole cabinet-load of bottles and blister-packs that filled the panniers of Des's bike. He never asked what they were for, and Norman never told him. But he noticed that, as soon as the routine was started, Norman seemed to exaggerate his immobility, never stirring from his green velvet armchair when Des delivered his medicines.

DES'S mother was nearly ninety, but still compos mentis. In fact her mentis seemed to be getting more compos with every year that passed. She had recently become a voracious reader. She was reading, she told Des when he cycled over to visit, a book a week. 'Sometimes two.'

'Reading's a good thing,' said Des, 'that's what they're always saying in the papers. They're always trying to get young people to read books. And there was something about reading helping to prevent Alzheimer's.'

'Too late for me,' Des's mother joked, 'but the doctor said it as well. He told me you have to keep your mind active, and reading is one of the best ways. Reading or crosswords. But I don't like crosswords, or any puzzles. Never have. The doctor said if you don't keep your mind active, it might just waste away. Watching telly's no good. It doesn't exercise your mind like reading. But by that reckoning people must have been much more intelligent before the telly was invented, because they read all the time. But when I think of my family, and all those stupid uncles and aunts of mine, it just doesn't make sense. Why have you got your trousers tucked into your socks?'

'I've got a bike,' said Des.

'A bike? What's the matter with the car, has it broken down?'

'No. It's in the garage. But I was thinking of selling it.'

'Have you gone mad? You can't get rid of your car just like that, it would be irresponsible . . .'

Des's mother got to her feet, as though the car was nearby, a weak and defenceless creature, and she was about to leap to its rescue. As she stood up, Des recoiled inwardly, as he always did, at the sight of her hunchback – the one disfiguring sign of old age that no amount of mental agility could disguise. He might pass over her crisp, ridged skin, her sunken eyes and wavering voice. But he couldn't ignore the hump on her back, the creeping curvature of her upper vertebrae that seemed so insistent in its yearly progress that he wondered whether his mother would end up tied in a knot.

'I'm beginning to wonder why I ever bothered with a car,' said Des, once his mother had settled herself back in her chair. 'Even our weekly shop doesn't fill the boot. They're opening a new cycle path that leads to the supermarket. I could get all we need on the bike.'

'I'm wondering,' said Des's mother, 'how I ever managed without the mobile library. They stop right outside the house now, every week, a great big lorry full of books. The lady comes out and lends me a hand up . . .'

Soon the mobile library was cancelled – part of a swathe of local council cutbacks that also saw the closure of two swimming pools. They said the huge new swimming pool five miles away made up for it, but not everyone had a car to go all that way. As for the mobile library, they said not enough people were using it to justify the expense.

Des's mother was heartbroken.

'Just when I've found something to make my life worth living, they have to take it away.'

And so Des took on a new duty – cycling to the library every week to return his mother's book and take out a new one for her. It was an enjoyable chore. The librarians even sent Des's mother a list of books they thought she might like, and she could reserve them with a telephone call. The library was made of scrolled terracotta and was surrounded by trees, which were rare in that part of the city. When the Edwardians had built the library, they imagined it as the centre of a village-like community, along with the swimming pool (recently closed down). In their uncomplicated way, they'd built temples to the mind and the body on opposite sides of the main road, facing each other.

And so Des got fitter, and his mother's brain got fitter, and Des's brother's health was maintained by the bicycle, and the pills and tonics it helped deliver. Soon Des began to feel that the kinetic energy of the bike, his feet turning the pedals, the pedals pulling the chain through the derailleurs and thus pulling the wheel, was also connected, by an invisible chain, to his brother's heart and his mother's brain, and that by his sweaty toil and endurance, he was making those turn as well.

IT was when his mother started asking about shopping errands that Des began to feel the strain. He could manage the doctor and the library, but a trip to the shops and back, panniers full, wobbling with carrier bags hanging from his handlebars, was difficult and slightly dangerous. After a few weeks people began to notice how the errands were taking their toll.

'Des, you look a bit peaky,' his mother said. 'You look like you might drop dead. The way things are going, either your heart's going to burst or you'll cycle into a tree.'

On the days when Des wasn't running errands for his mother

or his brother, he began staying at home, not taking the bike out. He felt he needed the days off to recuperate, and he'd been cycling every day for several months now: he'd explored every street, alleyway and cul-de-sac within the twenty-minute radius. But it still felt bad to let the bike go unused in the shed, even for a single day.

Yvette seemed relieved when Des suggested they take the car to the supermarket to do the shopping 'just this once'. She leapt at the chance to make her own suggestion.

'Why don't we do your mum's shopping at the same time? Then we could drop it off on the way back home. It wouldn't take ten minutes. We could change her library book, and get Norman's prescriptions, all in one go. It would save so much aggravation.'

It seemed to Des like an awful betrayal of the bike. It was the bike that had set up these new duties and responsibilities, rekindling valuable old relationships. The bike had done all the hard work, the car was going to get the credit.

IT all came to an end on the cycle path back from the supermarket a few weeks later. Suddenly a rhythmic thumping, like a distant drumbeat, vibrated through the body of both the bike and Des. A moment later, he began losing control and swerving around the path, only just managing to avoid falling off completely. The bulletproof tyre of the back wheel had got a puncture.

Des could remember his father mending a tyre in what seemed a matter of minutes, but the puncture completely baffled Des. In his eyes the bike became something hopeless and tragic, like a bird with a broken wing. A simple injury, but impossible to mend. He wheeled the bike home along the path for two miles, astonished at how slow the process of walking now seemed from the perspective of his cycling days.

THE bike stayed in the shed for nearly three years after the puncture. Des agonised about it at first, wondering if he was merely using the puncture as an excuse to give up cycling. He felt guilty and ashamed. It was as though he'd locked up a physically deformed son in the shed. He felt like one of those Victorian patriarchs who shut their pregnant daughters in the cellar for ten years. He carried on with the errands for his brother and his mother, but they didn't seem as grateful now that he delivered their things by car, and he didn't feel so generous in helping them out.

Then, within six months of each other, they both died.

By this time Des had nearly forgotten about the bike. He got rid of it when he was having a clear-out.

Hygiene

YOU get to know people in a job like this. Or at least you think you do. Take the other day, for example. A man came in I hadn't seen before and asked for a cup of coffee. So I took a polystyrene cup from its sleeve, tipped in a spoonful of Nescafé (the electrostatically charged cups cause the coffee granules to dance about like fleas) and filled it with hot water. He gave me the exact money, which I sprinkled into the till. Then he set about customising his coffee.

He was the type of person who does this at the counter. Some people pick a handful of sugar cubes, milk jiggers, a spoon, and tiptoe (so as not to scald themselves) to a table where they can sweeten and whiten their drinks in relative privacy. Others like to do it at the counter, and some of them, like this man, are a long time about it.

They've been talking about sachets for ages but for the moment it's cubes. Think how long it takes a cube to dissolve. Some people feel they can't leave the counter until they've stirred the rubble at the bottom of their cups to nothing. With tea it's even worse. There's the tagged bag to let brew, to press the juices from with the agitator, to flip into the bin. Then there are the milk jiggers to open – a little hangnail of foil waiting to be picked. I have a regular customer who'll take twelve jiggers of cream for a single cup of coffee (six go into the cup, six into his pocket, just because they're free); another wraps a little stack of sugar cubes in a napkin and smuggles them out like uncut diamonds. It is the ones who take their time at the counter who are likely to want to talk. Some people talk easily. They talk as easily as thinking. There's a man who comes down from the Mathematics Department at half eleven each day and natters all the way through his transaction. 'I'll have one of these guys,' he'll say, meaning a mini-pack of biscuits, and he'll always find something new to say about the hot chocolate. Then he'll mutter about his cash, draw a handful of coins from his pocket and apologise for not having the exact money. (I'm not sure why this bothers him so much. It doesn't bother me. That's the way with mathematicians. The numbers have to add up.)

Anyway, this man was filling his coffee with sugar, tipping in his UHT, stirring, so I asked him, as he seemed set for a long linger, how things were for him.

He shrugged, then said he'd been to Spain, as though it wasn't something of interest. How sad, I thought, to go to Spain and have nothing to say about it. So I asked him what he did there, and he said he didn't do anything much. Then he chuckled. 'Got drunk,' he said, 'lay around in the sun.'

Then he told me about fishing. How he'd fished from the stone jetties of the old town, with the locals, men in late-middle age like himself, how the water was sharply clear but empty, you could see the stones on the bottom, the seaweed waving.

He told me about the bait he used (I can't remember what, I'm not a fishing man myself), and mimed how he fixed it on his line (his hands deftly tying a knot of nothing), then he mimed casting off (a quick flick of both hands, one on top of the other) and how suddenly the fish appeared, shoals of little silver ones, like sardines (he used the fingers of both hands to describe their sudden, darting, criss-crossing arrival, their equally sudden, ghostlike disappearance), how the old Spaniards around him had bells hanging from their rods that chimed prettily when the fish were biting. Then he mimed the reeling in of a hooked fish (his right hand describing quick circles), the recasting, reeling in again (more flitting shoals with his fingers), and for those few moments with his hands he'd transformed my little snack bar into a pier, buttressed against a warm, thriving sea with a high Mediterranean sun beating down.

Not many people talk, though. Mostly they take their purchase, give me some money, and that's that. And sometimes that's enough; the physical contact, the moment of touching. Cash is the one medium of our exchanges. You only have to touch someone to leave a trace of your DNA on them. Enough dead cells and sweat come away at the point of contact to leave a mark on everyone. I think sometimes about how I've spread myself about in that way. How we all have. I'm not implying that I'm unhygienic. No. I have a sink at the back, a wall dispenser of Kleen-O-Tex hand sanitiser, a stash of paper towels, a cleaning rota, to which I religiously adhere. I'm just talking about the natural broadcast of genetic material. You could say every time someone hands me coins I've cloned myself. Alternatively, there is the way I accumulate traces of my customers. Each little pawing of change into my hand adds its stamp to the passport of myself. Or, to pursue the stamp metaphor, each exchange adds a franked postage stamp to the stamp album that is me.

I say you get to know people in a job like this. What you really get to know is their touch. What they feel like. Those with the warm, soft, moist palms, long pocketed, that arrive in your own hand like steaks that have spent too long in cellophane. Rough, stale hands, hands like the mitts of babies grafted on to a grown-up's wrist. Hands that are all claws, that nip and scrape you with lacquered nails. Hands that jab at yours, as gracelessly as birds taking up seed. Arthritic hands that make a creaking noise when they move their twenty-seven bones and thirty-three muscles. Shaky, trembling hands that drop change, that fail to find yours. Cold hands, hands that are icy even in heatwaves. Hands all downy, like rabbits' feet. Lucky hands, all rings and gold and bangles, that arrive like chevaliers, rich and dashing. Raw hands, wounded hands, hands all blisters and scuffs and scratches. Torn, ragged hands. Hands that are fragile, breakable things, or like the open face of a cut-into loaf.

Here is what she felt like. The charmingly rough pad you might find on the prehensile hand of a chimpanzee. That apelike abrasiveness was such a shock. Her Mount of Venus was a parched desert, the heel of her hand was like the rounded crust of a cottage loaf, her lifeline was a barren gulch. But her face was so softly sweet, so milkily white and her body, though always clad in fleecy tops and jeans, was so invitingly full. Her face had a simian beauty I hadn't seen in a human being before. It was sheer, indeed it was slightly hollow, and her eyes, round and sad, were set evenly and flat, like those of a sloth. Her nose was a cute, retroussé comma of flesh. But it was her mouth that drew my attention. The way the lower lip protruded sulkily, a little heart-shaped bolster of strawberry-coloured skin. That pout was also the legacy of her ape ancestry. Another generation and they might resurface fully – little hairy babies hanging by their tails.

I was more than happy to feed her. She always had a baked potato which I would fill generously with a filling of her choice – Cheddar, cottage cheese, tuna mayonnaise or coronation chicken.

She enriched me with currency. I would convert her over-folded fivers into a little palmful of nickel silver. I say over-folded – her purse was a tiny little leather pouch, about the size of a mouse. A five-pound note had to be folded down to little more than the size of a postage stamp to fit in, and it could barely fit a 50p. I once asked her why she bothered with a purse so small. 'It was my grandmother's,' she replied softly. Sometimes, so small was her purse, she had trouble finding it. She would go through her pockets, through her rucksack, taking out a smaller handbag from within, unzipping compartments of that. Sometimes I felt her money had come to me from deep inside her person, reminding me of the seven layers that need suturing after a Caesarean baby is delivered.

A lot of people are like that with their money, tucking it away in pouches within pouches, pockets within pockets.

So she delighted me, though we barely exchanged a word, this little ape girl. Her smile was enough. She came to me every day, alone, and always bought something. She always smiled, and that was that.

Otherwise my days are long dull stretches punctuated by bursts of frantic activity. There are busy periods in the mid morning and then again at lunchtime. The afternoons are often quiet, the few people that come in only have cups of tea, or a game of pool. I sit listening to the snap and rumble of the pool table and wait for the close of day to come.

Then there is the cashing up. The till, which in the morning I fill with its float of change (£30), will have swollen (on a good day) to two or three hundred pounds, (mostly in notes, it has to be said, most days I am starved of coins). The money that has gathered in the till is its own succinct résumé of my day. It is my life in money. If only those coins and notes carried some visible tag, like a colour, that identified their owners, I would have a complete record of my daily contact with human beings. As it is, I have little stacks of coins which I bag in clear bags, stacks of notes which I also bag, put inside a larger bag (the float) which goes inside my takings bag which our security man, Ian, comes for at five o'clock. Then I quickly lock everything away (the microwave, crisp display, confectionery stands), padlock the fridges, sweep up, wipe down the surfaces, and that's my day.

I was disappointed when she didn't show up on Monday. I had a string of coffees and the potatoes were starting to soften. The vending-machine man had just called to fill the multi-snack and the Klix machine, my inert, computerised competitors. These are new machines only installed last summer, to satisfy the needs of customers after I've closed up (though now that they've lowered the prices on certain items I find queues forming for the machines while my counter is empty). Some people, I know, enjoy being served by machines. They prefer them to human vendors. It is the simplicity and privacy of it that attracts them. There is no obligation to smile or make small talk. The machines these days are quite chatty, in a very one-sided sort of way. The multi-snack has a liquid crystal display which offers such friendly remarks as *Welcome to the Maths Tower*, or *Enjoy your snack*. I have to admit that, to nine customers out of ten, I will say even less than the multi-snack.

It is only when something goes wrong that my human skills come into their own – if a paid-for bar of chocolate dangles on the cusp of its row, for instance, refusing to drop. The frustrated customer will ask me if I have a key to the machine, which I haven't. Why can't they understand that these machines have nothing to do with me, that they are the outposts of some mysterious company in another city? But, obligingly, I will walk over to the machine and give it a friendly nudge, a pat on the shoulders or a punch in the ribs, which is usually enough to make the chocolate fall.

But she didn't come in for her usual potato. It was a good day for potatoes. They went quickly. By one o'clock I only had three spuds left. I was confronted by the dilemma of whether to put one by for her, but at half past one, with one potato left, another regular customer came in, a winsome teacher of Fluid Mechanics who looked like she should be herding geese, asking for something she quaintly called 'spuddies'. The potato had to go to her. Cutting into the warm, plump vegetable was like slipping a knife into my own heart. I filled it with the last of my pre-grated Cheddar. I filled it until it looked like an open wound. The fluid mechanic took it away and scoffed it with a plastic fork.

The next day she didn't come either. I was left with a bundle of unused potatoes that filled and melted my bin bag.

On the third day things were quiet. I only used a fraction of my potatoes. The rest were binned. And then the manager arrived with two health inspectors.

No warning. No nothing. Just this couple in long white coats with white trilby hats and hairnets. They had the silky, gauzy look of bridesmaids. Or phantom used-car salesmen. The two, a man and a woman, said nothing to me as they began their inspection. They came behind the counter and stepped into my territory and I felt as quietly affronted as if they'd stepped into my own bathroom while I was naked in the tub. My manager looked sheepish. She was a rare visitor to my snack bar, which was one of twelve satellites in stationary orbit around the main refectory. That was fine by me: when I didn't know about something I needed to know about, she couldn't blame me.

'There's been a complaint from a member of the public,' she said, 'probably nothing.'

The inspectors were rummaging through my fridge. They asked to see my temperature record sheets which, as is common practice among staff, were products of a repetitive imagination. The man took from the pocket of his white coat not the stethoscope I was half expecting but a thermoprobe, an electronic thermometer with a metal rod attached via a lead to a digital display box. He slid open the fridge and inserted the rod between two cartons of orange juice and waited. The woman asked me to heat a sausage roll in the microwave. I took one of the rolls from the fridge, a cold, rigid, pale thing of latticed puff pastry, opened the pleated end of its cellophane wrapper and popped it in the white oven. We waited while the sausage roll cooked, viewing together its revolving, silent agony. Then, when the microwave had pinged, she extracted a limp, dark brown, quietly sizzling length of meat and pastry and stuck the end of her thermoprobe into it. She noted down the registered heat, showed it to her colleague and together they whispered.

After poking intrusively into every corner of my workspace, noting every corner that was beyond the reach of brooms, noting the cobwebs behind my dry-storage cabinet, the accumulated crumbs beneath my chiller, they came finally to my potato oven. This was a small, tabletop contraption of dimpled copper and steel, with moulded cast-iron lettering meant to evoke, for reasons I have never fully understood, an era of Victorian industrialisation. Did the Victorians have a special fondness for the baked potato? I had no idea. My oven is rather old anyway. The main door is held in place by a piece of string tied to the smaller warmer door above, where the cooked potatoes are stored. They took out one of my last potatoes and the woman, placing it carefully on the counter with her white-gloved hands, inserted carefully the wiped needle of her thermoprobe into its heart. Had they pinned me down on the counter myself and stuck their probes into me, I could not have felt more the cold ingress of heat-sensitive metal. I felt like St Sebastian multiply skewered, my body reduced to a bureaucrat's chart of recorded temperatures.

Finally, blissfully, they failed to find anything wrong with my snack bar or myself. The woman gave me a look up and down as she left, suspecting I concealed somewhere about my person, beyond the limits of her jurisdiction, filth of some kind.

In and out they breezed (if they could be called a breeze, they were closer to fog), and in their wake left nothing but a few perforations in my food and in my heart. Of course it was my ape girl who'd complained. It had to be. She never returned. But a couple of weeks later, my manager came over, glowing as she showed me the report from the health inspectors that had found no fault whatsoever with my unit, and even went so far as to offer mild praise for its hygiene. And I glowed personally for several days afterwards, if I am not still glowing. I think it may have left a permanent lustre somewhere about me. I was clean, you see. Officially clean. I have never felt so clean in my life.

A Visit to the Fat Man

WHEN I was little my mother used to take me to visit the Fat Man. He lived at the other end of our road in a house that was almost identical to ours. I never really understood what the connection was between my mother and the Fat Man, but they seemed to be old friends. Or perhaps it was his wife that my mother was friendly with, I don't know. His wife wasn't fat. She was quite slim, in fact. I remember her as a quiet, gentle, kind woman. She wore clothes that were twenty years out of date even then, which meant she dressed like a woman from the 1940s, and had the same sort of hairstyle – curled and waved and backcombed. They had a dog as well. The dog was called Bonny and was a sheepdog-type of dog, black and white. She was also very gentle and friendly and, though quite big and strong, gave the impression of being incredibly light, as if she might float away.

Whenever we talked about the Fat Man and his wife, my mother and I referred to them as Bonny's Master and Bonny's Mistress, so I never knew their names. But to myself I always referred to Bonny's Master as the Fat Man.

I don't remember ever saying anything much on our visits to the Fat Man. Bonny's Mistress would make a brief fuss over me, then I would sit in a chair and do nothing for the half-hour or so that we were there. My mother did most of the talking, and the conversations she had with the couple passed completely over my head. Sometimes I would play with Bonny. We didn't have our own dog and I remember being fascinated by her mouth. The length of it. That fact that it was packed with all these sharp teeth; and the peculiar bacon-rasher tongue that fitted so neatly in among them all, and that would sometimes drape itself across the sharp teeth, so that you could almost see the impression of the teeth showing through the flesh of the tongue. I imagined how much it must hurt when a dog bit its tongue. I remember that we once took Bonny a present, a plastic pork chop that would squeak when you pressed it. Bonny was really excited by this chop, and would jump up enthusiastically and try to snatch it out of our hands. Bonny was very careful not to touch me with her teeth. As though she'd been trained to be gentle with children.

The Fat Man would usually be sitting on the couch, and if he was sitting on the couch there wasn't room for anyone else to sit there. He was exceptionally fat. He bulged in places you wouldn't expect a person to bulge, as though he had cushions stuffed under his clothes. He was fat everywhere except for his ears. He wore thin cotton shirts that must have been tailor-made because they fitted him well, not straining at the buttons as you might imagine. His face always had a freshly scrubbed appearance, quite rosy and boyish in a way, and he was nearly always smiling. He wasn't bald, but his hair was thinning, and he used to Brylcreem it and comb it back until it sat smooth and flat on his scalp like a swimming cap. Sometimes my mother and Bonny's Mistress would go into another room and I would be left alone with the Fat Man. I would be sitting on my wooden dining chair; he would be sitting on the couch, smiling at me. If I caught his eye he would sometimes wink. Sometimes he would say something like, 'How are you doing, Chuck?' Apart from the winks, he wouldn't move. Sometimes I would try not to look at him, but feel conscious, out of the corner of my eye, of him still smiling, and looking at me. He never stirred from the couch. He was always there, sitting in the same position. It was as though someone had made him, and left him there.

THE Fat Man got fatter over the years. I was older, but still little, and the Fat Man had become so fat that he had moved from the couch to the bed. He was just too big to get up. So when we went to visit now, we had to go into the bedroom. There, the Fat Man would be lying on top of the bed. It didn't matter how many times I saw the Fat Man, I was always surprised by the size of him, the shape of him. On the bed he looked fatter than ever (which he was), and he had taken to wearing nothing but an enormous pair of boxer shorts, because (I supposed) getting dressed and undressed was becoming too difficult. Sometimes he would be lying on his back, sometimes on his front and sometimes his side but he never changed position in my presence. When he was on his back, the enormous dome of his belly was visible, and seemed, from my young, seated perspective, almost to reach to the ceiling. His breasts flopped to the side, each pap as bulky as a big baby. And at the end of this great mass of swaying, rippling, undulating flesh, the Fat Man's head seemed small and puny, though it still bore an almost permanent grin. His head always made me think of a little village situated at the foot of a mountain. In the samc way that the villagers might not be fully aware of the mountain towering over them, because they could never see it properly, being too close, so the Fat Man's head never seemed to me to be fully aware of the size of his body. If he could have stepped out of himself and taken in the view of his little head and his big, sprawling, whale-like body, then he would have got a big shock, I am sure.

SO now when we went to visit the Fat Man, we spent most of the time in the bedroom. The most remarkable thing about this room was that it contained a collection of swords. They were proudly displayed on the wall, resting horizontally on special brackets. There were three columns of swords on the wall, and there were many different types. Some were straight and flat-bladed, like King Arthur swords. Others were thin-bladed foils with round hand-guards like they use in fencing. Épées, they're called. Then there were the curved scimitars and the samurai swords; the shorter, dagger-like swords. Some were richly adorned with decorative metalwork and jewellery. Some had leather tassels hanging from the handles. I have to say I loved looking at them, but the odd thing was, nobody talked about them. You would think that, with a child in the room, they might want to talk to me about the swords, because I was very interested, at the time, in things like battles. We had a teacher who could make history lessons come alive with his descriptions of the Battle of Hastings. I remember him telling us how he'd seen a re-enactment of it once on the telly. He told us that, during this programme, someone took a swing at a pig to demonstrate the effect of a sword-blow on the human body. A fully grown pig was, he said, very similar in anatomy to a human body. So they got this dead pig and hung it up, and someone took hold of one of those big, straight two-handed swords they used then, maybe a claymore, something with a lot of weight. And the teacher asked us how deep we thought the sword went into the pig's body. Hands went up and most people said an inch, or two inches, or six inches. And the teacher surprised us by saying no, the sword went right through the pig's body, cut it clean in half. Even making allowances, he said, for clothing and armour, and the fact that you wouldn't always be able to give the sword a full swing, there must have been an awful lot of half-bodies left lying on the field at the end of the Battle of Hastings. And even more severed arms, legs and heads. What a sight that must have been. And the amount of blood. The field must have been drenched.

But we never talked about the swords in the Fat Man's bedroom. I suppose they had been up there for so long that the Fat Man and his wife didn't notice them any more. But I noticed them. You couldn't help it.

THE only time the swords were mentioned was on my very last visit to the house. Bonny's Mistress and my mother had gone into another room to talk about something. I was left alone with the Fat Man, who this time was lying on his back. This meant he was facing the wall with the swords on, and I could see he was looking at them. He was lifting and craning his neck to see round the dome of his tummy. He would look at them, and then he would smile at me and wink as he always did. But this time he also said, 'Chuck, will you pass me one of those swords?'

The Fat Man had a high-pitched, soft, fluty voice.

I stood up, hesitantly, not sure if I should really be allowed to handle the weapons. I wondered what my mother would do if she came back in and found me with a sword in my hand. So I looked at the Fat Man again, at his little, smiling head. He raised a thick, quivering arm and gestured for me to go over to the swords, nodding eagerly. So I went over to the wall with the swords. The Fat Man was pointing.

'That one,' he said, guiding me, 'no, up, up again, there, that one.'

It was one of the big, heavy-looking claymores.

'Careful with it,' the Fat Man said. 'All you got to do is put one hand under the blade, one hand under the handle, and lift.'

I did as instructed. Even in the warm bedroom, the iron of the sword felt cold. But when I lifted it, I was startled by its lightness. It was as though it was made of plastic.

The Fat Man could see how I'd misjudged its weight.

'Lighter than it looks, isn't it?' he called from the bed through a half-laugh. I nodded, though I still felt the need to be very careful with the sword, and even nodding seemed a bit risky. Even with the flat of the blade in my hand, I could get a sense of the sharpness of the edge as it rested against my skin. I walked carefully over to the Fat Man, as carefully as if I was carrying a dish full to the brim with a precious liquid that I didn't want to spill.

Using both hands, the Fat Man took the sword by its handle. He held it vertically for a moment, still lying on his back and looking with one eye down its length. Then – God Almighty – he started swinging the thing around. I could hear the blade whoosh through the air, see it flash in the dim light, and I could feel the air stir against my cheek. I had to jump back. The Fat Man was really giving it some, whirling the great claymore around, tightening his face with the effort, and his whole body shaking and rippling with exertion. I'd never seen him do anything energetic like that before. His body was shaking and rocking so much it was like he was going to erupt; he went pink all over, and the sweat broke out almost immediately over his body, and there was a bitter tang in the air, but still his muscles worked. And his tits were flying and big folds of skin were flapping and banging against each other and ripples were moving through his body as if he was an enormous lake of flesh and someone had thrown in a great big stone.

Then suddenly it stopped. The Fat Man stopped swinging his sword back and forth, the creaking noise the bed had given came to a stop, although it took a while for the movement in the Fat Man's body to settle down, and for his body to become still, rather like (I remember thinking) the rocking horse in the children's playground which would go on lurching back and forth for a good ten minutes after you got off it.

The Fat Man was out of breath, and was puffing. He was holding the sword vertically. A great big blubbery knight. He then lowered the sword into the horizontal position and said, 'There you go, Chuck. You can put it back now.' I carried the sword in the same way that I had carried it before, and returned it to its place on the wall.

I didn't see the Fat Man after that. My mum carried on visiting, but I'd become too grown up to follow my mother round. Sometimes I'd see Bonny's Mistress taking Bonny for a walk.

Then, about five years later, when I was a teenager and had almost forgotten about my visits to the Fat Man, something rather odd happened. Bonny's Mistress became convinced that their house was going to be knocked down. She would stop people in the street, asking them to sign a petition. She got my mum to sign it. My mum asked her about it and she said the council were going to knock their house down. Why? The woman wasn't specific, she just said the council wanted to knock it down. It seemed strange. Her house was just one of many in the street, nothing special about it. Why should they want to knock that particular house down? My mother got in touch with the council. The council said they had no plans at all to knock the Fat Man's house down. It got into the papers. The council insisted they had no plans, and were unlikely ever to have any plans to knock the house down. But that didn't stop the Fat Man's wife. She walked around the town wearing a placard that said 'Save Our House From Council's Demolition Men'. Outside the house itself, she put a sign up that said 'Council = Nazis', with a big swastika underneath it.

No one said as much, but the Fat Man's wife seemed to have gone mad. Eventually she was found unconscious in her front garden and was taken away in an ambulance. She was put into a hospital and never came back. With no one to look after the Fat Man, he had to go as well. I wasn't there at the time but I heard they used a big delivery van, specially adapted. They had to knock out part of the door frame to get him through. I don't know where they took him. Eventually the house was sold, and new people moved in. I don't know what happened to the swords. Or Bonny.

Firemen

ERICA was woken in the middle of the night by the sound of burning, which came through into her dreams, strangely, as the sound of running water. She had dreamt she was in a vast, complicated public convenience, something like the changing area of the old swimming pool she used to visit as a child, with its broken yellow tiles and walk-through footbaths. In her dream, the cubicles had only low walls surrounding them so there was no privacy. She remembered hunting all over for an enclosed lavatory, but all she could find were exposed ones, some of which were clogged with excrement. She ran up and down little flights of tiled steps with increasing desperation, and eventually steeled herself to use one of the low-walled lavatories, looking carefully to see if there was anyone around. In the distance, some men in vests were gathered at a washing trough. At this point, as she prepared to undo her trousers, she woke up.

It was a dream she'd had several times since her split with

Paul. The desperate hunt through a confused complex of exposed lavatories. The odd pile of shit here and there, a brass tap left running, men in vests shaving. And a continual sound of water trickling and gushing. As though the lavatories were on permanent, automatic flush.

She sat up. Having escaped the anxiety of her dreamworld, she had been thrust into a far more dangerous one, and for a moment she thought the house might be on fire. It took only a few moments to realise this was not the case, and that the fire was outside rather than inside. Looking at the curtains, she could see that there was an orange glow beyond them, and a sense of jerky flamelike movement. It was probably another car on fire. It had happened twice since Christmas in her street. Gale and Phil had had a burning car directly outside their house only a couple of weeks ago. The heat had been so intense that the glass in their living room window had cracked.

Erica got out of bed to take a look. It was at times like these she most regretted throwing Paul out of the house. Having to deal with stuff like this, on her own, at night, was one of the worst things about being separated.

She parted the curtains and peeped through. It was like a sudden, unexpected glimpse of sunrise. Something bright was in the small front garden. It couldn't have been a car. More likely it was a wheelie bin. They were regularly set on fire by local kids. Once the plastic itself started burning the fire could get very intense. But they were usually left to burn on the pavement. This one was alarmingly close to the house.

She hurried downstairs and into the living room. It was like stepping into a theatre in the midst of a performance, but with the curtain still down. From gaps in the living room curtains dead-straight shafts of orange light crossed the ceiling, and on all the walls there were shadows leaping and falling, as if produced by a troupe of dancers. It made the room look very welcoming and festive.

She approached the curtains cautiously, remembering the cracked windows of her neighbours' house. She felt slightly awkward about opening them. It was a bit like walking up to the curtains in a changing room when you're not quite sure if there's anyone in there, fearing you might expose someone struggling into a dress two sizes too small for them. Instead, she reached through the curtains with her hand to touch the window. The glass was warm rather than hot, so she opened the curtains fully. There was the fire, barely three paces from the front of the house. A heap of burning matter – it could have been a wheelie bin, it was impossible to tell. There was no danger that it would reach the house. She was more concerned that it would set fire to the high privet hedge. There was nothing else in the garden worth worrying about. It never got the sun and they'd never taken much care of it. It was just a stretch of cracked concrete; they'd covered the two flower beds with gravel to stop the weeds.

Erica phoned the fire brigade. She realised she was shaking now, and for the first time felt frightened. The reality of the situation was beginning to register. Someone had decided to pick on her front garden for a fire. It was an act of violence directed at her and her property. Although she tried reasoning with herself that it was just a random act of vandalism, she couldn't help taking it personally. Some kids had chosen her house, picked it out from all the others in the street, as the place to dump their burning wheelie bin. She was afraid to go outside in case they were still there, and once she'd phoned the fire brigade, she felt a need to draw the curtains, so that she couldn't be seen. Having the fire in the front garden was like being stared at. Before closing the curtains, however, she removed the ornaments and other items that were on the front windowsill. A hand-painted beach pebble they'd brought back from Greece. A terracotta seahorse from the same holiday. Hardly combustible things, but she felt the need to remove them anyway.

The fire brigade took their time coming. When they arrived, the fire had started to die down, and Erica felt embarrassed about having called them. A woman on her own, she didn't want the firemen to think she was one of those desperate divorcees who call out the fire brigade just to get a handsome man into the house. She pulled her dressing gown tight as the engine rolled up the street, a great crimson chariot. It lit up all the neighbouring houses with its revolving blue lights. In their Roman gladiator headgear, the firemen seemed to have arrived from an impossibly distant age of chivalry and heroism. Erica couldn't help gasping at the sight.

The fire was out in seconds, the engine giving a mighty and powerful groan as its pumps discharged. Steam rose. The firemen lingered, though. One of them told her that they had to 'make safe', in other words check that the fire was properly out, that there weren't any embers or sparks that might reignite the blaze. They also had to ascertain, as far as they could, the cause of the fire. A report had to be written. They had to check for smoke damage. They hoisted a rig of spotlights on to the top of the engine which washed Erica's house and garden in bright, clear light. They asked to see inside Erica's house, just to make sure. They swaggered through the place leaving wet footprints on the carpet.

'I feel a bit stupid,' said Erica to the person she imagined was the chief fireman. 'It turned out to be such a little fire.'

'No problem,' said the chief fireman.

'Do you know what it was?'

'My boys are just having a look. There was a strong smell of petrol out there, did you notice?'

'No. I didn't go outside.'

The fireman's walkie-talkie gave a sudden burst of incomprehensible monologue, to which the chief fireman replied with equal incomprehensibility.

Another fireman stepped inside the house and spoke to the chief fireman quietly.

They turned and conferred over something the fireman had found in the garden.

The chief fireman looked over his shoulder at Erica, with something like embarrassment on his face.

'Is anything wrong?' Erica asked, feeling she was being left out of some important meeting.

The chief fireman spoke.

'You say you were woken up by the fire. So you didn't hear anything beforehand?'

'No,' said Erica, 'I was woken by the noise of the fire. It sounds strange but I thought it sounded like water . . .'

The two firemen nodded to each other, as though they too had noticed how fire can sound like water at certain times. They must know so much about fire, Erica thought. All the different types of fire and the different sounds they make.

'We need to bring the police in on this one, madam,' said the chief fireman, reaching for his walkie-talkie again, then speaking into it, which meant he didn't hear Erica's subsequent questions. 'What's wrong?' she asked. 'Is there something going on?' She could tell the firemen were behaving oddly. Other firemen were coming into the house, carrying charred material that they showed to the chief firemen. He waved them back to the engine, and called out, 'Get a cordon round this lot now. I don't want another foot set on that place.'

'Are you going to tell me what's happening?' said Erica. The chief fireman had barred her way as she tried to pass through the front door.

'I don't advise going out there, madam.'

Over his shoulder Erica caught a glimpse of another fireman doubled up. It looked as though he was vomiting. The chief fireman could see that Erica had noticed this spectacle, and did his best to explain.

'We believe that a person was involved in this fire tonight.'

'What do you mean, "involved"? Do you mean . . . ?'

'We believe someone set fire to themselves in your front garden tonight.'

ONCE, Erica remembered, Paul had said something funny about firemen. He had said that the word 'fireman' suggested someone who started fires, rather than someone who put them out. He had said this after reading a book about a tribe in Africa that had weird and wonderful customs, one of which involved priests who divined the future from ashes. They would start a little fire, put it out, and read signs in the embers. These people were called firemen, at least that's how the author had translated the word. And that had made Paul laugh a lot. The author hadn't seemed to notice the silliness of sentences like, 'They asked the firemen if it was a good time to get married' or, 'The firemen would tell them when was the best time to plant crops.'

'What should you call firemen then, if it's the wrong word?' Erica had asked.

'Isn't it obvious?' Paul had said. 'They should be called "watermen". Help, there's a fire, call the watermen! Phone for the water brigade!' He could be very funny, Paul, sometimes.

'What you don't want, if there's a fire, is a lot of firemen adding to the blaze.'

Should she have forgiven him? He'd had two chances already. Three strikes and you're out. Those were the actual words she'd said to him. So when he did have a third affair, she'd stuck to her guns. It pained her to think of it now, but she had taken all his shirts down to the bottom of the back garden and had set fire to them. Paul had this thing about shirts. He treasured them. He was a little bit obsessed with them. He had them specially made at an old-fashioned tailor's in the centre of town. He even ironed them himself, not trusting his wife. He could spend a whole evening ironing his shirts. At the time, it had given her great pleasure to have him come home from work, walk out into the garden calling 'What are you up to?' and catch a glimpse of a silk sleeve or one-hundred-per-cent cotton cuff waving at him before drowning in flames.

'My shirts – you bitch!'

It had stolen her thunder a little bit that he immediately walked out of the house never to return. She had wanted the pleasure of pushing him through the front door, of hearing him plead for forgiveness. But that came later.

'If you were on fire I wouldn't piss on you!' she had called to him.

A week later the phone calls came, then the knocks on the door. Then the pleading letters. In the end, she'd had to get a court order against him. The letters were awful, full of self-pity and accusations that Erica was being cruel and heartless. The restaurant was doing badly. He said it was all her fault. He no longer had the will to charm his customers, and it was his charm that had been the restaurant's greatest asset. That was how he'd managed to get three of his waitresses into bed.

* * *

IT wasn't difficult for the police to establish Paul's identity from the heap of ashes in Erica's front garden. His teeth would have done it on their own, the two gold inlays and the one crown having survived the little inferno. But so had his wedding ring, engraved with '*Two Becomes One*' on the inside. Erica sobbed when she saw it at the police laboratory, in a little plastic evidence bag. She'd never dreamt Paul would do anything like this. The detectives seemed far from surprised, however. They soon uncovered a little horror story at the restaurant. Paul had been on the verge of bankruptcy. The detectives talked about Paul as though his life had followed a familiar and predictable pattern – loss of marriage followed by loss of livelihood followed by loss of life. They'd seen it all before, men going downhill like this. They seemed to suggest Erica was lucky. Quite often they feel inclined to take someone with them, usually the spouse, or in the worst cases the whole family. But Paul and Erica had never had children. Just as well, the detectives seemed to think.

SO Erica was left with the fireman. The chief fireman who'd 'made safe' that night. She did wonder if she was doing something indecent in seeing him, the man who'd extinguished her husband's conflagration. Perhaps there should have been a respectable interval – but what the hell, a man like that comes along once in what? five years? ten years? a lifetime? He could have walked straight out of a Coca-Cola advert. Lantern-jawed with designer stubble, warm, twinkly eyes, safe brown hair. Tall, with shoulders like she'd never seen before. Shoulders so straight and powerful, so solid and square, you could have used them as a mantelpiece.

There was just one problem. Erica so strongly associated the fireman's uniform with a male striptease artist she had once seen that she could not look at her fireman, who was called Tony, without seeing him onstage, gyrating. She'd only been to a couple of girls' nights out with male strippers, but the raunchy fireman had stuck in her mind. At the time, she had laughed with the rest of them, but now she was struck by the indignity of the whole thing. How would she have felt if it had been her own husband or father, even, up onstage?

And there was something else that was not quite right with Tony. She felt it when she was taken to a top-notch restaurant for dinner one evening for their first proper date. The confident, handsome fireman seemed suddenly out of his depth, as though he'd never had to deal with anything more sophisticated than a Happy Eater menu before. Erica felt herself cringe at the way he tried to deal with his embarrassment by adopting an over-casual, wilfully indifferent attitude to everything in the restaurant. 'Yeah, I'll have a bit of lamb, whatever.' 'Bung it on!' – when the waiter offered some rarity of an accompaniment. The man who walked through flames for a living was foundering in a sea of etiquette. 'We normally go for a curry after a middle shift,' he said, by way of explanation.

I like a man who can carry himself in a difficult social situation, Erica thought to herself. Paul could charm his way through any situation imaginable. He could have made the Queen feel she had to mind her p's and q's. At the same time, he could have rubbed shoulders with a crew of road sweepers and been one of their brothers in brushes. But she made allowances for Tony. He was a hero, after all. He was a man who routinely saved lives. He carrried people out of fiery buildings.

'It must give you a fantastic feeling,' she said, that evening in the restaurant, while Tony tried to work out how to cut his piece of meat, 'to save someone's life.'

Tony shrugged, and chewed.

'I mean, to save lives day in, day out, as part of your daily routine, docs it ever feel like – so what?'

'You'd be surprised,' Tony said, 'how unusual it is to get called to a fire where life is actually in danger. The sort of house-fire where a family is trapped upstairs, you maybe get one or two of those a year, if you're lucky . . .'

'Lucky?'

'Well, not quite the right word, I suppose, but we become firemen to save lives, so sometimes you're longing for the opportunity. A lot of the lads in the station have yet to see their first dead body.'

Erica remembered the fireman being sick in her front garden. It was the smell, she supposed. Not until you knew that it was a human being burning to death did you realise that the faint aroma of roasting lamb was not the usual aftermath of a Sunday dinner somewhere down the road, but the smell of sizzling human flesh. It had made her sick as well, though she hadn't vomited. Not physically. She had vomited in her mind. In her brain.

'Sheds, cars, wheelie bins,' said Tony, 'those are the sorts of fires we're most likely to see.'

'My husband made this joke once,' said Erica, 'that the word "fireman" suggests someone who starts fires rather than puts them out . . .'

She didn't know why she suddenly felt this need to test Tony. To see if he would get it. Why should she care? It was just a silly little thought.

'Why?' said Tony, pulling a face.

'It doesn't matter.'

Paul had that sort of mind. The sort of mind that would notice things like that. He had such an eye for detail. He once saw an advert on the telly where someone was screwing the lid on to a tube of toothpaste, and he noticed that the cap had a left-hand thread rather than a right-hand one. 'That can only mean one thing,' he said. 'That after they filmed it, they decided to flip it over. Now why would they do that?' But Tony was still keen to talk about fires.

'Funny thing: most domestic fires start in the kitchen – chip pans, that sort of thing. But most deaths from fire occur in the living room and bedroom. Why do you think that is?'

'Because people are more alert when they are in the kitchen, so they can get out in time?'

Tony looked surprised and a little disappointed that she'd found the answer so quickly. This meant, she supposed, that he'd been baffled by the fact when he'd first heard it. It diminished him again in her mind. The thought of him labouring over the paradox – *most fires break out in the kitchen, but most deaths from fire occur in the living room or bedroom – how the hell can that be? It just doesn't make sense. For crying out loud someone explain it to me!*

But it didn't really matter, Erica thought. He might lack a certain depth. He might not have the same quirky sense of humour as her old husband. But he had other qualities. He was almost embarrassingly handsome. As he drove her home that night, she couldn't help saying to herself, as if to help her prepare for an impossibly important event, 'I'm going to be fucked by a fireman. I'm going to be fucked by a fireman.'

Perhaps they should have gone back to his place. He seemed awkward from the moment he stepped through her front door. Was there some taboo, Erica wondered, in firemen visiting socially the dwellings they'd once saved from burning? Had some boundary of professional etiquette been breached? She didn't see how it could have been. But she wondered at Tony's hesitancy, even when she led him by a finger upstairs to the bedroom that she still cowered in at night, watching, stupidly, for any flickering glow from beyond the curtains. She faced him and pushed his jacket back over his shoulders, then yanked at the suede knot of his tie. He stood impassive for a moment, then reached forward and took hold of her breasts, giving them a rather rough going-over, as though testing to see if they were real. Then he fell on to her neck, golden bristles digging into her skin, and began gorging. The wetness of his saliva gave her a chill, the soft biting of his teeth was ticklish. She laughed and they fell backwards on to the bed. Thank God, Erica was thinking. Thank God he's loosened up. But she was alarmed a moment later by a new type of wetness. Tears were falling on to her face. The fireman was making a noise that she mistook at first for chuckling, but was in fact deep, heavy sobbing. And the tears were falling like the ingress of rain she remembered in that leaky old kitchen of her and Paul's first house.

'What's up?' she said.

When the fireman had collected himself, sitting up on the side of the bed, his head in his hands, Erica stroking his shoulders soothingly, he said, 'How can you do it?'

Erica sat back, feeling worried.

'Do what?'

'You know . . .' The fireman seemed to find the subject too distasteful to talk about, but he managed. '. . . do this, only a couple of weeks after . . .'

'Oh.' Erica felt a wave of disappointment crash through her body and extend its foamy reach right through into her furthest memories. What she had taken to be so strong and solid was in fact fragile and delicate. It had collapsed before her eyes. She couldn't say anything. Tony went on.

'I just don't know how a woman can watch her husband

burn to death, and then sleep with the fireman a couple of weeks later. I mean, I can still smell it. In this house. Can't you? The smoke. That smell . . .'

He stood up and began dressing.

'I'm sorry,' he said. 'Like I was saying, we don't actually get to see many dead bodies. And I've never seen anyone as badly burnt as your husband was that night. I mean, he was completely carbonised – don't you remember?'

'You wouldn't let me look.'

The fireman shook his head pityingly.

'All I can say is – I haven't been able to get it out of my mind since that night, and I didn't even know him. What sort of person must you be – actually *married* to him, and you don't even seem bothered about it?'

'What? You're trying to say I'm heartless? We were in the middle of a divorce. He'd been a complete bastard to me. Of course I get nightmares about the fire, but I want to move on. I have to live here night after night . . .'

But Tony was on his way out. Within seconds she was alone. She went to the bathroom and dried her neck and face with a towel.

She spent a long time crying that night. For about two hours the tears flowed, and by the time they stopped, she was asleep.

She had a dream. In the dream she was with Paul again, and he was like he was when they first met. She could see him in every detail. The mullet of hair cascading down behind his ears, which they'd laughed about in later years. The white jacket with the sleeves rolled up to the elbows (how did they always stay up?). The thin red lamé tie. And he was being his smooth, romantic self. He gave her a red rose, said he'd plucked it for her specially from his great-aunt's garden. They were in a restaurant. There were lobsters in glass tanks, their pincers bound with rubber bands. She was indescribably happy. Paul's skin was pale and smooth. Even in his mid-twenties he couldn't really grow a proper beard. They sat at a table holding hands and smiling into each other's eyes. There was romantic music playing. Chris De Burgh. 'Lady in Red'. The song they'd fallen in love to. And then Paul lifted something out from under the table. 'This is for you,' he said with his sweet, beautiful smile. A large parcel gift-wrapped in silver paper and with a big bow on it. 'For me? Paul, I'm so flattered.' She pulled at the bow and undid the string. The paper fell away. Diners on other tables were looking on with interest. They were the centre of attention. Within the paper was a white box, which she opened and looked inside, squealing with delight – 'Paul, Paul, how do you do it? How do you always know exactly what I want?' She reached in and lifted out the gift. A chamber pot, antique china with a motif of flowers (forget-me-nots), and a big handle on the side. 'I hoped you'd like it,' said Paul, leaning across the table to kiss her. 'Why don't you use it now?' 'Shall I?' Paul nodded eagerly. So she placed the chamber pot carefully on the floor beside the table, stood up, pulled down her knickers and squatted over the thing. Erica peed into the chamber pot, filling it to the brim, as guests all around the restaurant applauded.

My Husband's Dream

ONLY when I'd allowed her to convince me that her husband was long gone did I let Lucy take me to her farm. We arrived in the dark and spent the night making love in her rattling double bed, by the light of several scented candles whose perfumes, unfortunately, sent me into sneezes.

When I woke up, Lucy was already getting dressed. It was morning, and beautiful white light was pouring in through a small window in the thick farmhouse walls. I could still taste the marmalade tang of Lucy's body on my tongue. I ran it round my mouth as I watched her getting dressed, wondering if she could still taste me. I supposed not, as there was a toothbrush sticking out of her mouth, and shortly she drifted back to the bathroom and finished doing her teeth.

I looked at my watch and laughed, because it was still on my wrist. Had I really kept my watch on all through that long night of passionate lovemaking? What for? But now it said half past seven.

'Why are you getting up so early?' I said as Lucy came back into the bedroom, her hair wet from the quick wash she'd given it.

'I need to feed the animals. This is a farm, remember?'

I suddenly found myself filled with childish excitement. I had forgotten that we were on a farm. But it was so quiet, there were no animal sounds to remind me.

I walked naked to the window. I couldn't see any animals. There was a small, untidy yard, then a low stone wall, and then a stretch of poorly drained marshland, ditches brimming with bright, motionless water that led to the dykes, a few hundred yards off. Such land couldn't support sheep or cattle, who would sink into the peaty earth. The grass was poor – mostly marrams and thistles. Beyond the dykes I could see the tops of vast container ships heading inland up the estuary. As no sea was visible, it seemed as though these immense vessels, precariously stacked with their boxed cargoes, were sailing over dry land.

'What sort of animals do you keep?' I said, having to shout above the noise of a hairdryer. Lucy didn't hear me and I walked across the room to the other window. This was at the front of the house and showed the small driveway that led to the main road. Again there was no sign of livestock, nowhere to stall, feed or shelter animals.

Lucy was on her way down the narrow wooden stairs, which creaked and rasped loudly beneath her weight. I grabbed my clothes and followed, fastening my jeans as I went down, calling out, 'Hang on, I want to help you feed them.'

I followed Lucy through the crookedly flagged kitchen, past her warm range and, after she'd unlocked the back door with a huge key, out through the little glass-enclosed porch into the yard.

Still there was no sign of animals. Some rusted machinery, building materials, a wheelbarrow, a bath. Further off, the other side of the low stone wall, was an expensive-looking sports car with a dilapidated caravan attached. As I looked closer, I could see that the sports car was rather dilapidated as well. It was a Ferrari S2. It had no wheels and was resting on brick stacks. There were rust spots that leaked streaks of brown over the paintwork. The windows were blind with dust and leaves, and there was a faintly green, mossy tinge to the whole thing. The caravan, a five-berth Riviera Rimini with a blue flash down the side, was in a similar condition. Lucy vaguely dismissed these objects as her 'husband's toys', which he had since discarded.

'I sold the wheels to a farmer's son who wanted to put them on his little Peugeot 205. The car itself is worth quite a lot of money, so I'm told. If my husband ever comes back it'll be for that.'

Lucy was heading towards an enclosure a little way away. Among some thorny bushes there was a tall fence of wire netting that surrounded a space the size of a couple of tennis courts.

'I can't see any animals,' I said. 'Do you really have any?'

'I have thousands,' said Lucy, smiling as she fiddled with the latch to the gate of the enclosure, 'tens of thousands. I couldn't count them, really.'

I was expecting, at the best, some sort of battery farm, chickens in little cages or something (though there hardly seemed room even for that), but within the enclosure there was just a series of rectangular, raised wooden beds, each about the size and shape of a single human bed, arranged radially, like spokes, around a large sycamore tree. The rectangles were filled with dark soil, which was heaped up to a shallow peak in some of them. Others had covers on – scraps of old carpet – which made them look even more like beds. I wandered among these structures for a while, feeling somewhat disappointed (they were so evidently for growing something – so where were the animals?), poked a finger now and then into their cool, crumbly soils, while Lucy busied herself with a wheelbarrow and a spade, shovelling something from a heap on the floor into the barrow. Though there were no animals about, there was a strong smell of animal manure, and it was this that Lucy was filling her barrow with, then spreading it over the beds.

I enjoyed, for a few moments, the spectacle of Lucy as a manual labourer. I couldn't help but see, in the way she handled that spade, an echo of the way she'd handled me in bed the night before. The strength, energy and dexterity were all there, but on a larger scale – and the same curve of the back, the same hanging forward of dark strands of luscious hair, the same determined pursing and pouting of the lips. There could hardly have been any drying off between the sweat of last night and the sweat she was working up now.

Lucy must have known, when she caught a glimpse of me watching her, what was going through my mind, because she gave me a secretive smile that thrilled me, and I thought how lucky I was to be here, now, on her little farm with its invisible animals.

'You were joking about the animals, weren't you?' I called. 'What do you grow here, mushrooms?'

'I'll show you,' said Lucy, and she led me over to one of her carpet-covered beds. She removed the carpet. 'I had to extract these yesterday as the man's coming for them this morning. There's always a fear they'll run off if they're extracted too soon, but it was a dry night, luckily.'

The contents of the bed puzzled me at first. It seemed to contain one of those vast ropes you see on old sailing ships, a great thick knotted loop composed of thousands of lesser threads, the whole thing twisting back on itself in a series of coils that packed the wooden bed to its edges. There was no soil in this bed, and nothing alive, or so I thought. And then I saw that the rope was moving. Some of the tiny threads, hanging loose, were waving slightly, as if disturbed by a breeze (there wasn't any wind). And a strange, gentle clenching and unclenching seemed to be passing in waves along the length of the rope. Barely perceptible contractions. The whole thing was alive.

'You can help me get them in the sacks if you like,' said Lucy.

Once I'd sensed the close presence of a powerful, muscular body, I instinctively withdrew. It was as though Lucy had pulled back the covers on a hospital bed to reveal a patient horribly mutilated, without limbs or head, but still alive. The great body of what had seemed rope was writhing, flexing, bracing itself – a Promethean presence, naked in a tub.

'Some people are physically sick when they first see them,' said Lucy. 'My last lover was. Stupid. They're only worms.' She took a garden fork, eased it down between the mass of worms and the wooden side of the bed. As the rusty metal tines of the fork touched the tangled worms, I noticed a reflex contraction as the worms sank from the metal's touch. This set up a response in the interlinked worms and sent a muscular ripple down the length of the worm bed.

'Can you get one of those sacks for me?' said Lucy, pointing to a stack near the fence. I did, and watched as Lucy gently raised her fork until a sizeable clump of worms began to separate from the bed, slowly disentangling, appearing to snap, until there was a coherent ball of matter at the end of her fork, which she tipped into the sack I was holding open.

'You are looking at my husband's dream,' she said. 'The biggest worm farm in Kent. Not that it has a lot of competition. God knows where he got the idea from. He gave up everything for this. He had a good job. Merchant fucking banker – I know, it's laughable. Everyone thought he was mad. I was happy to go along with him. I thought it would bring us closer together. We'd be working side by side, I'd see more of him . . . Perhaps that was the problem. Anyway, as soon as we were here and had our first crop of worms, he seemed to change.'

Lucy had another forkful of worms, added them to the sack, which was nearly full. I asked her if there was much money in worm farming.

'Not much, but enough. The good thing is they don't take much looking after, just dollops of manure now and then. You have to thin them out, separate the adolescents from the breeders. My husband built up a good client network – he was good at that sort of thing. Do you feel sick yet?'

'No. Not at all.'

'Not like my last lover,' Lucy grinned, showing her slightly and attractively protruding teeth. But the second mention of her last lover in so short a time irritated me. It reduced me to just one among many. Lucy poked her fork into another heap of worms. I could see a tiny mouth reaching out for something to bite into, its gritty lips banging up against the steel of the fork and withdrawing. I watched the way Lucy gently loosened the worms so that they slid off the fork and into the bag, imagined I could see thousands of tiny limbs reaching out desperately as they fell.

By now we had filled two bags, and we wheeled them, in

another barrow, out to the gate at the end of the track, to be collected.

LUCY claimed that, six months ago, her husband had simply walked out. He had done it before, the sudden disappearance, but usually he was back after a few days, a fortnight at most. He had never been gone this long. She said she used to hang on the front door waiting for him to come home, but not this time. This time she was glad he was gone. She hoped he was never coming back.

'And now I'm waiting for my worms to do the same thing,' she said. 'Worms are migratory creatures. I bet you didn't know that. One of the things you have to watch out for, on a worm farm, is a walkout. That's what they call it,' (she laughed), 'a walkout. Suddenly, without any warning, a whole bed of worms will crawl out and make off. It only ever happens on a wet night. I saw a walkout once: they were spilling over the side of the bed like a liquid, pouring down the side, spreading out on the floor. We had to scoop them up and put them back.'

We walked back to the farmhouse. After she locked her gate (why lock it, I wondered, did she really expect thieves to come for her worms?), Lucy put her arm around me, gave my waist a squeeze, nuzzled right into me as we walked slowly across the yard to the back door.

Having seen the worms, I somehow felt I had seen everything about Lucy. I had seen all her qualities in one moment. The thought briefly occurred to me that I was arm in arm with a murderess, that she had slaughtered her self-absorbed husband, having been driven to despair by his obsession with worm farming. Perhaps she had actually become jealous of the creatures. Maybe she had fed them her husband's dismembered carcass. And then I thought that, in fact, she was some kind of saint, incapable of cruelty, devoting her life to the healing of the sick. I didn't really care. I was going back to bed with her. She was beautiful. I couldn't wait.

I caught a glimpse of the red Ferrari and its caravan, rusting and unloved in the grass.

Cleopatra

I

THAT odd thing happened on the train back from London Bridge, when you find yourself sitting opposite someone and you can't stop looking at them. The woman sitting opposite me was not unattractive, though her face was slightly pouchy with age, but she had these beautiful eyelashes that fluttered and waved as she read her book – and since her face was downturned in reading, these lashes were really the only thing I could see of her eyes. That was, until she lifted her face and caught me staring at her. Normally in these circumstances I would look away, but this time I couldn't, at least not for a second or two, and neither could she. For a short moment, we were both caught in each other's gaze, and this could mean only one thing – that we recognised each other.

We kept catching each other with our eyes as we trundled through the suburbs of south-east London. I tried my best to look away from her when I could, out of the window at the back gardens that passed by in an endless parade of lawns. I pass the same gardens twice a day, five days a week, but I still find them fascinating. You look at them and it is like looking at a series of faces, some old and worn out, some young and healthy, some pretty, some ugly. I often wonder if the householders' own faces resemble their gardens, and I wouldn't be surprised if they did. Sometimes you would glimpse a child on a trampoline, or a man in a vest at a bathroom window, or a couple helping each other fit new curtains, and you would think how close-packed the lives of Londoners seem, all taking place within a couple of bricks' thickness of each other, and also on a series of islands, with vast spaces separating them.

Once, many years ago, I was watching the houses from the train in what must have been winter because it was dark, and I glimpsed, through an uncurtained window in the back of a typical brick-built house, a woman having a bath. She was sitting up, her hair in a towel-turban, squeezing a sponge and letting the water spill over her enormous pink breasts. The vision lasted maybe three seconds. Three seconds. I couldn't even see the woman's face, but somehow the memory stayed with me, as one of the most beautiful things I have ever seen from a train window. Perhaps because it was offered in such a surprising, sudden and unexpected way. In the thousand or more times I've done the journey since, I've seen nothing like it.

Eventually, and to my surprise, the woman sitting opposite me spoke.

'Excuse me,' she said, 'I know this sounds like a really crap chat-up line and it's not meant to be, but don't I know you?'

'I think we've met before,' I said, or something like that, and there followed a discussion that took us through several stations, where we tried to find some point of intersection in our lives. We had gone to different schools and different universities, we'd worked for different companies and had different dentists. But we had once lived in the same part of London at the same time. In fact, we'd lived in the same flat for the same two years in the mid seventies. It was at this point that the woman suddenly snapped her fingers and said, with a squeal of triumph, 'I've got it! You're my first husband.'

'That's it!' I replied, almost simultaneously. 'You're my ex-wife.'

WHAT else had I forgotten in the twenty-three years since I'd married Sophia? It wasn't that she even looked that different. Those eyelashes should have told me straight away that I was sitting opposite someone I'd once shared my life with. I thought back to Sophia's face as it had been then. It had been the eyes and their lashes that had attracted me in the first place. She was too clever for me though. Or I was too stupid for her. She had a good mind. She'd already spent a year in New York as an intern on the *Village Voice*, writing reviews of gigs and films. Then she'd gone out to the Far East for a year, helping famine victims in Cambodia, or somewhere like that. I couldn't keep up with her. Shortly after we married, she got a job with the BBC, a researcher for the *Today* programme. It meant she was almost constantly at work, and when not at work her life was an endless stream of media parties and gatherings, the launch of this, the opening of that. Oh, how the memories came flooding back. I'd embarrassed her at several of these events. I can remember a dinner party once, the wife of the American ambassador asked me what I did. I said I worked as a waiter in a pizza restaurant. She was completely knocked back by that. She looked at me, blinking, her long earrings twinkling, trying to think of a follow-up. The best she could manage was, 'Is that good work?' I had to feel sorry for her. Luckily the economics editor of *The Times* chipped in with some witty remarks about the service economy, and the ambassador's wife was saved. There had been many incidents like that. There would be long arguments in the taxi home where we would accuse each other of being snobs. 'You don't like me working in a pizza restaurant, do you?'

'It's not that I don't like it. It's just that someone like you shouldn't do it, unless you're making some sort of ironic or satirical point.'

'I'm doing it because it's the only job I can get.'

'You know that's not true.'

I had recently tried for a job in the Civil Service. They had a gruelling three-part selection process. I'd had to go to a mansion in the middle of the New Forest and spend two days role-playing with the other applicants. In one exercise we were each given a report and told to use it to build a bridge between the protesters, contractors and residents surrounding a projected bypass. As team leader for the task, I took it all too literally and insisted that everyone use their reports to help build a model suspension bridge, with the additional help of Sellotape and string. It was a magnificent structure, and could bear the weight of a stapler and two ballpoint pens. It also made me a laughing stock for the rest of the weekend.

'I told you they wouldn't take me,' I'd said to Sophia when I got home. 'Fast-track, slow-track, they didn't want me.'

I'd had vague hopes of working for the Foreign Office, or the EU. In an embassy somewhere hot and exotic.

Eventually Sophia went off with one of the editors of the 'Today' Programme, and I was more upset by the humiliation than by the sense of loss – the awful experience of listening to Brian Redhead droning on, and knowing that, just a few feet away from him, was some creep in a black collarless shirt who, the night before, had had Sophia dancing on the end of his prick. Perhaps she was in there with him – probably promoted from mere researcher now, probably editorial assistant, probably sitting there next to him, probably giving him a handjob under the mixing desk while they watch Brian Redhead interviewing the Chancellor of the Exchequer: 'Let us have a minute's silence while the nation mourns the death of your monetary policy, and you compose an apology for presuming to know how I cast my vote . . .'

('Oh yes, that's so good, Brian, that's got the listeners by the balls . . .')

Eyelashes, that's all it was. That's what the editor of *Today* liked, the flutter of eyelashes against his glans, the vampish sweep of them up and down, up and down, curled and set and gooey with mascara (so they seemed, she never did anything to them, didn't need to). That's what I told myself. And when I first saw a picture of Brian Redhead, I was horrified. The man should never have grown a beard. It didn't suit him. It looked as though it had been Sellotaped there, and had slipped. It looked like the sort of beard a woman would grow, if she could.

Sophia, with your headphones round your neck, turning down the volume on the voice of the nation . . .

WHEN I mentioned it now, on the train, she spoke of it as though she hadn't thought about it for years. She even seemed surprised

I remembered. Their relationship, she said, had barely lasted a year. The editor had turned out to be an obsessive compulsive, the sort of person who has to touch every button on his shirt before he posts a letter. He was like that with sex as well, Sophia said, smiling.

She asked me what I was doing now.

'I'm a career criminal,' I said.

'Oh really? What line?'

'House-breaking. But I want to move into bank robbery.'

'Why?'

'Because that's where the money is.'

I looked out of the window into the late-evening twilight of the back gardens. Then, in a shaft of light, I caught a glimpse of an old man peeing into a milk bottle.

'And is that how burglars dress these days, in a suit and tie?'

'The world moves on.'

'And is that your swag bag – that smart little attaché case on your lap?'

'We have to be presentable.'

Sophia eyed me through those velvet curls, then shrugged.

'OK, you don't want to talk about what you do.'

'And what about you? What are you now, editor of *Newsweek* or something?'

Sophia wrinkled her nose in bewildered disgust.

'*Newsweek*? Why on earth would I be editor of *Newsweek*?'

'Married with three or four kids?'

'Yes, I'm married. No kids. Hey – did we ever get properly divorced? I don't remember.'

'Oh, I'm sure we did. If we didn't then I'm in big trouble . . .'

'But you don't sound sure.'

She was right, I wasn't sure. So much had happened in the last twenty-three years: parents dying, children being born, jobs to apply for, promotions to be sought, bonuses to be worked for, houses to buy and sell and let, cars to be bought and repaired and sold, holidays to be taken. Where, in all this gouged and mine-shafted landscape of transactions and dealings, were the little wilting flowers of our divorce papers? I couldn't remember ever seeing them, but that didn't meant they weren't there somewhere.

'I remarried twice. Two kids by the first marriage, they're grown up now. Second marriage is going through one of its difficult phases at the moment, but we'll soldier on.'

'You mean third marriage.'

I still can't think how Sophia had managed to disappear so thoroughly from my thoughts. Perhaps it was because we had owned so little. Whereas my second marriage had ended in a hideous tangle of property disputes and custody battles, Sophia and I had come apart as if held by the weakest of glues. A few paperbacks and LPs had to be divided up, and I'm not even sure we bothered much about those.

The train was stuck at a faulty signal for a while. We sat there for a long time, Sophia and I, with the darkness outside. To my horror, our conversation became so dry that Sophia at one point returned to her book. Twenty-three years of our life to catch up on and there was hardly enough to talk about. Out of the window I could see a living room brightly lit in the darkness. Through its patio doors a family were sitting around a table, but in the twenty minutes or so that I was stuck with this view, the family didn't say anything to each other, just sat there, at an empty table, staring.

I got an invitation from Sophia. Of all things, an invitation. She said she lived in a little place in South Wales, near the coast out beyond Cardiff. If I was ever down that way, I should let her know. That was hardly ever likely to happen, I thought. I'd have to make a special journey. Did she expect me to bring my wife, too? What would her current partner make of it? She hadn't said much about him, only one thing, just as I was leaving to get off the train. She said this thing I could hardly believe. Her husband, she said, was a policeman.

2

It must have been about a year later, because it was dark again on the train home, the orange-lit suburbs drifting past the window, masked every now and then by the inkiness of a cutting or tunnel. I'd been going through a spell of overwork, taking the early train in, falling asleep on the train home. Sometimes the trains home were full of dozing commuters, especially towards the end of the week. Exhausted office personnel nodding in and out of sleep. Once I was the only one awake in a whole carriage. So I don't know if I dreamt this or not, but I remember stopping at a signal, opening my tired eyes and looking out into blackness, except for this one lit and uncurtained window, which revealed in yellowy tungsten light a woman preparing her bath. She had a towel wrapped around her body and another one in a turban around her wet hair. What makes me think it might have been a dream was that she seemed to be filling the bath with milk. She had these copper churns that she was picking up and tipping over, one by one, and warm steamy milk was pouring out of them. This went on for a few minutes and I was willing the train to stay where it was so that I could watch the whole process. After about three or four churns, the woman tested the milk. She stirred it with her hand, then lifted her hand to her mouth and licked her fingers. She was an extraordinarily beautiful woman. She seemed satisfied, and began undoing the loose knot of her towel, where it was fastened above her bosom. And it was at that moment that the train jolted into motion, and the woman, her back to me, the towel slipping slowly down, was drawn away into the greater darkness of the city.

3

SOPHIA lived in an old terraced cottage in a fishing village. She had left the media world altogether and had retrained as an occupational therapist. She said she had simplified her life and had been very glad to have escaped the London rat race. She found her present life, and her job, much more fulfilling.

'I live within sight of the beautiful Ceredigion coast, with the Black Mountains within half an hour's drive,' she said in one of her letters. I wondered why she'd felt the need to add that 'beautiful' to her sentence. Perhaps I shouldn't have added the adjective to my account of my own patch. 'I live within sight of the beautiful North Downs,' I'd said in one of my letters. As if we were in competition with each other to see who could live the most exquisitely. If so, then Sophia had probably won, I had to concede. Her bulging, crooked-roofed fisherman's cottage was lifted straight from a postcard. By comparision, my Barratt home, although roomier and plusher, never really stood a chance.

But it was poky inside. There were low beams, and jutting mantels. A small settee and an armchair swallowed up nearly all the living room. Her husband, a big man, seemed like a giant in the restricted space. As though he'd drained the bottle that said 'Drink Me'. Barry, he was called. A man of strong opinions. So unlike Sophia, or at least the Sophia I had known. Yet, she seemed quite in awe of this man. Whenever she said anything that was the least bit ambiguous, Barry would hold up a wagging finger and say, 'Remember, Sophia, woolly thinking.'

And Sophia would put an apologetic hand over her mouth.

Nothing Barry said had anything ambiguous about it. He saw the world in black and white. He was a member of a local debating society. I laughed when I heard it. I didn't think such things still existed. But apparently, on the first Tuesday of every month, Barry and his fellow debaters discussed some profound topic or other, formally, with speakers for and against, eventually voting on a proposition. Sometimes they discussed current affairs, sometimes philosophical or religious or ethical issues. 'Last month the proposition was "Art has no use in our society",' Barry told me, when we'd settled down for dinner at the tiny yellow dining table.

'And was that passed or not?'

'What do you think?'

'I think,' said Sophia, chipping in, 'that it shouldn't have been passed.'

'And why do you think that, my beloved one?'

'Because art does have a use . . .'

'Such as?'

'Well, some of my patients . . . In occupational therapy we use art all the time, whether it's painting or ceramics. We even pay artists to come in and help, and the patients get a lot out of it.'

'OK,' said Barry, rocking his head thoughtfully from side to side, 'perhaps it does have a use in that very restricted, and limited context. What about in a wider sense? Do you think art has any use in society generally?'

'It makes you a better person,' said Sophia, then bit her lip. 'I need to be more specific, don't I? I need to apply the argument. I'm sorry for being woolly, but if people aren't made better through the perception of beauty, then what hope is there?'

Barry sat back and smiled a most patronising smile.

'A very interesting point,' he said, leaning forward and casting a shadow over the whole table as he did so. 'In that case let me talk about a certain artist I'm thinking of, Austrian-born, a great admirer of the Romantic school of landscape painting, who was twice turned down by the very conservative Vienna Academy of Fine Arts, on the recommendation that he should be studying architecture, who made his living by selling paintings, who painted, according to some estimates, over two thousand paintings by the age of twenty-five . . .'

Barry broke off and looked at me and Sophia, smiling.

'You know who I am talking about?'

We both nodded.

'So did art make Adolf Hitler a better person? If you think it did, then I hate to think what he would have been like without it . . .'

This was the way with Barry. He didn't talk, he debated, or lectured. I noticed a framed certificate on the wall. While Barry and Sophia were clearing away the dinner things, and I was left alone in the tiny living room with a glass of port, I looked at it up close.

This Certificate is Awarded
To Sgt Barry Hillier
Of the Glamorgan Police Force
For exceptional Bravery
In the line of duty

It gave no specifics about what this brave deed might have been, and I didn't get any clues when Barry caught me looking at the certificate on his way through the living room, though I nodded towards it and asked for an explanation.

'What's this all about?'

His reply was a slow shake of the head with eyes closed, much as a parent might gesture to a child who is asking too many questions. 'All in the line of duty,' he said. 'They give these things out for telling the time. All in the line of duty.'

Shortly, Barry went upstairs to do some work in his study. I had seen this study on the little tour I was given on my arrival, a cramped space with an antique roll-top desk and a computer. The shelves were filled with heavy reference works: encyclopedias and books of quotations, *The Times Atlas of History, The Guinness Book of Records* (several editions), *The Family Britannica.*

For the first time, Sophia and I were alone, and could talk more freely. She came through to the living room and sat on the couch. She kicked off her shoes, and I found myself staring at her feet, and at that darker section of nylon at the tip of the foot, enclosing the toes. I wanted to talk to her about so many things, but first I had to ask her about the certificate.

'Wouldn't he tell you?'

'No.'

'I'm not surprised. He hardly tells anyone. He'll be very cross with me if I tell you.' She looked up at the ceiling, above which was Barry's study. 'We should keep our voices down, he could easily overhear us.'

'I won't let on.'

Sophia dipped her nose into her Chardonnay, thoughtfully.

'OK,' she said, in a quieter tone, 'but promise me you won't say I told you.'

'Promise.'

'Well, it's quite simple really. He was shot. Twice. He was part of a raid on a house – I don't know all the details myself. Someone took shots at him. He was wearing a bulletproof vest, grappled the gun off the man. They let him keep the vest as a souvenir, he's got it upstairs in his study. The bullets had to be taken out for forensics, of course . . .'

'Quite a story,' I said.

'Yes, not many people can say they've been shot, or know what it feels like to be hit by a bullet.'

I had this image in my mind, of Barry as a breastplated warrior, the spears pinging off his blazing armour, an unstoppable force.

'How long have you been married?' I asked.

'Nearly four years.'

'Happy?'

Sophia looked down into her glass again, and I got that beautiful perspective on her face – cheekbones and eyelashes, and the crown of her head all glossy with hair. The gauzed feet stirred uncomfortably.

'Ecstatic,' she replied, eventually. I couldn't decide if she was being ironic or not.

'You've changed,' I said.

'Of course I have. It's been twenty-three years.'

'But in odd ways, Sophia. Listen, you're not like the woman I knew.' I was talking hurriedly, urgently now, as if I feared Barry might suddenly return. 'In those days you were spirited, confident. You could do anything, you could out-argue anyone, you had a thirst for knowledge, but now you're always kowtowing to that man. He treats you like a little girl . . .'

Sophia was looking at me in open-mouthed wonder, I hoped

at the sudden realisation of an uncomfortable truth. But I soon learned it was from shock at my audacity.

'You can't sit in my living room and talk like that about my husband,' she began.

'But you know it's true, don't you?'

'I just cannot discuss my marriage with you, it's totally inappropriate, you'll have to leave –'

'OK. Sorry.' I held up my hands, pleadingly. 'Sorry, but you invited me here. Surely we can talk openly together –'

'Yes, as long as Barry is in the room. I'm not going to discuss him behind his back.'

'Fair enough,' I said, 'but I can see you're not really happy. That's all I want to say, so we can stop talking about it.'

Instead of denying it, Sophia sighed exasperatedly, shaking her head. I went on.

'There's something else I wanted to say, and the main reason I decided to take up your invitation. Do you remember what we talked about on the train that day?'

'What? We talked about lots of things.'

'About our never getting properly divorced.'

'Oh. But we did, didn't we?'

'No, I don't think we ever did. I have thought back as hard as I can, and I cannot remember us ever getting divorced. Can you?'

Sophia was silent again, thinking. Her silence was enough to tell me that, like me, she had no clear recollection of any formal separation.

'Well,' she said, 'it's not a problem. After twenty-three years of living apart, it'll just be a formality.'

'You're forgetting that we are both bigamously married. That could have rather awkward consequences. I've only just started thinking about them, but already I'm overwhelmed by the legal implications. My two subsequent marriages are null and void. My ex-wife isn't my ex-wife at all. And my children, you could say you're their stepmother. Perhaps you'd like to meet them some time.'

'This is ridiculous,' said Sophia. 'It's just a legal anomaly, it can be easily sorted out.'

'Don't be so sure,' I said. 'Bigamy is a crime, whether it's done through oversight or not. And how are we ever going to get divorced without bringing our bigamy to public attention?'

'What are you saying?'

'I'm saying there could be all sorts of problems. What about Barry? He's a policeman. If it's discovered he's bigamously married, he could lose his job.'

'Not if it's my fault . . .'

'But who's to say it's not his fault as well? He could be in on it.'

'To what purpose?'

'For any number of fraudulent purposes. It won't look good whatever happens. As for me, I could end up in prison.'

'Don't be crazy.'

'It's true. It's taken very seriously.'

'No. A good solicitor will be able to sort it out. I suggest you look for one as soon as you get home.'

'So you're going to let Barry know you're still married? How do you think he'll take it when you tell him your marriage has been a complete sham?'

I was pleased that this gave Sophia pause. She had been about to dismiss the whole thing as a fuss about nothing, but now I could tell she was starting to have doubts. 'If you like,' I said, 'I could tell him now, when he comes downstairs.'

'Don't you dare,' said Sophia. 'We need to think carefully

about this. Think it through. That's why we need to talk to a good solicitor, each of us.'

'It could be a good excuse for a fresh start,' I said.

'What do you mean?'

I moved over to Sophia, leaving my armchair and joining her on the couch. It was the closest I'd been to her all evening. I could feel the breeze from those big, fanning eyelashes of hers, and the eyes within them were staring at me, tinged with fear.

'You and me, Sophia. A fresh start.'

Her eyes drew away from mine and moved down my face to my mouth, as though she was trying to see the words I had spoken, as if they might drift like smoke from my lips.

'What about your wife?'

'I told you, we're probably going to separate. Funny, isn't it? I thought I was pretty bad at relationships, but it turns out I've been married for longer than I've been married, if you see what I mean. I think we might have to stay married for ever. Just so we don't rock the boat.'

There was a short silence. Then, from above, came an odd rasping sound. It could have been a floorboard creaking, but it wasn't. We were directly under Barry's study, and I am sure that what we heard through the low ceiling was a fart.

4

It was thanks to Barry's use of the room upstairs as a study that there was no spare bedroom in the house. I was given the couch. It was only then, unable to sleep on the lumpy cushions, that I thought about the inappropriateness of my visit. It had been a kind of madness between us – her offer of the invitation, my acceptance of it. I really didn't know why I had come. There had been no intention, on my part, to salvage anything of our long-lost marriage. But somehow, now that I was in the cottage, and could see how Sophia had been beaten down beneath the granite self-confidence of her policeman husband, I found stirring in me a desperate longing for us to be together again, fuelled by that odd fact I'd discovered – that we were still married. I couldn't fathom it – the so easily forgotten loves and desires. To forget an entire marriage so thoroughly, to the extent that one doesn't even remember to get divorced . . . Had my life really been so crowded with incident that such a thing could have been overlooked? It almost made me fear for my sanity, and I wondered if my longing for Sophia was really a longing for the restoration of my own memory and sense of who I was and had been. But perhaps that is a definition of love anyway.

I woke early, keen to be up and dressed before Sophia and Barry appeared. I washed and shaved in the little downstairs bathroom that was beyond the kitchen. Barry had one of those big badger-bristle shaving brushes, rather redundant for the purposes of a bearded man like him, and I thought about using it myself, but baulked at the roughness of the thing when I tested it in my palm. But I did use his shaving cream. I never use shaving cream myself, and was interested to know what it would feel like. It was horrible. The stuff burst out of its pressurised nozzle with a lisping, seething sound, and filled my palm with a reeking white goo that I could hardly bear to put on my face.

I hung around in the living room after making myself a cup of tea (there seemed to be no sugar in the house at all), and eventually Sophia appeared in a purple dressing gown. Belted at the waist, this garment showed off her figure magnificently. The previous evening, I'd thought she'd filled out into a middle-aged shapelessness, but here she was, with a waist and hips curved and voluptuous. Her hair was loose and pleasingly dishevelled. She gave me a smile as she passed through into the kitchen.

'Help yourself to – oh, you have. If you want some toast . . .'

She went into the chilly bathroom and began running a bath. I felt unable to settle, experiencing that discomfort you sometimes feel as a guest in someone else's house, not quite knowing where you should be or what you should be doing. I couldn't sit down and so drifted between the kitchen and the living room with my mug of tea, listening to the quiet roar of Sophia's filling bath. She remained in the bathroom. The door was still open and I could hear her pottering around.

Then Barry appeared, with nothing on but a towel around his waist. His upper torso was dense with hair, like a doormat, turning grey. He had big puffy nipples and was wearing a thin gold chain. His eyes were sleepy and half closed, and he barely acknowledged me as he walked past, even though he was close enough to nearly brush against me. He went into the bathroom as well, and the door was closed behind him. I heard the click of a bolt being drawn across.

Alone in the kitchen, I listened to the noise of their mutual ablutions through the bathroom door. The only sound was of water. Barry and Sophia were silent. I couldn't help but picture them together, naked in that little bath (it hadn't seemed that big to me). Why did they do it? As part of a sexual game? A sacred rite? To save hot water? I tried to picture Barry's big podgy hands wiping soap across Sophia's breasts, or her doing the same to his candlestick cock. Occasionally I heard a murmur. Not words, but perhaps half-words – an 'Er, huh-huh' and then an 'Er, er, mmm, yer', then a splash and trickle as a limb was lifted out of the water for washing. As I listened, my ear almost to the door, the noises seemed to become thicker, and heavier, big slurping and sucking sounds, as though they were bathing in syrup, and their wordless murmurings became less and less human. In the end it seemed as if, behind the bathroom door, were two amorphous creatures struggling in a lagoon, or a single beast that was a hybrid of many parts, multi-limbed and double-headed, flailing in a morass of perfumed mud.

And it was at that point I decided to leave, while they were still in their bath, probably doing each other's backs (I caught a trickling laugh from Sophia as I went out of earshot). I picked up everything I had, put it in my canvas bag and left as quietly as I could.

Gardening

MIKE had got some friends from work to help him with the garden. Since he was their boss, they couldn't easily refuse him, not without a good excuse. But even so, he was pleased with the turnout. He'd laid on free beer for the afternoon, and his wife Jill had prepared a cold spread.

Pete, Mike's assistant, was helping with the organisation. He handed round the beers, and divided the volunteers into two squads, one for making the pond, one for the bark chippings. The pond needed digging, and the spoil wheeled down to the end of the garden. Although it wasn't a huge pond Mike had in mind, it was surprising the amount of earth that needed shifting. Still, Mike reckoned that Ian, Raj, Charlie and Leo, four big strong lads from the warehouse, could get it all done in an afternoon.

Some wives and girlfriends had come along, and their presence gave the afternoon a party atmosphere. There were even a few children running around. Some of the girls who worked in the office had brought their partners to help with the heavy work. Brian was the husband of Brenda, who did some of the admin upstairs, and Stuart, a civil engineer in his late fifties, was married to Maureen, one of the cleaners. Mike knew Stuart quite well. He'd given Mike a lot of help a few years ago when Mike was planning his extension. Stuart knew all the building regulations, and practically designed the extension for Mike, as well as advising him on the planning application.

Mike wasn't exactly frightened of Stuart. He wouldn't have said that he was frightened of anybody. As his teenage daughter once put it, rather shockingly: 'I ain't scared of no fucker.' (Not true, in her case, as beneath a streetwise exterior she was terrified of most people.) But Mike did feel rather in awe of Stuart. He had such command, such self-possession. He carried immense responsibilities so lightly. Mike had only a vague understanding of Stuart's line of work, but had a sense that he was responsible for the structural soundness of entire cities, that he built bridges that carried a million people a month. And yet he appeared untroubled by such onerous duties. He strolled casually around the garden, beer in hand (work hadn't started properly yet, they were waiting for the bark chippings to be delivered), looking relaxed, and chatting with Mike about cars. All morning Mike had been mesmerised by Stuart's new car, a black Jaguar XJR supercharged V8 with heated seats and walnut-burr veneers. Stuart must have been earning a bomb, and yet his wife cleaned the toilets at Mike's office.

Maureen was a small, plump, noisy woman with curly brown hair and heavy bags under her eyes. She would creep up behind Mike in the men's loo while he was at the urinal, then clang her bucket down loudly behind him, causing him to piss all over his shoes. She had a foul mouth and a vulgar sense of humour. And she had seen his prick in full flow.

'Don't you go working my fucking husband too hard, you old bastard,' she yelled at Mike as she passed the two men, carrying a trayful of coffee mugs. 'Boss or no fucking boss.'

Mike laughed, as though this piece of verbal abuse was actually funny, and smiled politely, though he found it hard to believe that comic intentions lay behind its deafening vitriol. She was always like that. Mock rages so authentic they were disconcerting. What was she doing cleaning the toilets? She didn't need to work. Her husband was rich. Did she really sweep the piss out of the porcelain gutters because she wanted to? It seemed to Mike a little disgusting that someone could take pleasure in work like that.

It was silly, but Mike really felt like going up to Stuart and saying, *Look, you're a good-looking, successful, educated, professional man. Is the best you can do for a wife that slutty little dumpling of a woman who goes around my garden effing and blinding, and who cleans shit out of the toilets because she likes to have something to do? What went wrong, Stuart? For the love of God, what went wrong?*

Mike looked across the lawn and caught a glimpse of Maureen talking to his own wife, Jill. The contrast between the two couldn't have been stronger. Compared to frumpy little Maureen, Jill's beauty and elegance was doubled. What must it be like to come home every night to that sweary little tart, that little rubber ball of a woman who'd spent her day up to her elbows in tampons and sputum?

Mike couldn't help it but he was actually growing to hate Maureen. Another memory flashed through his mind – a memory of when she'd burst in, as usual, while Mike was quietly peeing at the urinal. She'd given a giggle and walked straight out again, and he heard her calling to the girls in the office, 'It's all right, darlings, there's nothing to see in there . . .' A short pause was followed by shrieking laughter from the girls. Mike presumed that, in the pause, Maureen had made a gesture, probably using finger and thumb, to describe the length of his penis.

It was in his power to sack her. The next time she makes a joke about my cock, he thought, I'll have her out on her arse. If only. Mike shuddered at the thought of the din she would kick up if he did such a thing. She was just one of these torments one had to endure. She was even shouting at him now, right across the garden.

'What are you standing around for? Why don't you do some bloody work for once? . . .'

Mike put a hand to his ear mockingly.

'Could you speak up a little bit, Maureen? I couldn't quite catch that . . .' Then, under his breath and through a smile, 'Why don't you wriggle off back to your sewer, you disgusting little rat?'

THE tipper truck arrived, carrying one and a half tons of bark chippings, which it shed with a thunderous roar, a mountain instantly forming in Mike's back garden. Jill and Pete distributed rakes, forks and shovels, but there weren't enough of these. They started giving out mops and old snooker cues, anything so that the party could begin levelling the mountain, spreading the chippings around to cover the dug-over part of the garden.

'Beats grass,' Mike said to Pete as they raked side by side. 'No more pissing about with mowers or sprinklers. Don't have to worry about weeds or moss or leaves or moles or any of that. Self-maintaining – bark chippings. Looks after itself; like concrete but prettier.'

'Yeah,' said Pete, whose own backyard, never in the sun and permanently soggy, was the scene of a perpetual struggle, between himself and the various forces that Mike had just mentioned, for the soul of a ten-by-five patch of lawn.

'I've got these mirrors,' said Mike. 'Just found them in one of the alleys behind the office. A barber's shop had closed down, being turned into a bookie's. They'd slung out their mirrors. I put them all in my boot. I saw this programme on the telly where they put mirrors in the garden. You can put them behind your pond and it makes it look twice as big.'

'That's a clever trick.'

'It works for flower beds as well. You can double your flower bed with a mirror. Brilliant.'

'Funny idea really,' said Pete, 'putting mirrors in your garden. They're indoor things really, aren't they? Like carpets. You wouldn't put a carpet down in your garden, would you?'

Mike thought, raked some chippings, then thought some more.

'No, not carpets, no. But then in this same programme they painted a fence. A bright colour as well. Not just staining it with creosote, but painting it yellow or purple.'

'Painting a fence?' said Pete, laughing cautiously, unsure if Mike was joking, then adding, 'Could look good, I suppose. Are you going to paint yours?'

Mike wrinkled his nose to indicate he'd thought about it but was now having doubts. 'Might look silly, a purple fence,' he said. 'Doesn't go with the other gardens, does it? Seems wrong somehow, like wallpapering your garden wall, or having a telly out on the lawn.'

'Mind you, now you mention it . . . Perhaps it's the latest trend to have everything inside out and outside in. Frank in Despatch has got a fountain in his living room. Not a big gushing one, just a little trickly one, with lots of big old stones and gravel. Looked quite good, come to think of it.'

Mike straightened his back and looked around. Everywhere there were people raking the bark chippings, working back and forth. The garden was full of laughter. Mike was a little bothered by the smell of them, however. En masse the smell of bark chippings was faintly ammonia-like. They smelt of piss.

'It's funny what the world is coming to,' he said, bending down again. 'One of my wife's friends has got a vegetable patch in her bedroom. The floor's covered in soil and she grows carrots, lettuce and spring onions down beside her bed. She just reaches out in the morning, grabs a carrot for breakfast . . .'

'What about all the watering?' asked Pete. 'Has she got some sort of waterproof lining on the floor or something . . . ? Oh, you're joking. It's a joke, isn't it?'

Mike raked silently, then said, 'How will we know when we're outside and when we're inside? That's the problem . . .'

MAUREEN'S powerful voice suddenly assailed Mike across the swathe of bark chippings.

'Look what you've done to my husband,' she yelled. 'I told you not to work him too hard.' She pointed, glaring with mock severity at the recumbent figure of her husband as he sweltered in a deckchair, a hat over his face.

Maureen's mock rages were often of an unsettling ferocity. Mike recalled the time she'd carried her mop and bucket into his office while he was taking a rare and well-deserved nap, and how she'd exploded in pseudo-fury, but then worked herself up into such a splenetic humdinger of a rage that her little frame went stiff, her face puffed up like an angry cat's, her eyes dribbled and her temple veins bulged. 'Of all the fucking nerve!' she'd screeched. 'Sitting here with his fucking feet up on the fucking desk while I've been on the go non-stop since half past five in the morning cleaning up all his fucking mess . . .' and so on and so on and so on. These diatribes were always as though spoken to an unseen third party, an angry little commentary on the situation. Hard to tell, sometimes, if she was joking or not. Surely one couldn't expend that much emotional energy on a mere joke?

She was like that now, red-faced and big-veined, shrieking at him across the half-formed garden. Mike was getting fed up with it. Funny or not, being hollered at by this harridan in his own back garden with his neighbours listening, being hollered at by a common little woman who was good for nothing more than sluicing lavatories, began to anger him so much that he felt compelled to return her invective and started yelling back, doing his best to disguise his anger as good humour. 'Why don't you get that lazy bastard of a husband of yours to do some work for once, he's never done a day's work in his life, he doesn't know what hard work means . . .' And other jibes of that nature. Yet the effect of these was to crank up the woman's harangue even more, and so these exchanges went on for some time, Mike, determined not to be got the better of in his own garden, trying to shout over Maureen's vituperation, until Pete nudged him.

'I think you'd better listen to what she's saying . . .'

Mike fell silent, allowing Maureen's words to become intelligible in the otherwise quiet garden.

'You've fucking killed him, you bastard, you've killed him.'

And it was true, as Mike slowly and reluctantly realised. Stuart, the civil engineer in his deckchair, was dead.

IT was the last time Maureen did any shouting, as far as Mike knew. She was a changed person after her husband's death.

The transformation was so complete it was almost frightening. To Mike's amazement, she turned to him for help with the sudden mountain of administrative chores that appeared after Stuart's death: dealing with the insurance people, the mortgage people, the credit-card people, dealing with her husband's boss who, like Mike, took a while to believe Stuart was dead. Mike had to take the death certificate over to the Borough Engineer in order for him to release all wages owing with outstanding holiday pay and other benefits. The Borough Engineer was deeply embarrassed, mainly because he'd left an angry message on Stuart's answering machine, which let it be known that he was getting fed up with all the time off Stuart had been taking in recent weeks.

So Stuart hadn't been quite the high-flyer Mike had imagined. He'd never had the power and authority Mike had assumed was his. He was just someone who worked in an office, with a boss like everyone else. Someone who could be ordered about and harangued. Mike felt a bit disappointed, as though at the sight of a fallen idol. But why had he assumed Stuart had been someone with power and high standing? Was it just because he drove those flashy cars? That, in combination with a naturally authoritative and confident demeanour, seemed to have been enough to convince Mike. This fact made him feel foolish.

And then, at the funeral, Mike finally got to drive Stuart's car. It was a perfect car for a funeral after all, being jet black and with the lines, almost, of a limousine. Mike got the car washed and valeted for the funeral, and drove Maureen and her family with respectful slowness the sombre route from her house to the crematorium, all the while nearly weeping at not being able to open the car up properly, to feel the surge of those eight cylinders.

The car was another problem for Maureen. She couldn't

drive and had no use for it. Mike offered to handle the selling of it for her, and in the meantime she allowed him to have full use of it. He could drive it as though it was his own.

If he could have afforded it, Mike would have bought the Jaguar himself. As it was he delayed selling it for as long as he could decently manage. And then Maureen started troubling him with queries about her husband's debts. They were huge. Stuart had been spending far beyond his means. That was how he'd managed to buy the car, by borrowing the money, far more than he could afford to pay back. Within weeks of her husband's death, Maureen was being troubled by debt collectors; she was seeing debt counsellors and insolvency advisers. The sale of the car became urgent, even though it would only pay off a small portion of the overall debt. It looked as if Maureen was going to lose her house and everything in it. She phoned Mike nearly every day with a new problem for him to sort out. He went to see her every day after work and spent an hour or more going through the latest batch of paperwork.

'You need to get a good accountant on to this straight away,' he said. 'I'll see if I can get Bernard to look at it.' Bernard was the firm's own accountant.

'I'm only the office cleaner,' said Maureen in a quiet voice. 'I don't suppose he'll have time.'

'Well, don't worry about it,' said Mike. 'I'm sure it can all be sorted out.'

'You're a very kind man, Mike. I know you've got a lot on your plate.'

'It's no trouble. It's the least I can do.'

'But you've got the firm to run. I saw all those papers in the car when you pulled up. You're taking them home to work on, aren't you? I'm just another burden.'

Well, the man did die in my garden, Mike felt like saying. He died trying to help me rake all those bark chippings.

'Stuart never had much time for his own garden,' said Maureen, as though Mike had spoken those thoughts out loud. 'If you take a look out the back you'll just see a lot of overgrown grass. He could never be bothered. But he was very keen to help you with yours. Very keen.'

Mike craned his neck to see if he could glimpse the garden from the couch where they were sitting. He could make out the gnarled branches of fruit trees. He stood up and went over. A scruffy lawn framed by overgrown shrubs.

'Well, it was very good of both of you to come round that day. I'm just sorry it turned out like it did.'

Mike recalled the horrible afternoon that followed. The gardeners crowding round Stuart's body, the young bloke from Logistics, whose only medical training had been watching *Casualty* every week, trying to bump-start Stuart's heart as if he was a clapped-out Ford Anglia. Then the air ambulance that came and hovered over the house for what seemed like hours looking for somewhere to land. At one point it looked like it was going to touch down in the garden and blow all the bark chippings away. The road ambulance arrived while it was still circling.

'Perhaps we can organise something for you along the same lines,' said Mike, the thought suddenly occurring to him. 'You know, get a few of the people from the office to sort the garden out. I mean, if you do have to sell this place (and let's hope not) you want to get the best possible price for it, don't you? We could muster a little work party to sort the lawn out . . .'

'Bark chippings,' said Maureen, enthusiastically. 'My Stuart was really impressed with those bark chippings of yours. He said he never thought of it himself, but how, like, they could be put down and you'd never have to worry about mowing the lawn or pulling up weeds again.'

'They're self-maintaining,' said Mike, staring out of the window, 'just the job. We could sort that for you, Maureen, no problem. A couple of tons of bark chippings and you'll never have to worry about the garden again. I'll sort it, don't worry.'

Mike felt triumphant. He imagined the day, a few weeks in the future, when this event might take place. Ian, Raj, Charlie and Leo digging over the old lawn, all the others milling around with beers in their hands. He himself would be the stand-in host, because Maureen would be too weak and frightened to deal with everyone. She would be encouraged to take a seat, perhaps a deckchair, while everyone else would do the work. Eve might bring her kids over again. A party atmosphere, like a village fete. Fun and games. Then the bark chippings would arrive, another thunderous roar from the tipper truck. They would have to be unloaded on to the concrete round the side of the house this time, and they'd have to get a couple of wheelbarrows to take it all through to the lawn. He'd order extra chippings, completely swamp the fucking garden in them. Have them a foot deep from fence to fence so that no blade of grass or straggly little sprig of ragwort would ever dare to show its face again. And would she care, Maureen? When they left afterwards? Leaving her alone in her little living room, sitting in her little armchair with her cold cup of coffee, looking out of the window at what used to be a garden, and just seeing bark chippings going on for ever, no flowers, no grass, no nothing. The apple trees would have to be cut down beforehand. After all, you don't want dead apples landing on bark chippings and rotting away. Just bark chippings, nothing growing. And then watch her try her old trick of telling him he didn't do any work. Just let her try her shrieking again, her hollering and mock bollockings. There'd be no chance of her going back to her old ways. It'd shut her up for good. Shut her up for good.

Chickenpox

IT was 1979, and you were infected. Somehow you'd caught a children's disease – chickenpox. But you were a grown-up, an adult. Well, seventeen. Not exactly a child.

I went round to your house: 15 Peacock Walk. I loved that name. Not a peacock in sight, not a peacock to be seen, though there were always pigeons on your roof. The tiles were splattered with their crap. You said they woke you up by having sex above your bedroom window.

Your mum let me in. She was talking to me at last, if you could call it talking. And your Norwegian stepdad, well, he wasn't exactly talking, but then he never did. Your mother asked me if I'd had the chickenpox. I said I had, when I was little. I've still got the scars, little silver dots on my chest (she didn't ask to see them). She said I could go up. We hadn't seen each other for a week and you were over the worst. I found you in your bed, with your 1920s nightgown on (white silk), and you were radiating heat like a two-bar fire. There were some pustules on your face. You kept looking at yourself in a hand mirror, and every time you looked, you dropped the mirror and moaned in a way that made me laugh. You reminded me of that tapestry with the unicorns.

Your bedroom was long and narrow, and you shared it with your little sister. She was getting ready for a bath. I could see her across the landing, pulling towels out of an airing cupboard. She was naked but for a large towel wrapped around her. When she lifted her arm to reach into the airing cupboard she exposed part of her breast. I couldn't help looking and you could see that I was distracted by something. Then you turned and saw what had been distracting me. And you mouthed words of disgust at me – 'She's only fourteen!' – jumping to conclusions. But it was the smoothness of her skin that fascinated me. Nothing else. You were covered in pox. You were disease-ridden. You were poxy, pustuled, scabbed, carbuncled. They were on your face, on your neck, on your shoulders. You had them on your breasts (you showed me), your belly, your thighs. And yes, you had them on your cunt (you didn't show me those). Papules, lesions. Ulcers. It was as though someone had taken the measure of you, a tailor who worked in flesh, marking you up for a new skin. You had used calamine lotion to ease the itching and dry up the pustules. The lotion took on the colour of your skin, but wrinkled as it dried, which made it look like your skin in seventy years' time. Little bits of old skin all over you. And the temperature. You were hot, sweating, and curls of hair were stuck to your forehead. But still I had the nerve to ask you, after a week-long absence (that in those days felt like a lifetime) – any chance of a fuck?

As if we could have done it there in your room, with your sister in the bathroom and your parents downstairs. In your room that still had all its soft toys, though now demoted to your little sister's bed, from which they viewed you reproachfully. Your dressing table with its hopeful arsenals of cosmetics – strawberry-flavoured lipstick, strawberry-flavoured soaps, the futuristic radio alarm clock that sprang into life with the voice of Tony Blackburn every morning (so you said). I'd bought you a gift, the LP of *Armed Forces* by Elvis Costello and the Attractions, with its horrible pastel drawing of charging elephants on the cover. Who could have imagined my surprise when you replied, yes, let's fuck.

Then the long-drawn-out process of doing it without being discovered. We had to leave the door open so that we had forewarning. If the door was shut, someone could have burst in at any moment. With it open, we had a view of the landing so we could see anyone coming up the stairs. And we had to stay dressed, of course. Your little sister was safely in the bath. She would be in there for ages, you said. Somehow we managed it. Nothing exposed, nothing given away. Your little sister was splashing in the distance, and we stopped every now and then to listen for noise on the stairs, giggling when we heard a voice from somewhere down below, your stepdad telling everyone to get ready for the big film on the TV that night (Humphrey Bogart). He called for your little sister, but she was in the bath. We were still fucking when he came up the stairs. You didn't notice him, because you were facing the wrong way, but I saw him, his blond Teddy-boy quiff and his steel-rimmed glasses, his blotchy face emerging from the stairwell. He had a sleeveless T-shirt on that showed off his show-off biceps and that stupid tattoo, the bleeding heart.

We were at the point of no return in our fuck and I couldn't bring myself to withdraw so I carried on. My head was burning with what was happening between us and I wondered if this was what it was actually like to have sex with a virus. Then your stepdad went in, just like that. Turned the handle of the bathroom door and stepped into the bathroom. Closed it behind him. I didn't really think about it because I was so bound up, and you were starting to gasp and make ecstatic noises and I had to put my hand over your mouth, and then your stepdad came out of the bathroom. I heard him say 'The film's starting now' in his quiet, polite, monotone voice. How he mumbled for a grown man. A real mumbler.

The lock didn't work on the bathroom door. You'd said because he'd tampered with it. I didn't tell you I'd seen him go into the bathroom while your little sister was in the bath. But I spent the next hour doing your scabs for you. Dabbing them with calamine lotion. I felt suddenly desperate for them to heal. And I dabbed them all. All of them, knowing I would never do this again. You had the antibodies now.

Milk

I

THIS could be the start of something big.

I am perfectly situated on the corner of Milwain Road and Cotton Street, the bus station on one side and the market on the other, with all the human traffic in between. Every few minutes, at peak times, a double-decker will swing into one of the yellow bays, unfold its doors and produce a random selection of humanity. From there, weary and thirsty, they will pass my transparent frontage.

I've done a count. A thousand people an hour. Inevitably they will be tempted. Who wouldn't be? I've a hundred glasses clean and sparkling, a hundred fluted goblets, Corinthian-lipped, of viridian-tinted Venetian glass waiting. My interior is the last word in upmarket café design: walnut veneer, cut-out all-in-one chairs hitched to chrome-steel frames, round tables of tortoiseshell-pink Formica, each one decorated with a smoked-glass vase containing a sprig of subtly unrealistic buttercups. The floor is violet lino, the walls mint-green ceramic tiling intaglioed with cows. At three and a half feet the tiling gives way via a black dado to pink plaster on which hang a series of Lichtensteinesque pop-art paintings of cows, grass, fruit, igloos, bees and pint bottles of milk. At the back is my servery – steel and glass with pink fittings, a spotlit display of cold bain-maries brimming with sliced fresh fruit, slender cylindrical jars of chocolate shavings, carafes of runny honey, cinnamon shakers, censers of allspice, jugs of cream. The centrepiece, however, is my Schweinfurth-Burmeister MkIII LactoMixa – glass silos of milk, chrome jugs like fairground mirrors, and the triple-headed, five-speed carbon-spindled loops of my power-whisks.

As I look at it now, an hour before my grand opening, I feel I am witnessing the last moments of its virginity. Those unstressed chairs. That spotless floor. It will never look like this again. Not quite. Over the coming months and years, these pristine surfaces will slowly accumulate the traces of usage, the marks, scratches and stains that are left even by the purest and cleanest of customers. But it will never look dirty, tacky, threadbare or rundown. It will never look old.

It will be the mother of replicas in neighbouring towns. In two years I will have a branch in Manchester, then Liverpool, Leeds. I will spread across the north of England like a sweet epidemic. And then I will move south. As I said, this could be the start of something big. An empire.

Business empires are always built around a single idea. Mine is this – quality milkshakes. Milkshakes for the milkshake connoisseur, for those discerning milkshake drinkers who are disgusted by the pink gunk of the seaside promenades, the puréed bubblegum of the burger bar, or the syrup-based strawberry froth of the greasy spoon. My milkshakes are a rethinking of the milkshake. They are made from the best-quality milk (full, half or fat-free), real fruit pieces (strawberry, raspberry, banana, blackcurrant, kiwi, melon, mango as well as other seasonal soft fruits), sweetened with heather honey, seasoned with spices, thickened with cream, garnished with any of a wide range of toppings (mocha, aniseed, crushed cloves, white-chocolate leaves, fresh mint, lemon balm, chopped pistachios). Each milkshake is individually tailored to a customer's wishes. Each milkshake is a gourmet experience, a celebration, a festival in a glass. I have reinvented the milkshake.

So that is my idea. Such a simple idea. So simple it barely merits being called an idea. To be honest it wasn't even my idea. Nor was it Mary's idea. Mary is my ex-wife. She left me the day I put the idea to her.

2

'YOU'RE what?' she said, her voice dangerously quiet, her nose shrunken with disgust. She was holding Theodore at the time. He was gently pounding the side of her head with a corduroy frog. I repeated what I'd said.

'I'm reinventing the milkshake, like I said. I'm going to totally rethink this unsophisticated beverage and I'm going to transform it into the designer drink of the nineties. It's never been done before; quality, specialist, haute-cuisine milkshakes. Milkshakes for grown-ups . . .'

Mary snatched Theodore's frog and threw it at me. I let it hit me.

'How could you?' she hissed. Only Theodore's presence was preventing her from screaming. 'Milkshakes. How could you?'

'What are you talking about? I'm doing this for us. You'll be able to give up work –'

'This was her idea, wasn't it?'

'Whose?'

'Janet. That cow.'

'No . . .'

Theodore blew a raspberry. Mary wiped spit from her reddened cheek. Our marriage was over in that instant. I had overlooked one essential fact when laying the foundations for my business empire – Mary my wife, my sweet ex-wife, detests, loathes, is repulsed by that simple, white, nearly odourless substance: milk. Where most people see a harmless, innocent liquid, Mary sees phantoms, disease, decay. No one can really explain this, least of all Mary. She and I always assumed she had an unpleasant experience involving milk as a child, although she can't recall one. And she was right about Janet. It was her idea. *Janet, that cow.* I wonder if Mary was, in the last few seconds of our marriage, making a joke there. Janet, you see, lives in a cowshed.

3

MARY and I first met at art school. I discovered her lactophobia the very first time I invited her back to my hall-of-residence hovel and offered her a mug of hot, sweet, milky, flesh-coloured tea. She peered into the mug as if into a hot abyss and withdrew sharply as the steam hit her face.

'Could I have one without milk?' she said, her voice taut with self-control. She went on to describe the revulsion she felt at the very idea of milk. She'd never tasted it. To be in the same room as milk was only barely tolerable. The thought of drinking it induced nausea. Once, a clumsy tea drinker had squirted a jigger of UHT over her, and she'd had to rush home and shower. I laughed, thinking her to be trendily neurotic, endearingly eccentric, original in her phobias as in her art.

Later that same sultry north London afternoon she unfastened the fish-shaped mother-of-pearl buttons on her white silk blouse to reveal those firmly ovoid breasts – twin treasures with salmon-pink nipples at which I was to drily suck for the next twelve years.

In those days she still had the legginess, the spidery clumsiness that was the last trace of the child in her body. After an awkwardly bumpy session of lovemaking I made the first of thousands of cups of black tea.

It quickly became routine. Two teas – milk for me, none for Mary. Ordering coffees in cafés it became automatic to say 'two coffees – one black'. Perhaps once a year her milk-attitude became the subject of a brief, playfully teasing conversation along the lines of:

– How can you not like milk, it's got no taste?

– It's disgusting.

– How can it be disgusting, it doesn't smell?

– It smells like blood.

– Was your mother frightened by a cow?

– I've never asked her.

– A milkman?

– I don't think so.

– But you like cheese, yogurt, butter . . .

– But I hate cream, blancmange, rice pudding . . .

– But you like ice cream . . .

– It doesn't matter if it's derived from milk, what matters is if it's milky, if it has that horrible, milky, yukky quality . . .

And she would perform a series of theatrical retchings, extending her tongue and hawking up invisible vomit.

We'd laugh.

4

BUT I turned into something of a disappointment in Mary's eyes. When we finished art school I became suddenly and briefly famous – the New Contemporaries, the Whitechapel Open, the John Moores, and then I was taken up by a Cork Street gallery. Colour photospreads of my work appeared in the glossies. I was profiled in the Sundays. My paintings began selling for four figures, then five figures.

I'd developed a reputation as the artist who paints sewage farms. Water-treatment works. Purification plants. To me they were charming little clearly bordered territories filled with ellipses, parallelograms, cubes and pyramids. I was fascinated by their boundedness. I painted sewage farms in Fauvist reds and greens, sewage farms populated by zebras and giraffes, I painted sewage farms as sites of carnal bliss, abstract sewage farms, sewage farms floating in the sky. The public lapped them up. My reviews were rapturous: 'He sees the sewage farm as a site of elemental renewal, of bodily resurrection, as a place that processes dead matter to produce rivers of life . . .' said one, under the title 'Fra Filippo of the Filter Beds'.

I wasn't surprised by my success. I felt an arrogant sense of entitlement, of expectations fulfilled, of satisfaction. I had the swagger of an innocent youth who's jaywalked the boundaries of the art establishment and pitched a shabby tent there. To have shown surprise or delight at my own achievement would have been to admit that my gift was not embroidered into my very chromosomes. That I was not a natural.

It all went wrong at my first major one-man show which, set as it was for touring to New York, LA and Berlin, should have sent my fame to uncharted heights. But as the show approached I felt a need to change direction. I'd been painting nothing but sewage farms for nearly five years. I'd painted all I could paint about them. I felt it both prudent and daring to change my subject. I painted racecourses.

Chester, Fontwell, Aintree. To me they were a logical development. I painted racecourses in Fauvist mauves and oranges, racecourses on which zebras and giraffes endlessly competed, racecourses whose green furlongs provided lush sites for exotic lovemaking. But above all, as with my water-treatment works, it was their boundedness that attracted me. These fenced-in, measured spaces.

The show flopped.

'Having abandoned the richly fertile ground of the sewage farm for the sterile and pointless looped turf of the horse-racing circuit, he could be said to have pulled up at the first fence . . .' wrote one cheaply punning reviewer.

My reputation evaporated. Did they expect me to paint sewage farms for the rest of my life? Some collectors of my work even tried selling my sewage farms back to me, seeing them shed layer after layer of investment value.

I could no longer support Mary and myself. We agreed that she should take a teaching job in Leeds while I put my career back on track. We both saw the sense of it. It wouldn't be long before my work was selling again, and Mary could leave teaching and concentrate on her own painting.

We settled in the gritstone isolation of Ravendale, the Pennine mill town Mary had grown up in, and I rented a studio in a disused woollen mill. Traces of fleece, little tufts and wisps, could still be found in its crevices.

The hills around us were dotted with reservoirs; some of them were great, elevated seas, others little more than ponds. Every fold and hollow of those wet mountains, it seemed, had been dammed and allowed to fill, the water piped to the towns and cities below. These quiet, sequestered, liquid harvestings became my new subject. I painted reservoirs in constructivist greys and browns, reservoirs like glass menageries, liquid beds (the site of aquatic lovemaking), reservoirs sailing in the sky tethered by spindly streams to the ground.

My early success didn't return. A decade had skipped by. People who were still in nappies when I was entering art school were now being hailed as the future of art. Painting was proclaimed dead. Landscape irrelevant. I tried to laugh it off as the transience of fashion, but my laughter had an echo in it. It came back to me. It bounced off the white walls of my studio. The empty walls.

And then Mary had a baby.

5

LITTLE Theodore showed me a path out of the white fortress my artistic career had become. Slowly I forgot about making paintings and became instead a househusband.

I'd watched Mary's skin slowly burnish itself with fine and lush hair, her dome become drum-tight and hard as marble, and I'd watched her breasts stock themselves with milk.

Mary was not troubled by the prospect of pregnancy's bodily cataclysms. Her only fear was that of being a milk-bearing creature. I pitied her and tried to imagine the horror she must feel at the notion of her body as not only a repository but a manufactory of that substance she considered more toxic than cyanide. She believed she was becoming a depot of vileness, and feared she would develop a need to suppress her own milk production, to escape her own body, to sever her own breasts.

But when it came, sealed up and present only as a weight in those antenatal weeks, she felt at first an indifference and later a pride in the new, pert stance of her breasts. And when the miraculous puppet, more bird than person, of our baby appeared, and the engine of her milk was, after several false starts, started, she felt no repulsion as she filled the intestinal loops of Theodore's tiny gut with her pure white thread.

For a while we wondered if her lactation might erase the horror she felt for cows' milk, and that we might enjoy a future of shared milkiness, of creamy desserts, rice puddings, blanc-manges. But her attitude towards cows' milk didn't change, and she could still feel a repugnance, though mild, if her own milk found its way back to her, if it leaked and dripped on to her skin, or if Theodore brought up a posset of her partly digested self, or more vigorously vomited, bearding himself like a curdy Father Christmas.

I continued making black coffees and black teas. I once tried whitening mine with Mary's milk, but it rose to the surface in oily droplets. I suckled at her once only. It was like drinking sweetened olive oil, carpeting my mouth wall to wall, floor to ceiling, with fatty deposits.

And this is where Janet comes in.

6

WE'D been in Ravendale for three years and I had made no friends. Mary saw chums from her childhood and had an adequate social life around the Leeds college where she continued to teach. I had spent my time in the white cube of my studio watching my canvases shrink and fade to nothing. There were other artists in Ravendale, a surprisingly large number in fact (there was even an area of back-to-backs and converted engineering workshops that called itself the Bohemian Quarter), but they were mostly young and I found their ambition and optimism relentlessly depressing. I felt a need to meet people unconnected with me or with painting and so, from the meagre list of social activities pinned to the noticeboards of Ravendale Library (UFOs, feng shui, tap dancing), I chose to join the Ravendale Archaeological Society, which met fortnightly.

At first the membership didn't look promising. Aged ladies with grey hair set in stiff, meringue-like waves, post-adolescents whose faces were pinned and ringed with silverwork like out-of-use noticeboards, self-consciously anachronistic gents with mutton-chops and tweedy, damp-smelling clothes. Janet presented a dazzling contrast to this motley assembly as we listened to a guest speaker discourse at length on Greek Revivalism in the mill chimneys of Ravendale Valley and surrounding areas.

Janet had a freshness, a newness about her. What, I wondered, was something so colourful and alive doing at a meeting of antiquaries, whose interest in dust and rot I was already finding dull. Neither did she look like the farmer's wife she claimed to be, not with her bobbed blonde hair and lunulate earrings, her zebra-skin leggings and leather jacket. As we milled about with cups of tea after the lecture, she shimmered towards me, a beacon casting its light on a lost ship. I was expecting welcoming pleasantries from her – *Nice to see a new face,* or *How long have you been interested in archaeology?* Instead I got:

'Were you breastfed as a child?'

'I think so,' I replied, although I had no idea. 'Why do you ask?'

'You have a glow about you.' She moved her hands – palms out, fingers fanned, in contrary directions around the surface of my personal space, as if warming them there. 'Only breastfed children have this glow. It lasts them all their lives.'

I had not thought of myself as a glowing person before. People had often commented on how Mary glowed during her pregnancy, but I was never thought of, in any way, as luminous. If anything, I thought of myself as something shined upon, and therefore a producer of shadows.

As Janet's hands lifted, completing their loop of my radiant aura, her leather jacket opened to reveal her tightly T-shirted torso, the low neckline of which half disclosed her lifted breasts. They were not young breasts. Her body had aged in a way that her face had not. I found this slippage of synchronicity strangely exciting.

Surrounded by the sluggish chatter of physical historians, she told me everything about herself. How she was married to Jack Tilley, who managed a herd of twenty-three Friesians on the pastures between the precipices of the valley and the heather of the moorlands. How she'd provided him with two children, twin boys, both of whom had gone into dentistry. How Jack had failed, over twenty-seven years of marriage, to see any real difference between his wife and his cows.

'I was just another of his herd. I happened to walk on two legs, live indoors, make interesting food and produce human children. When I left him, his way of tempting me back was to convert an old cement yard at the back of the farmhouse into a lawn. He seemed to think that I'd always wanted a lawn. I just laughed at him and he became very, very angry.'

She'd left him only to a distance of three hundred feet. She'd moved into an old cowshed, built of gritstone and roofed with Jurassic rock, which they'd previously converted into a cosy holiday cottage for letting out to tourists. She let it out to herself, permanently.

Jack never fully understood why she left. He took to pounding on her stout oak door all through the night, posting scrawled messages on torn paper through her letter box (*The herd's not right since you left, their milk smells of onions. You trying to ruin me? You got to come back, love*). He was not a violent man and never threatened her physically. He whimpered that he couldn't manage the kitchen. Eventually he turned sour, claimed he'd never wanted to marry her in the first place, said he was happy alone at the farmhouse. They lived totally separate lives on the same farm. She only ever saw him as a tiny figure in the distance, fetching his cows, sweeping slush, making silage, filling his quotas. Occasional bouts of loneliness caused him to knock at her door and beg for her return. She always stood firm but was not cruel and tried to comfort him when she could.

She took me to her cottage that evening after the lecture in her battered orange 2CV. The car climbed the steep, dark lanes, past the derelict church of St Simon, followed the Möbius strip of the track that led to her farm, chased the beams of her headlights into the farmyard. On the journey we talked about archaeology. She'd become interested in it when a team came to excavate some tumuli on her land. They found a skeleton, an Iron Age chieftain's wife (no sign of her husband), with a horse buried alongside.

'It fascinated me to watch them uncover her, but it made me wonder – is it right for us to dig these things up? To disturb what was once a sacred site? I wept when they began lifting her, bone by bone, out of the dust. It was her right, surely, to be there for ever. There's always a dilemma between knowledge and preservation. We can't know anything without damaging it, no matter how careful we are. But I can see you have a special, historical sensitivity . . .'

Her voice was melodious, soft, grassy.

The interior of her cottage was an odd conjunction of the rustic and the bohemian, as was Janet, I suppose. Above the lovingly restored black range hung a stuffed zebra's head. Over the nested teak tables in one corner, the face of James Dean was outlined in blue neon. The varnished flagstones of the floor were adorned with zodiacal rugs.

We made love for an exquisite hour in her bedroom. The cows, in their modern shed, thirty feet away under a roof of corrugated iron, coughed and shuffled.

At midnight I returned to Mary, already asleep in our bed. I sensed her flinch unconsciously as I entered, as though she could already smell my contamination.

7

OUR affair developed slowly after that first night. Our meetings were brief. By day I spent my time filling Theodore with the milk Mary had expressed, bottled and stored in the fridge. I would supplement this with formula, sterilising the bottles in a plastic tank, scooping the sulphur-coloured powder into a measuring spoon, levelling it off with a knife. I'd rock Theodore to sleep and then phone Janet. We'd talk about history, animal husbandry, the mysteries of human relationships. She told me how Jack had taken to baking complicated iced cakes which he offered to her as sweet, pointless gifts. She told me how he'd started having singing lessons.

I saw him from Janet's window, sometimes, in the brief and occasional evenings I spent at her cottage. He represented for me a figure of complete isolation, a tiny little man in blue overalls, so small I could cover him with the nail of my little finger, a blue dot in the green pastures. Once, wellingtoned, he clumped right past the cottage and I was suddenly shocked by his near-presence, the magnification of his body, as he swaggered beneath me.

Sometimes, as Janet and I lay in a post-coital stupor on her bed, the cows would be grazing in the field at the back of her cottage. The only sound would be the tearing of grass, the relentless pulling and ripping up of young shoots. I felt an odd sense of envy. I envied the cows their hunger.

I entered into infidelity with an ease that shocked me. I looked upon the deceit as a form of invention. Of creativity. The lying was a species of fiction-making. It didn't seem difficult. And if I felt any guilt, it was at not feeling any. I wondered why I didn't feel bad about what I was doing. I began to think of myself as a rather skilful adulterer. Until Mary said to me one day:

'Are you having an affair with Janet Tilley?'

Mary had known Janet since childhood and had never liked her.

'Who? Janet? No. Janet who? Oh, that Janet. No.'

I wondered how such clumsiness had found its way into my denial. Something in me wanted to tell her. When I noticed a shadow of disappointment cross her face, I couldn't tell if it was because she believed me or disbelieved me. I went for belief. Mary needed a reason to get rid of me. I was nothing but a burden to her, a morose failure lugging around the sack of his missed opportunities. I felt I'd been given coded permission to continue and develop my affair with Janet.

8

AND then my mother died.

You don't need to know anything about her. All I will say is that she admired Mussolini for his multilingualism and violin-playing, but wouldn't comment on his politics. She bought a house with my father (now ten years dead) in 1949 for next to nothing that was now worth a bomb. My share of it came to sixty thousand pounds.

'We need to think very carefully,' said Mary after reading the solicitor's letter over breakfast (two teas – one black, one white; three bowls of cornflakes – two wet, one dry), 'this might be a way out.'

'Of what?'

'This mess.'

'Yes,' I said thoughtfully, adding, 'which mess do you mean?'

'I mean the mess of us having no life. Me working all the time and never seeing Theodore, you with Theodore all the time and never working. Which mess do you think I mean?'

'That one. You're right. I was thinking – I could set myself up in business. I could find some way of supporting both of us.'

'Business? You?' she said, without intending any insult.

'Why not? Something on the arty side, I mean. An art shop with gallery upstairs, picture framing . . .'

'I don't want you to take this the wrong way,' said Mary with the quiet authority she'd developed over her years as a teacher and which I found rather frightening, 'but you will tell me, won't you, before you spend all this money on some half-baked scheme. It's not that I don't trust you, but I'm beginning to think you have a fear of success. Every time something you want is within reach, you kick it further away. Don't feel frightened of this money, don't feel you need to rid yourself of it . . .'

Theodore, in the midst of some wild game, thumped his cereal bowl and flipped it upside down, showering us with cornflakes.

9

I mentioned my inheritance to Janet. We were in one of Ravendale's coffee bars spooning cappuccino froth into our mouths. We were surrounded by goateed young men and angular, attenuated young women sitting in stern silence with their espressos.

As if developing an idea that was latent in the beige-and-black decor of the bar, she poured forth the whole concept of a milkshake parlour for Ravendale. In a few minutes she had detailed everything from the recipes for the shakes to the dairy-and-fruit-themed design of the interior. She convinced me that there were enough writers, artists and media evacuees in Ravendale to support it. There would, she pointed out, be an interest in it for her. She could supply the honey. I'd seen the little cluster of hives in the field behind her house, like a row of clapboard cottages wherein the heather of the moorlands was refined and processed into the sweetest honey of the Pennines.

I began experimenting that afternoon. I bought four litres of milk in plastic bottles and filled Mary's Moulinex with chopped fruit, honey, cinnamon and anything else I could think of. I hacked my way through strawberries, bananas, kiwis, pineapples and melons, and tipped them into the graduated beaker, pressing the button and watching with great pleasure the pink and yellow vortices, those torrents, tornadoes, maelstroms of milk and fruit trapped within. All that afternoon I spun milk and fruit while Theodore watched from the high chair, laughing, although the frantic engine of the mixer frightened him at first.

I poured out the inflated liquid, upholstered a glass goblet with it and drank. It felt as though I was drinking liquidised tropical gardens, fluid flower beds, flowing blossoms. My drinks were the concentrated essence of sheer beauty. I knew then that I'd discovered a beverage that couldn't fail. A drink that would change the world.

It was when Mary returned from work that evening to find the kitchen a yogurty mess of fruit peelings and splashed milk that I broke the news of my milkshake parlour and she reacted so badly. Her whispered rage soon gave way to shrill anger. Theodore put his small hands over his ears.

'Why are you doing this?' she shouted. Her voice was so strange. It was almost as if she was singing. I felt scared. She seemed on the point of losing control. Theodore was trying to climb down from her. For a moment, in her crimson, swaying anger, I thought she might throw him. I moved towards her, my arms extended, to catch any hurled baby, to contain any explosion that might come. She drew back, her nose as wrinkled as a walnut.

'Get away from me, don't come near me, ever!' Her 'ever' was said with such force it was as though she'd vomited the word out.

I haven't touched her since then. I tried everything I could think of, including the abandonment of milkshakes, the confession and renunciation of my affair with Janet, the promise of exemplary dad- and husbandhood, to make Mary stay. But she was gone that evening with Theodore, first to her mother's at the other end of the valley, then to a female colleague's in Leeds.

10

So now I am fifteen minutes away from my grand opening. In my fridge are two pergals of milk and a further two quart bottles from the Co-op dairy in Huddersfield. They sit there in the dark – marmoreal, cold, unchanging. I've fruit, spices, honey. The honey is from Safeway. It is not Janet's honey.

Although she helped me, comforted me, encouraged me as I set up my milk parlour, something had changed in our relationship. I wanted to move in with her, but she said her cottage was too small, too 'hers'. I asked her to move in with me, but my house was too big, too 'mine'. But she found me this property, the old wool shop on the corner of Milwain Road and Cotton Street, perfectly situated. And she helped me with all the admin – sorting out the rental agreement, business rates, insurance. We worked together on the design, carefully thinking through every last detail. We scoured the glass catalogues of the world for just the right tumbler, which we found in Iceland (Norglass Inc.). But a week before opening, I went to her cottage and she wasn't there.

Puzzled, I hung around the filthy, splattered farmyard, wondering at the silence. It wasn't just the silence of her cottage, my knuckles echoing on her stout oak door, but the silence of the farm itself. There was something missing. Then I realised it was the cows. They'd gone. It was their clumsy footsteps, their coughing and snorting, their nervous shuffling that was missing. Neither were they in the fields. The sound of tearing grass had stopped.

Just then, from round the corner of the steel byre, came the clumping weight of Jack Tilley; blue-overalled, wellingtoned. His head was down and he was walking purposefully towards me. I thought he might walk right through me, unaware of my presence, but he stopped when he was just six feet away and looked at me without any surprise in his face. He didn't say anything. Neither did I. We looked hard at each other's faces for perhaps fifteen seconds, both of us curious to take in every detail of what we'd seen only distantly before. I noticed the stiff, coarse texture of his skin, flecked with broken capillaries, the blond wickerwork of his eyebrows, the moistness of his eyes. As I looked into his face, I knew that she was back with him. Jack Tilley walked past me.

I got a letter a couple of days later in which she tried to explain. Jack's herd had fallen to the disease that was yet to become famous. The disease that grew in their brains like rot, that caused them to stumble like drunks, that poisoned their flesh. Jack's herd had gone to the abattoir, the carcasses piled and fired, the first Pennine cows to be culled.

'Jack's ruined . . .' her letter read, *'he's lost everything. I can't abandon him now, not when he needs me so much. I hope you understand . . . our cows. I keep thinking of the smoke. The black clouds our cows made . . .'*

MY family has become people I visit occasionally in a city the other side of some mountains. Theodore fills the loo with paper when I arrive. Mary is busy but she says she'll try and come over for my opening if she can. Imagine that – Mary in a milk parlour. I'm sure if she actually saw what I've managed to put together here . . .

The floor needs one more clean. You look at it, think it's spotless, a minute later it's thick with dust. It's the same with the windows. I've cleaned them twice this morning but they still look filthy. That's the trouble with glass. It shows up the dirt so easily. I remember my mother saying that about the windows at home. Even though no one ever touched the windows, they needed regular cleaning. So where did all the dirt come from? I asked her once. She said the dirt was just made by people living, people breathing and sweating, stirring up dust. She said a man could stand stock-still in a room doing nothing but breathing, and the windows would still get dirty.

I'd better give them just one more go.